RANDOM
SHOTS

THE WANDERINGS OF A MONTANA WRITER

RANDOM SHOTS

THE WANDERINGS OF A MONTANA WRITER

John Holt

ABSOLUTELY AMA**Z**ING eBOOKS

ABSOLUTELY AMAZING eBOOKS

Published by Whiz Bang LLC, 926 Truman Avenue, Key West, Florida 33040, USA.

For information contact
Publisher@AbsolutelyAmazingEbooks.com

ISBN-13: 978-1949504200 (Absolutley Amazing Ebooks)
ISBN-10: 1949504204

The Mountains of Youth they would always be for me; and when I wondered sleepily, would I be seeing them again? Soon I decided; and the sooner the better...

- R.M. Patterson, *Far Pastures*

RANDOM
SHOTS
THE WANDERINGS OF A MONTANA WRITER

TABLE OF CONTENTS

GETTING TO THIS
Introduction

SO HOW DID THIS book come to be? How did this collection of articles and stories wind up in one place in this book? One fine October afternoon I was standing out in front of Sax & Fryer bookstore in my hometown of Livingston, Montana. I was talking with a couple of writer friends, which is not unusual in this place. There are so many quality writers living in the area that all of their published books would make for a fairly decent public library in itself. The conversation turned to compilations of people's work and do they have any merit. We decided that "Yes, they do." When arranged by theme and chronologically these books give people a chance to both read some things that they were unaware of, and also they might see the changes, maturation and, hopefully, improvements in a writer's style and voice. Then one of them said "Holt, you should round up some of your older stuff. Probably nobody remembers Grizzly Dance that you did for Gray's or all of the environmental rants you did for Fly Fisherman." The other guy in this triumvirate had never read Grizzly Dance, a short story that I wrote 30 years ago. When I showed him the thing a few days later, he read it then asked if I had more like it. I said "Yes." He shook his head and the conversation drifted off to brown trout as it will do around here in the fall.

I'd never considered the notion of doing a collection until now. I thought about this idea for several days during my morning walks along the Yellowstone River and finally

i

Random Shots:
The Wanderings of a Montana Writer

decided "Why the hell not?" I ransacked my collection of magazines and found around 30 stories that I liked, then arranged them in sections and in the order they were published. They begin in 1988 though I'd done many more before this time even when I was working for small dailies in Beloit, Wisconsin and Kalispell. What surprised and pleased me to some extent is that all of them stand up to the passing of the various years, especially the environmental ones, though I'm not sure this is good. It means that nothing has really changed or improved and threats to good country are more prevalent than ever. Still, I figured, the book would give some readers a chance to see what I've done over the years, and maybe I'll even make a buck or two. After all, if anyone starts running down the tired "Art for art's sake" number, walk away for your own sake. You're probably speaking with a disingenuous fool. A writer who doesn't want to make money most likely doesn't have much to say and has little if any faith in his work. And we all have to pay bills. I broke the book up into sections called Long Running Madness, The Environment and Big Sky Journal. Before each story I added a brief explanation of how it came to pass, public reaction, random thoughts, and/or various pratfalls that occurred along the way.

I've only made a few minor changes in some of these selections, though the early ones sometimes seem strained, at times hackneyed, and primitive. The changes are mainly slight word and punctuation improvements, and I combined shorter paragraphs wherever possible to make larger ones for visual enhancement in book format. But I wanted to have a book I could look at and see the gradual and admittedly slight improvement in my abilities as a writer and a storyteller. Still a very long way to go, but unlike an athlete who is usually finished by 40, writers can continue to grow and mature provided they work at it and don't bow down and worship the twisted god alcohol as I did some years ago. I'm still alive, mad as a hatter, mad as hell about the destruction of wild country and still trying to learn how to speak my native tongue.

\- John Holt
Livingston
Spring 2018

SECTION ONE

Long Running Madness

GRIZZLY DANCE IN GLACIER'S OWN TIME

Gray's Sporting Journal – 1988

This short story was inspired by a late-summer day I had along the western edge of Glacier National Park. I was driving the inside park road along the North Fork of the Flathead River. Coming up on the North Fork Road before cutting east at Polebridge and across the North Fork I had already spotted seven grizzlies – a sow and three cubs, a male working along a ridge eating huckleberries, and then another female and a lone cub wandering downriver from me as I cast enormous streamers to visible bull trout of 10 pounds or more at the tails of huge, sapphire-colored pools (I managed to take one fish). The inside road winds through dense lodgepole pine forest, open stands of Ponderosa and across grassy meadows. In an hour's driving I saw six more of the great bears. So I took that day's remarkable experience and blew it sky high. Shortly after Gray's (at the time a wonderful sporting publication, though getting paid was a sporting proposition) published the story an officious official (I can see this bozo applying for the job saying he'd like to have this glorious position because it's his life's dream and then being handed a No. 2 pencil and the Official Asshole Aptitude Examination by some career fool) from Glacier Park called me at my home in nearby Whitefish. He said, in a voice that reminded me of some twisted teachers I'd had and one puerile managing editor I'd worked for in Kalispell, that I had totally misrepresented the facts concerning grizzlies in Glacier and that it was impossible to have seen that many bears. He went on to say that my work was irresponsible and misleading. This led me to immediately consider applying for a job in the park. When I told him that the story was an act of fiction, a short story, a flight of fantasy, this bright bulb said "Oh" and hung up. These are the clowns we trust to manage magic places like Glacier, Grand Canyon and Yellowstone. I'm encouraged. How about you?

~ ~ ~

"Alas, peaceful man may be unnatural man, a fairly bleak prospect in the atomic age."

- Robert Traver

"THERE GOES ANOTHER ONE!" screamed my companion, madness making an appearance in the cracking, high-pitched whine of her voice.

But she was right – another grizzly, this time a five or six-hundred pound bear.

The bears were everywhere. Not the usual "Once-in-a-lifetime,-oh-my-God-I'm-going-to-die-if-I-don't-get-my-act-up-a-tree-quickly" rag.

This was the real thing.

Since we'd started up the trail towards Kintla Lake in Glacier National Park, grizzlies had appeared constantly, downhill to the right of us, loping past us in two's, three's and four's or meandering through the pines.

Not one of them acted like they had seen us, gotten wind of us or if they had, there were apparently bigger doings in the woods this day.

Running into a grizzly in the back country of Glacier goes with the territory. It is part of the charm of hiking in the park. Every season some hapless visitor from Peoria, Illinois is chased up a tree by a bear, then usually hauled back down and chewed on to the tune of 100 or so stitches.

Deaths are rare – only a half dozen, give or take, in the park's history – and the end result is normally a photo of the victim in a hospital bed and a lengthy interview in one of the local papers about how a crazed 35,000-pound, deranged animal attacked the innocent bystander without provocation.

Sometimes the injured party sues the Park Service, hoping to make a killing (having only recently avoided a similar fate at the paws of the bears). A media-type attorney handles the case, which draws a good deal more attention from the press, but life goes on for the bears and the park in general.

So what the hell was going on today? A late-summer spectacular in northwestern Montana? Nothing was out of the ordinary. The sky was a perfect, deep blue. The temperature was in the low 80s with a light breeze lending a soft counterpoint to the peculiar situation.

The two of us had already seen over 30 of the legendary creatures – more than we'd sighted total in our lives.

Stranger yet, the bears ignored our presence. Even sows with cubs, usually a deadly combination, were unconcerned.

True, the park was overrun with hikers, neophyte nature freaks, twisted health fanatics and assorted other crazies. And, yes, the bears had lost their fear of humans, but what was taking place in this part of Montana today was not normal.

"I don't get it. We should be dead by now. I've never been that close to a bear before."

"Strange days in the park," said Anne with an expression that was glazed and confused. "Damn, there go two more."

Just up the trail a couple of medium-sized males ambled across the trail and down to Kintla Creek, flowing with benign indifference not far below us in the dense lodgepole.

"I'd say let's get the hell out of here, but I don't know where that is. Bears to the right of us. Bears to the left of us. Stuck in the middle again."

"Cut the comedy. Do we go up or down?" Terror had apparently made a slight exit from Anne's life sometime in the last few minutes. "The bears have gone crazy and if they haven't, we have. So what's the difference?"

Desperate times call for desperate measures. I cracked open the bottle of bourbon I'd carefully stashed in my pack and took a healthy blast before passing it over to my tightly-wound friend.

It was a half-gallon bottle, but this was intended to be a four-day trip and the potential for things to turn ugly was now ever-present. Eight ounces of whiskey per day per person was cutting things a bit thin, but both of us had known adversity before.

No bears sighted in the last 10 minutes. Maybe their bizarre behavior was over. No one would believe what had happened today, whatever had happened.

Grizzlies are known for their unpredictable behavior. They had killed two 19-year-old women on the same night in August 1967 in different parts of Glacier – only the second and third bear-related fatalities at the time.

The bears will also gather on Huckleberry Mountain in pursuit of the hill's namesake. And some animals will converge on McDonald Peak in the Mission Mountains just south of here in pursuit of army cutworms – a social event of mammoth proportions in better bear circles everywhere.

A park ranger who knew this area as well as anyone had been dragged down by a female grizzly in a surprise attack a couple of years back.

He had been looking for an airman on leave from Mamlstrom Air Force Base in Great Falls. He was thought to be either drowned in Bowman Lake or making a damned good effort at making things look that way – an elaborate mountain AWOL.

The bear came out of the brush with a vengeance, smashing the ranger down and holding a vicious grip on the man's leg. After what must have seemed like an extended trip to hell, and aren't they all, the bear was driven off by of all things a punch to the nose.

Fending off an enraged grizzly with a pop to the chops seems as likely as putting out a lumber yard fire with a garden hose. But who can argue with success. The ranger escaped with a badly mangled leg and his life. The bear vanished back into the high country.

"Oh when I'm dead an' in my grave
An' no more whiskey will I crave.
On my tombstone let this be wrote,
'Ten thousand quarts run down his throat.'

But that's a story best told when no one is listening.

Anne took another pull from the jug and passed it back to me while a huge cinnamon-colored bear, smelling for all the world like a high school locker room, padded by. The big guy stopped, looked us both over and let out a soft "woof" that seemed to have cynical implications – an apparent statement of fact in the eyes of the griz, who strolled on down the trail.

More whiskey. Anne just shook her head. This trip was beyond her control and she laughed before nodding off into warm afternoon serenity.

Glacier is magic country. Members of the Blackfeet people stayed away from its rugged interior – strong vibes or something. Only a few hardy and slightly deranged trappers and prospectors ever got to know the land on a first-name basis before the area became a national park. Lack of access and decidedly aggressive tribal members on the eastern front of the park kept all but the most determined white men at bay.

Ambushes, harsh winters and disease took their toll on these adventurous wayfarers, until whiskey and greed leveled the Blackfeet's hold on the land. Railroads, surveyors and homesteaders did the rest. Glacier's million-plus acres officially became a park in 1910. The opening of the Going-to-the-Sun Road in 1933 revealed the park's inner side to hordes of tourists who viewed this country through windshields and viewfinders. Less than five percent of the visitors ever see anything but what the highway offers and they rarely spend more than a day here.

These facts aren't lost on the grizzlies. In their own way they know what is left to them. The bears rarely go near the road, preferring to mind their own grizzly business in the secluded, glaciated heartland.

But trails were built – lots of them and the bears are having a hard time avoiding humans. Grizzlies may not fear humans, but they don't get a big kick out of being around them either. Humans don't often know what they're doing in the woods and they get in the way a lot – cutting down trees, starting fires, falling off cliffs, etc.

There are not a lot of grizzlies left in the lower 48 states – maybe a 1,000 and at the most 300 in the park, but with tourists scrambling over deadfalls and boulders at every twist of Siyeh Limestone confrontations are bound to occur. Several attacks each season and a handful of deaths so far are relatively small figures considering the fact that Glacier has about two million visitors per year.

Still, the Park Service comes up with stuff like the following concerning the bears' intransigent behavior "...the Park is preparing to take a harder line on any bear that has torn up camps, consumed other than natural food, or simply become overly familiar with humans...that such bears be trapped and immediately removed."

Every man's home is his castle, but what was once home to the grizzly in this small part of the state, is not anymore. Tough luck guys. Enjoy the view. Eat a few berries, but leave the tourists alone. They're not too bright, but they spend lots of money. Bottom-line wildlife management at its finest.

The bears probably don't see the situation in these terms. They just work harder at staying invisible, sort of a northern Rockies version of Ralph Ellison's fifties prototype.

Or do they?

For the last few years grizzly sightings have been on the rise. Trail closures are more common and a couple of bear-related deaths have occurred – a popular public outrage bursting into bloom. Maybe today's weirdness is a bear response to being pushed around or to the limit. "The hell with you people. Stay out of our way and you'll be fine. Get in our way and you may pay the price."

We shouldered our packs as a light afternoon breeze drifted down from the snowfields above us. Upper Kintla was a couple miles distant and the bears were popping out from among the trees with a now not so frightening regularity. We'd become jaded or perhaps shell-shocked. Ever upward was the theme for the remainder of the day's activities. Suspension of belief. No bear was going to kill us and if one or two of them did lay waste to our misdirected expedition, so what?

"Well, how did they die?"

"Some bears ate them in Glacier Park."

"Is that near Butte?"

See? No big deal.

It took an hour to cover the distance to the lake, bears blooming at every turn. Silver-tipped ones, brown ones, mangy ones. Alone or in groups of ten. Take your pick. It was a grizzly bear blast at the Upper Kintla Trail Bar and

Random Shots:
The Wanderings of a Montana Writer

Grill.

We had cameras (good ones at that), but we didn't bother exposing any film. The photos wouldn't have turned out and besides, none of this is happening anyway.

Anne talked freely with the bears and they just as freely ignored her. Sort of like trying to relate to inner city man somewhere. "Boy, you're not even here," despite protests to the contrary.

The mountains were their usual magnificent selves. We were the only ones at Upper Kintla, its smooth surface now reflecting the sky in full sunset regalia. The air was dead still. Several young grizzlies were slapping fish (cutthroat, bull trout?) out of the lake and onto a gravel bar not far from us. Fishing's easy when you're a member in good standing in this old-line, well-respected club. We caught a few small cutthroats on nymph patterns, cooked them over a small fire and washed them down with gulps of non-purified Upper Kintla water. After dealing with 400 grizzlies, the threat of giardia seemed a small cross to bear.

We lay down on our sleeping bags under a sky packed with stars. Bears were crashing about in the forest. Fish by the thousands broke the surface of the lake and splashed back. The fire eventually burned out. We eventually fell asleep, and tomorrow wasn't here yet.

MACLEAN COUNTRY

Fly Fisherman – 1988

Norman Maclean's novella *A River Runs Through It* has been running around in my head ever since I first read this brilliant piece of work in the late seventies. The word "brilliant" is carelessly tossed around, notably by sportscasters who describe a pedestrian six-yard pass completed in the flat or some clone golf professional draining a 12-foot putt for par as something akin to a painting by Botticelli. Maclean's story is brilliant in its conception, its succinct use of language and its wealth of feelings and images packed so easily into so few words. The movie done by Robert Redford (made a number of years after the following story appeared in print) impressed me as merely another bit of Hollywood hack work without soul or vision. Redford decided that the Blackfoot River so close to Maclean's heart was not good enough for him, so he filmed the thing on the Gallatin. The two rivers are entirely different in character and this showed in a film totally devoid of heart or integrity. In the early seventies I spent a good deal of time fishing the Blackfoot. It was beautiful and fun back then and remains so today. A group of musicians, used to have a place above the stream. One day I pulled in to visit before fishing and spotted a 16-foot aluminum canoe lying in the yard. It was totally filled with ice, Rainer (vitamin R) beer and champagne – a wondrous sight. One of the members had won the thing in a bar raffle in nearby Seeley Lake. The well-provisioned craft fueled a great day filled with music and laughter. These guys were top shelf players and they

9

Random Shots:
The Wanderings of a Montana Writer

were on this time around. Some years later, after reliving that youthful time in my head, I called *Fly Fisherman* editor John Randolph and pitched a story on this country. He liked the idea and so here it is.

~ ~ ~

"In our family, there was no clear line between religion and fly fishing. We lived at the junction of great trout rivers in western Montana, and our father was a Presbyterian minister and a fly fisherman who tied his own flies and taught others. He told us about Christ's disciples being fishermen, and we were left to assume, as my brother and I did, that all first-class fishermen on the Sea of Galilee were fly fishermen and that John, the favorite, was a dry-fly fisherman."
- **Norman Maclean, *A River Runs Through It***

WITH THAT DECEPTIVELY SIMPLE paragraph Norman Maclean begins his classic story. While most fly fishermen concentrate their efforts on the more famous waters in the southwestern corner of Montana, a strong case can be made for spending a couple of weeks (or months or years) fishing waters described in Maclean's book.

The country of Norman Maclean is as vast and varied as an angler could hope for. From the high plains lakes east of the rugged Rocky Mountain Front, to the wild waters of Glacier National Park and the Bob Marshall Wilderness, down through the heavily-timbered Swan River Valley and north along the North Fork of the Blackfoot River, countless permutations of fly fishing exist.

Perhaps the best way to gain an understanding of the possibilities of this remarkable country is to briefly describe some of the fishing, beginning with the Blackfoot River and working counterclockwise around the region.

The Blackfoot has its origin high in the mountains about 100 miles northeast of Missoula. . A meandering stream in its upper reaches, it then becomes a whitewater flow in the before turning into a classic deep-pool, glassy-run, long-riffle river for the rest of its course to its confluence with the Clark Fork River near Bonner.

The Blackfoot has always meant warm-weather, late-summer hopper fishing to me. Working a large floating pattern dead-drifted against pine-covered banks or in and around swirling eddies and large boulders often produces rainbows that head skyward at the first sense of pressure from the line.

Because of heavy fishing pressure, and few restrictions, there are not many large fish remaining in the Blackfoot. However, I spent an afternoon trying to coax a large rainbow out of the current and into shore after the trout had slammed my hopper and then tail-walked its way into fast water. The fish won the battle, the tippet snapping with a familiar twang.

When the fish are not rising I resort to a #4 or #6 Marabou Muddler with a small split-shot attached at the head of the fly on a sinking-tip line. The water where the fish hold is deep, and the pattern must reach bottom to entice them to strike. Sometimes it takes hours of casting and stripping to turn a fish, but the ones that respond are usually the largest in the river.

Concern for the Blackfoot may result in restricted creel limits and size constraints on the river in the near future, and if other state rivers are any indication, they should cause an improvement in the fishing within a few years. Access to the river is relatively easy. Public fishing sites are clearly marked by gray sings along Highway 200. Large pools are accessible from roadside turnouts.

If you head north and east on Hwy 200 at Clearwater Junction, you'll see the North Fork of the Blackfoot River, a fine, clear stream that meanders 22 miles through timbered mountains and for 14 more miles through open meadowland to its rendezvous with the Blackfoot. Its evening fishing is superb for rainbow, cutthroat and bull trout from early summer into autumn. The fish average 12 inches but frequently go much larger. Elk Hair Caddis, Wulffs, Adams and hopper patterns are effective in late summer, with sizes starting around #10 for all but the hopper, and decreasing gradually as the water level drops.

Every bend in the North Fork offers a number of technical problems – how to place the cast drag-free above feeding fish without looping the line over a snag, or how to approach one trout feeding in mid-stream without disturbing another working nearby. Walking back to the truck in the darkness, I've been amazed at how far up the river I've worked, totally lost in the rhythm of the water and the challenge.

The Dearborn River rises in the wilderness on the Continental Divide and flows for 20 miles through Forest Service land. It's mostly rainbow trout water with fish averaging about 11 inches. Below Hwy 200 the river has some large browns and is deep enough to float.

About 30 miles to the north on Hwy 287 you cross the Sun River, which from below Gibson Dam and on downstream is fine fishing for rainbows, cutthroat and browns that can reach several pounds. The upper reaches are in canyon country that is inaccessible by car, but fishing trails reach most of the water. It's an ideal place to hike, enjoy the solitude, and feel the power and peace of the land. Fishing often becomes a subordinate experience to the surroundings.

The lower river runs are in ranchland, but permission to fish is sometimes granted if you ask politely. The Sun is but a pale image of its former self following a vicious scouring of the streambed by a massive flood in 1964, but the fishing is still good in spots.

Fishing the Glacier High Country

The peaks of Glacier National Park are visible for miles as you approach from the plains on US 2, an imposing mountain wall that dominates the south-to-north skyline. In fact, the scenery is so spectacular that fewer than 10 percent of the park's visitors ever bother to fish the countless backcountry lakes.

To work all of the park's waters would take several seasons, but there are a number of quality lakes accessible from the road or by a brief hike on any of the hundreds of miles of maintained trails.

Just north of the small town of East Glacier are Lower Two Medicine and Two Medicine Lakes. The first contains rainbows and brookies that exceed 16 inches, and can be taken during summer evenings from shore. You can reach the upper lake by tour boat and then make a two-mile hike to the head of the lake. On times when I've walked along the north shore to the better water at the top of the lake, I've often stopped and spot-fished for trout cruising along the shore. I make soft casts well ahead of the imagined course of the fish and watch as the trout work ever closer to the waiting fly. Then suddenly, the fish spots the pattern bobbing on the surface and takes it in a rush, the line going taut, the rod bending sharply. Someday I'll reach the head of the lake.

But, if you can resist this shoreline temptation, walk up the north shoreline and you'll find fishing for fat brook trout that often rise for #14-16 Adams and Royal Wulffs or take streamers. There are campgrounds with postcard views at both lakes.

Moving still farther north through brushy grizzly country you'll find the St. Mary's entrance and the famous Going-to-the-Sun Road. Driving this is a heart-stopping experience. Frequently park rangers must drive visitors' vehicles back down the mountain, the sheer, dropping-off-the-end-of-the world views are too much for some people.

But if you persevere and reach the top of the road at Logan Pass, some interesting fishing for large Yellowstone cutthroats lies just a few miles up and over a rise at Hidden Lake west of the visitor center. You may see goats during the hike that takes you beneath mountain peaks, through bear grass and fields of wildflowers. Cutthroats cruise the shallows and drop-offs along the shore of this lake, but you'll need fine tippets and delicate casts to entice the fish into striking. I fish small. Dry patterns and nymphs from ice-out in mid-summer until the road closes in October.

The park's interior offers superb fishing for cutthroats and large brook trout, but some of the best waters require several days to reach and are in prime grizzly country – a natural danger of Glacier to take seriously on any outing.

Most of the park's streams are relatively barren of aquatic insects and, as a result, also of fish. But rivers like the North Fork of the Flathead along the western boundary are migration corridors for bull trout (related to Dolly Vardon) that can exceed 20 pounds. Cutthroats also roam the rivers, usually from June through September. Unless there is an obvious hatch situation (usually caddis or stoneflies), large streamers fished in the eddies provide the best results. South of Glacier and Hwy 2 lies the Bob Marshall Wilderness complex, which also includes the Scapegoat and Great Bear wilderness areas. Within these places you'll find hundreds of thousands of acres of unspoiled wilderness with some of the finest fishing for native westslope cutthroat found anywhere.

Cutthroats and Wilderness

The South Fork of the Flathead River above Hungry Horse Reservoir has mile after mile of emerald-clear water, pool upon pool and riffle following riffle alive with trout that often top three pounds. And recent changes in regulations have dramatically increased the numbers of large fish.

The first time I worked the South Fork, in the early seventies, an outfitter told me before I hiked into the country that the fishing was poor at the moment. I reached the river in three days, rigged my rod, and made several false casts before letting a large hopper smack on the water. Cutthroats dashed from every direction competing to hit the fly. I'd heard of fishing where you got bored after a couple of days because it was too easy, but I thought that you only found such angling in places like Alaska and Alberta, not Montana.

There are hundreds of other streams to choose from, and it's difficult to be disappointed in the area. A two-day hike or extended trip by packhorse. Arranged through one of the area's many outfitters, will take you into pristine country that has changed little since it was formed thousands of years ago.

Among the more popular streams are Big and Little Salmon rivers, Danaher Creek, Gordon Creek, Spotted Bear River and Youngs Creek. Most of these streams are fast-flowing. Whitewater fisheries and the floating capabilities of the fly are critical. The Goodard Caddis is my favorite, and its light color makes it easier to see on the water. Many of the streams also hold bull trout and mountain whitefish. Many of the larger lakes are overpopulated with cutthroat. Choosing a pattern requires little thought. Take your pick. I've experienced times on the South Fork when any pattern took fish on every cast.

The Swan Valley
The character of the country shifts as you head south down Hwy 83 in the Swan Valley to fish the river and its

many small tributaries. Although describing the Blackfoot, Maclean also pictures the Swan when he writes:

> *The voices of the subterranean river in the shadows were different from the voices of the sunlit river ahead. In the shadows against the cliff the river was deep and engaged in profundities, circling back on itself now and then to say things over to be sure it understood itself.*

The Swan is like that, bouncing along between two strong ranges of mountains, flitting in and out of the sunlight on a warm July afternoon. And many small creeks dance down steep drainages full of spring water and glacier-melt. The Swan used to be one of the finest cutthroat and rainbow fisheries in the northwest, but siltation from logging, development and over-fishing took their toll. Fortunately, concern for the watershed has led to improved management. The fishing is slowly recovering. You can catch rainbows, cutthroat, bull trout, mountain whitefish and brook trout from the time when spring runoff declines in late June through the golden-larch days of October. As water levels drop, caddis, stonefly and mayfly (including baetis) hatches increase in number and intensity. Larger streamers produce an occasional big bull, a nearly religious experience in a small river like the Swan.

Most of the tributaries headwater in remote, beautiful mountain surroundings and contain healthy populations of pan-size trout. The high mountain lakes of the Mission Mountains offer quality fishing in a secluded environment. There are golden trout in several of these waters, but the trails are rough and steep. Destinations are often 10 miles or more from the trailhead, and this is prime grizzly turf.

Late September or early October is a serene time to explore the many lakes of the Missions. On one day-hike, the family dog and I jogged up a trail to a chain of lakes nestled against a jagged mountain cirque. I fished (the dog chased marmots in the scree slopes) the upper lake for 12-inch goldens that were suckers for olive Woolly Worms. Then we strolled back down to the lowest lake where I caught a dozen dark-bodied cutthroat from shore with an Adams. The larch had turned flaming orange and the weather offered one last taste of the summer gone by, making for a perfect day in the hills, one to help carry an angler through a long winter.

Heading south again along the highway toward the resort community of Seeley lake, you'll discover the gentle Clearwater River that flows for about 40 miles to its junction with the Blackfoot. This small mountain stream passes through Rainy, Alva, Inez, Seeley lakes and Salmon lakes. There is sporadic fishing for brook, rainbow and cutthroat trout. You may occasionally latch into a spawning brown trout between Salmon and Inez during the fall run.

This tour is well over 500 miles long and takes in about 15,000 square miles of land that ranges from arid high plains to deep pine forest to mountain cirque lakes. Every type of freshwater fly fishing is available, and the waters mentioned represent a mere fraction of the possibilities available to intrepid seekers of salmonids. Maclean says it best:

~ ~ ~

Eventually, all things merge into one, and a river runs through it. The river is cut by the world's great flood and runs over rocks from the basement of time. Under the rocks are the words, and some of the words are theirs. I am haunted by rivers.

GOLDEN TROUT – LUMINESCENT FISH IN HARD-TO-FIND PLACES

The Flyfisher – 1988

Golden trout have always fascinated me with their technicolor-intense coloration, the fact that they swim in only the highest, purest and most difficult lakes and small streams to reach in North America. As the years passed in Montana I learned about more and more waters that held these unique salmonid that have been long since transplanted from their native waters in California's high Sierra country. I've caught large ones of five pounds or more in Wyoming's Bridger Wilderness and in some lakes in the Beartooth Mountains of southcentral Montana. And again some large specimens that I stumbled upon in an unnamed lake in the Whitefish Range, though they were frozen out some years back. But my favorite place to look for these curiosities is in a way-up-there lake in the Mission Mountains of northwest Montana. The fish don't grow large, but I'll always remember the first time I, along with my Irish Wolfhound Bonzo Dhogge (named after a bizarre Irish band of the time), staggered into this water after slogging through many feet of melting snow under a wicked late-July sun. The water was dead calm and the goldens were lazily circling around like gold ingots as they sipped very small bugs. We set up a modest camp, caught a few, kept a few for dinner. I fried them whole with the heads on in butter and seasoned them with sea salt, black

19

pepper and some lemon juice. They were excellent. Then I spent the evening sipping Rich & Rare around a small fire as Bonzo and I watched the stars come out and meteors flare overhead. I'll always remember that time and whenever I get the chance I head up to the high country lake and pretend that I'm young again.

I WAS BEGINNING TO WONDER ... to talk out loud to myself ... to answer my own questions. Were my friends right? Was I really crazy.

People had told me that the hike into this high mountain lake was a death march under the best of conditions and when they heard that I was going to make my third trip here in less than a month, they just stared, mouths open, or they turned away, too embarrassed for me to comment.

Why was I up here in these mountains in the chill of mid-October?

Spectacular scenery, solitude and the joy of self-sufficiency that comes with backpacking were all part of the attraction. But the real reason the steep 10-mile hike seemed inconsequential was right in front of me, swirling in the emerald waters, flashing in the clear light.

Golden trout, a lot of them, were casually dining on a hatch of small caddis flies. I was here to try and catch one, to admire its beauty and rarity. There are not many of these fish around and not many anglers have ever seen one, let alone felt one struggling at the end of the line. I was the last of the very few, if any, people who made it up here to see this lake before the rough winter winds and deep snows closed the trail for eight months.

A light puff of breeze pushed my small fly a few feet from its intended target and as the fluff hit the lake's surface, a 12-inch piece of gold rose up and sucked in the offering. The strength of the fish surprised me – quick, strong runs punctuated with vigorous waggings of the head, then brief soundings on the bottom. The fish came haltingly to shore, partially on its side, the fly hooked in the roof of its mouth. The body glowed in the sunshine. A bright crimson band ran the length of the fish through eleven bronze parr marks. Black spots covered its back and tail. The fins were orange tipped with white. A magic blending of yellows, reds, greens and black in perfect proportion.

The golden's appearance was stunning. The killer hikes were worth the sweaty, lung-burning effort. This was the most brilliant of trout caught in primitive surroundings – the rugged mountains of Montana.

To help understand this fish's allure an explanation of its life and history is required.

Goldens originated in the Kern River drainage in the Sierra Mountains of central California. Golden stock was exported to Colorado, Idaho, Montana, Oregon, Utah, Washington, Wyoming and as far away as England until 1939 when California passed legislation prohibiting the shipping of eggs and fish out of state. (The trout I just caught was the offspring of fish planted in the late twenties by a now old friend of mine.) The golden became California's state fish in 1947. Idaho, Washington, Montana and Wyoming still carry on stocking programs on a limited basis. Small populations remain in the Unita Mountains of Utah and the Pincher Creek area of Alberta. Goldens may be holding out in the isolated lakes of Colorado and Oregon.

"Our problem is that we don't have many barren lakes to stock them in," said George Holton of the Montana Dept. of Fish, Wildlife and Parks. "Over the years almost every lake has been stocked with fish (other than goldens) and that's why I advocate leaving barren lakes to provide places to stock fish like golden trout."

Goldens need their own secure water. One of the main

problems with establishing a fishery is that goldens will hybridize with other trout and lose their hold on a lake or stream. This was brought home last summer when after catching several westslope cutthroat with yellow-tinted gill covers and a distinct golden hue on their sides, I remembered hearing that this particular isolated chain of lakes had been planted with goldens in the 1930s. A call to fish-and-game a few days later confirmed this and also revealed that the lake had been recently stocked with cutthroat. It is obvious that cutthroats are taking over the lake and in a few more generations almost all visible traces of goldens will be gone.

"If we could get a brood stock going in a lake – they're very expensive to rear in a hatchery, plus there is a problem with genetics and inbreeding weakening of the stock – we could do a better job of planting goldens," said a fisheries biologist. " They're a very desirable fish."

This desirability probably led to a number of the colorful trout being transported "in coffee cans" from their original waters in California to neighboring lakes and streams during the 1870's by cattlemen who wanted goldens swimming in streams near where they tended their stock. One story has it that in 1876 a Colonel Stevens lugged a dozen of the fish from Mulkey Creek in the Sierra over a crest in the mountains and dumped then in Cottonwood Creek. The Colonel operated a sawmill in the area and the goldens no doubt occupied his spare time quite nicely.

In 1918 the California Dept. of Fish and Game began raising goldens in the Cottonwood Lakes at an elevation of 11,000 feet. Today eggs are still gathered there and transported to the Mt. Whitney hatchery before wilderness plantings.

Most people believe that the fish can only survive in lakes of high altitude. Goldens have been successfully transplanted as low as 3,000 feet, and in a number of lakes between 5,000 and 7,000 feet.

"They do almost as well on valley floors, despite their reputation as mountain fish," said Holton.

Most of the goldens caught today are technically known as *Salmo agua bonita* and are originally from the South Fork of the Kern River. Several other species of goldens exist in California. Among them are: *Salmo whitei* and *Salmo gilberti* of Coyote Creek; *Salmo roosevelti* of Volcano Creek; and *Salmo rosei* of the Culver Lake drainage. All of these trout are distinguished through minor variations in coloring and marking, but as Robert H. Smith states in his book *Trout of North America,* trying to compare them is "like trying to compare two sunsets."

Nobody knows for sure the evolutionary history of goldens, but some experts believe the trout may be descendants of redband trout, of which rare members include the Gila, Apache and Mexican.

How did goldens evolve into the brightly-colored creatures they are today? There are several theories:

First, their colors tend to mirror the environment of their native range, the reds and other brightly-colored gravels of the Kern Basin, making the fish difficult for predators to spot, even though there are few predators at the altitude where they exist. An interesting idea is that the intense light, unfiltered at high altitudes, produce deadly levels of radiation, and the colors of goldens may be a form of protection from this harsh light. Some credence is given to this by the fact that the trout lose their color intensity after prolonged stays in lakes at lower elevations.

Goldens can reach an impressive size, although the days of 11-pounders being taken from Cooks Lake in Wyoming are long past. A five-pound fish would be a truly large one. Today 12-inch fish are common, and in streams five to seven inches is average. Exceptions exist, but lakes that hold big fish are hard to find and get to. And once there,

Random Shots:
The Wanderings of a Montana Writer

the angler may find the goldens extremely selective (trout on English chalk streams have nothing on goldens in this respect).

The trout grow rapidly for the first three years, sometimes reaching 15 inches and more than a pound. After this, things slow down and a golden that is eight years old is an old golden.

So what does the fly fisher do if he wants to try his luck with these rare fish? Prepare to suffer. Ninety-nine percent of the water holding goldens is fished by less than one percent of the seekers of this gold. The reason for this is simple. Golden waters are remote and difficult to reach. Steep climbs (literally) are to be expected. And even with a good map, some golden lakes are almost impossible to find. Chasing these fish takes preparation and patience. Someone who is not willing to go the extra mile had better look to other trout for recreation.

There are specific tactics for goldens, Most of the time this means using small dry flies or nymphs. Aquatic insects are the most important food, especially caddis flies and midges. Shrimp and terrestrials (ants, beetles and grasshoppers) are also a key part of the diet. When the air heats up as the day progresses, winds sweep up ridges dragging with them helpless insects that live down below – a natural artificial hatch the angler should watch for.

One hot August afternoon warm winds from well below the lake I was fishing snarled my lines, but also swept hundreds of small hoppers onto the water's surface. Goldens went crazy, racing along the surface like surfers as they competed with each other for the unexpected gourmet offering. A quick switch to a #10 Joe's Hopper provided memorable fishing between tangled, eye-threatening casts.

To be safe the prudent angler packs in an assortment of caddis and midge imitations , among them: Elf hair caddis, Goddard caddis, Adams and Bucktail caddis in #14 and smaller, The Hare's ear nymph in the same sizes is also a good choice. Some patterns to try when the fish are acting selective are Muddler Minnows and Spruce flies in #8 and smaller. The ever-faithful woolly bugger, especially in olive, can be a life saver.

Presentation must be extremely cautious. A light, delicate cast that gently delivers the fly is needed. The slightest disturbance and a golden trout stampede with Bonanza overtones will result. Keep low and use whatever cover is available. Remember, these fish are *spooky* and you just risked a coronary to find them, so take your time and do things right. Almost all success with dry flies or nymphs and the goldens involves waiting – minutes at a time. Let the fly adjust to its water-borne situation for as long as five minutes (shorter with nymphs) . This is the *key* to catching the trout when they are being selective. After an agonizing wait, give the fly a slight flick. This often draws the ardent response of one or more greedy goldens for a solid take.

So what does the intrepid angler do when none of this works? Switch to the Spruce or the Muddler and cast near drop-offs and submerged boulders. Let the streamer rest a minute, then retrieve it in slow, short strips, with a couple of seconds between each strip. If this fails to work, shift to Woolly buggers or shrimp imitations using the above technique.

Still unsuccessful? Go back to camp, have a cocktail, drink in the scenery and try again later. High mountain fishing, especially for goldens, is never a sure thing. A number of trips I've made were slight excuses to indulge masochistic tendencies.

Fishing for goldens that October afternoon stayed good and special until dark, when I put my rod down and enjoyed a simple meal over a warm fire. Millions of stars came out as the wind disappeared over a snowy ridge. Another good year of fishing was over. When I went back down to the

Random Shots:
The Wanderings of a Montana Writer
valley in the morning, living seemed right and good. The way it should after chasing these golden fish way back in the mountains.

GLACIAL GRAYLING
Flyfishing – 1988

I've been captivated by grayling since the evening I watched very old films of grandparents on my step-father's side fishing for these fish in Alaska. We watched these in the den of their home in Lake Forest, Illinois more than 40 years ago. The flickering black-and-white images of them unloading their gear from what looked like a Fokker single-engine, overhead-wing plane, the wild mountains behind the streams they were fishing with bamboo rods, the blurry scenes of the fish thrashing along the surface when they were hooked and the brief close-ups of the grayling before they were released or whacked on the head with a rock and shoved into wicker creels – all of it. My grandmother fished all over the world in places anglers had never heard of way back in the thirties and forties, but she always said, and her eyes sparkled when she did, that catching grayling in the far north was among her favorites. The fish are unique to fresh water because of their large dorsal fins that are marked with carefree bands of turquoise spots. They eagerly take dry flies, fight fairly well, are beautiful and are excellent table fair, especially when smoked over cherry wood then stuffed in morel mushrooms that are sautéed in butter, dry sherry and minced garlic, then seasoned with sea salt and freshly-ground white pepper. Quite good -especially with sourdough French bread, unsalted butter and a decent bottle of white wine (not Chardonnay, please). I've had many fine and interesting times fishing for grayling. Like when I was working along a high mountain lake shore and

Random Shots:
The Wanderings of a Montana Writer

I started hearing Moon River being played on an organ. I thought that I was having one of my periodic episodes, but rounding a rock bluff I saw a camper with Minnesota plates pulled over on the side of the logging road that hugged this lake. A white-haired woman was playing a Farfisia organ powered by the rig's generator. Her husband was parked in a lawn chair working on a toddy and puffing a cigar. Ah, the good life. And a lake north of long-gone-trashed (all hail Ryan Zinke)Whitefish, Montana that always has nice, sizeable fish in it, though one time a few days after I'd fished It, a ranger discovered a body in a parked car near shore. The guy had apparently committed suicide. Perhaps his last sight of this world was the grayling dimpling the smooth, sapphire surface of the lake as they fed on midges. Perhaps.

THE BEST FISHING FOR GRAYLING is way back in the mountains – far up, sometimes above timberline, up there with the eagles and the clouds. Sure, there is excellent fishing at lower elevations in Alaska and Canada, but I prefer the high country of Montana. Tucked away beneath glacial cirques where avalanche chutes funnel tons of snow and rock down into clear, cold lakes – those are the places.

There is not much time to fish for grayling here. Snow, many feet of it, blocks most trails until mid-July. By late September the peaks have vanished from sight, hidden by dark, boiling clouds that hold the first storms of winter. When the lakes are open, swarms of mosquitoes and horseflies make tying on a #20 pattern a nightmare. Millions of minute insects flying just above the water or trapped in its surface film tempt the grayling. A perfect cast is often rewarded with sight of a maddeningly discriminating grayling sucking in a midge right next to the angler's cautious offering. A person has to be persistent, lucky and, most of all, driven to seek fish under these conditions.

So what is it about grayling that draws ardent admirers back over and over to these outposts of solitude? The scenery, to be sure, but there is something more. There is a magic spell that swirls around grayling.

The first time the power of the fish is felt at the end of a quivering, slender leader, the sight of the dorsal fin slicing through the surface of turquoise water, the shimmering purples and silvers – this, too, is part of the attraction, but only a part. Grayling addiction has many facets, Its grip on the angler, like all addictions, is tenacious.

Montana or arctic grayling (*Thymallus arcticus* for the fish's supposed thyme-like scent) is found primarily in streams, but adapts readily to lakes. The fast-flowing, frigid waters of Alaska, Alberta, British Columbia, Manitoba, the Yukon and Northwest Territories and Saskatchewan have large numbers of grayling, but if you want to find the fish in the lower 48 you'll have to come to the Rockies of Montana, Wyoming and Utah.

The ice ages of North America wiped out most species of fish. The massive sheets of ice ground up everything in their paths. The knife-like ridges and near-vertical cirques of Glacier National Park offer striking evidence of this tremendous gouging action. When the icecaps begin to recede, perpetual winter abated and fish gradually returned. Warm-water species carved out larger and larger territories as the climate warmed. But the grayling were here all along, surviving in near-freezing waters at the edge of the towering fields of ice.

The range of the species was extensive, from Michigan and Minnesota, cutting a wide swath through the Rockies into Utah then well into eastern Siberia.

Over the millennia they evolved into an elongated, muscular shape that was ideal for the fast currents and riffles of the headwaters they prefer. A large, sweeping dorsal fin provides stability and maneuverability, which is helpful during the constant search for aquatic insects and crustaceans, especially fresh-water shrimp. The dorsal fin is the grayling's most distinctive feature with irregular, but clear rows of turquoise spots. Occasional the fin's upper edge is tinged with white or pale pink. The tail, pectoral and anal fins are usually a yellowish color, but the pelvic fins more often than not have lengthwise stripes of black and pink.

As settlers spread westward, the grayling began to rapidly disappear. Outside of Montana and a few portions of Wyoming, the grayling are gone from the Rockies. Grayling used to inhabit most of the Missouri River headwaters, and were recorded by the 1803 Lewis and Clark Expedition as a "new kind of white or silvery trout." The last remaining native population in Montana is holding out in the Big Hole River drainage in the southwestern corner of the state. West of the continental divide the Montana Dept. of Fish, Wildlife and Parks has pursued a policy of stocking the fish in several lakes. Grayling can be raised in hatcheries, but they do better when reared in special lakes set aside for that purpose, then netted for transplant elsewhere.

Grayling naturally inhabit oligotrophic ("Scant nourishment" or "few foods") waters. These are deep, clear lakes that do not have much plant or animal life. Where trout struggle to survive or may even die out, grayling can exist, frequently producing populations that are far too large for their surroundings and resulting in stunted fish. Fisheries biologists have recognized this ability to survive in near-barren waters. This, in turn, has provided a fishery in pristine, backcountry waters that were formerly barren.

"We've given them substitute habitat, and that means lakes instead of streams," said George Holton of the

Montana Dept. of Fish, Wildlife and Parks. "Grayling can withstand low oxygen levels, and thus survive in lakes that would winterkill trout."

Many of these lakes have small, almost indistinguishable, outlets and inlets. This can be a problem because grayling spawn almost exclusively in small, fast-flowing streams. A number of the lakes are stocked annually, the fish sometimes packed on foot or, at other times, dropped from the air (a curious sight as thousands of silvery creatures are disgorged from the belly of a low-flying aircraft).

Most of these lakes require at least an overnight hike, usually up steep terrain. Because mountain weather can turn nasty in a matter of minutes, rain gear and a lightweight tent with a rain fly are necessities. Wood is often scarce or nonexistent, so a dependable (if there is such a thing) gas stove should be brought along. A number of quality pack rods are available that can be strapped to the backpack with only a slight increase in weight.

Most grayling mature by three years (often as early as two). At this age in Montana they are about a foot long. The female lays from 1,000 to 13,000 eggs in a territory defined by the male. No redds are built, but the males vigorously defend the breeding areas, repelling invaders with dorsal fins extended. The fin is also erect when the fish are hooked, perhaps as a display of anger or aggressiveness. Most grayling live less than six years and a fish over two pounds is considered a trophy in the lower 48. The largest grayling recorded in North America is 5 pounds, 15 ounces from the Katseyedie River in the Northwest Territories.

The fact that they survive at all is remarkable. Many waters in Montana are ice-covered in August. Consider a lake buried under 50 feet of snow and another four or five feet of ice, the water black and nearly lifeless underneath.

The grayling more than make up for winter's inactivity

with summer feeding binges. The vision of hundreds of swirls, fish leaping out of the water and crashing back, slurps, plops and gurgles amid clouds of insects, the air literally humming with life, is fantastic. At these times extremely small patterns – #18-22 – tied to 7X tippet are needed. Larger flies and tippets are blithely ignored by the fish. On other occasions a medium-sized woolly worm cast in the middle of a pod of fish will provoke a determined strike, while minute patterns are proving ineffective. It is prudent to carry patterns like the Adams, BWO, Black Gnat, Elk Hair Caddis and Hare's Ear in #14-22 and wooly worms #10-14 in olive and also black.

The fish are gregarious by nature and will feed in groups of three, four or more. Schools frequently work the shore, the rise rings marching towards the angler like some carefree, slightly lunatic infantry battalion.

On this day a frenzy is upon the grayling. No time to be that discriminating connoisseur who delicately sips emerging caddis from a perfectly smooth lake surface reflecting the hot yellows and golds of aspen and larch in autumn, a time when matching the hatch is important. And cast, nearly any pattern works right now.

The attraction of grayling is not only in the fishing. Nor is it exclusively the wilderness experience, that chance to escape the madness of cities and rush-hour traffic. It is also the sound of the fish feeding in the night, the sky blasting starlight on snowfields high above camp. The grayling moving to their own rhythms as they have done for thousands of years.

THE ETERNITY HUNT AT RED BASS LAKE

Game Journal – 1993

The following short story is a compilation of a number of things I experienced over a run of about 10 years. Everything in this number happened, but not in the short span of time covered by these words. Northern Wisconsin is excellent country to play in, at least it was many years ago. My closest friend in high school and I would stay at his family's second home, located on a peninsula above a lovely walleye, musky and smallmouth bass lake lying in birch and pine forest between Boulder Junction and Presque Isle, an area that is considered by many to be the nexus of musky fishing. We'd fish at all hours of the day – at night for walleyes, early in the morning for muskies and we'd wade sandy shores casting to feeding smallmouths. Grouse, deer, lynx and black bear roamed the forest. Geese and ducks dropped in on their way north or south. Eagles and osprey roamed the airways. There were brook trout in really isolated little streams that flowed through and off the Shields country both in Wisconsin and the adjacent UP of Michigan. Those fish were colorful, wild and some of them were big. The days we spent chasing all of this and then drinking beer and whiskey way into the night seemed like they had an eternal life. They didn't. My friend took his life while only in his mid-twenties. I've never been back to this country since. His death worked me over for many years until I finally decided to write this story. When I finished I felt that much had been put in better places and

I moved on from this segment of my life.(My friend's family hate this store and I understand. Death, especially this kind, is brutal, cruel and never-ending). This is not to be confused with closure. I've learned that there is no such phenomenon, either in life or death. I called my friend John Barsness who lives over in Townsend, Montana and asked if he would consider publishing the story in Game Journal. He'd recently become the magazine's editor. A few days later he called me and said that he liked the story a good deal and would use it. That completed the circle I call The Eternity Hunt.

THE DEER WAS DOWN, an easy shot: the animal lying across a tiny spring creek that flowed over a duff of brown, grey and yellow birch leaves, pine needles and moss. After twenty-six months of hunting this one animal I thought the killing would leave me exhilarated, shaking, unable to walk. It didn't just then, though all of that would show up in force later that night. Walking up to the buck, reaching down and lifting its heavy head by the rack, the touch of a cold breeze on my face and the crystal sound of the moving water, none of this felt real. I thought that was surprising back then, but not today.

For someone unaccustomed or incapable of exhibiting patience in situations requiring stealth or the consummate nuances associated with tact, still-hunting whitetail deer in the woods or, for that matter, fly fishing for brown trout, and raising a family, can be fraught with absurdity, craziness and even a touch of layered insight. This realization made its first tentative appearance at Red Bass Lake that crisp, lonely October day in northern Wisconsin more than twenty years ago, the subtle shadings of meaning gleaned from the hunt are only now discernible as I stumble and lurch through the harsh honesty of my forties – the wear and tear of many years well and hard spent don't brook many lies. While I know a little bit more than I did then, that was the first time I understood the interrelatedness of seemingly random events. How a conversation here, falling down in a wet ditch there and taking the fork going that way all added up to right now. Heady stuff for an irresponsible hipster back then, and still a little scary today.

Reaching the point where earthly truths were revealed and a deer was actually killed was the tricky part, made all the more so by two factors: Inexperience as a hunter and cocksure idiocy. I planned to hunt whitetail somewhere in the birch, poplar and pine woods up near Presque Isle just below Michigan's UP. It looked easy in a state where not running into a deer for a period of two weeks while chugging to and fro on daily and nightly errands of little importance is almost impossible. The deer are everywhere, I was informed several nights running by the boys nursing their schooners of Chief Oshkosh at the Sportsman.

For me, local opinion was dead wrong. It simply didn't apply. True, like anyone else who had ever hunted deer in the state, there had been the brain-dead, easy hunts where I walked into an area I knew held deer and waited for the does and forkhorns to come gliding silently out from the woods to feed along the edge of a clearing and then I pulled the trigger. Before the hunt for the buck at Red Bass, I thought this was the game. Not anymore for me, even if it still is for others, The journey to get that one deer nearly finished me as a hunter before I even knew what that meant. Yet that solitary, long-distance stalk covering a raft of whirling seasons, in some maniacal, demented way drove the fever of the chase into me with barbed permanence.

I was familiar with the country around Presque Isle. Had been for years. A friend owned a place on a narrow peninsula jutting out into a small lake filled with walleye that later gave way to the ravenous attentions of muskies. The predators found their way into the water via a new culvert connecting with Red Bass Lake. The large metal tube bridged a soggy gap between the two waters providing an excellent food source for the muskies and a swift end to some fine walleye fishing. This was upsetting, but I quickly learned to take my fishing where and how I found it and the muskies of Red Bass were large, aggressive and wild. No one but my friend and I ever fished for them. There were too many famous waters – Turtle, Flambeau, Rainbow, Spirit River – for serious guides and fishermen to bother with obscure lakes like Red Bass. We'd hauled an old, battered Grumman canoe into the lake, stashing the noisy thing in some cattails that clogged a small cove. We had the place to ourselves along with the ruffed grouse, osprey, lynx and the deer.

Three years into college my friend ended his life with a twelve-gauge Merkel for his own sad reasons. No one wanted the gun. I was offered the piece but declined. Too weird for me, but I kept coming back to Presque Isle and Red Bass Lake, camping in the thick woods for days on end, catching large muskies on hideous-looking streamers tied on mean, long-shanked hooks and casting an old red-glass Fenwick flyrod. Or I'd spend the day walking through the trees or just sitting by a small fire. I loved the place, but now there was a sense of melancholy emptiness sliding across the surface of the lake. Years ago my friend and I had filled an empty gallon Everclear jug with pennies as a hedge against the time when we might run out of cash for burgers and beer. I'd retrieved that heavy jar and set it in the hollow of an old stump.

One day staring at the copper coins got the better of me. I filled my pockets with the things, bound and determined to head into town and have numerous memorial drinks to my friend. (A sad state of mind, but we all arrive here sooner or later.) Coat and jean pockets bulged with god-knows-how-many-pounds of the things. I lurched down the faint trail like Jacob Marley's ghost (or my friend's?) towards the truck. Working up a slight rise, I tripped over a root, feel in a heap and rolled like a set of deranged barbells down into a wet, leafy gully, winding up face first in a rotting-black-mud bottomed creek bed.

Rising up on my elbows I thought "Oh shit. They'll love me at the tavern, especially with all of these damn pennies." I rolled over and out of the water. Lying on the ground looking uphill I saw the deer. A buck, its rack softly shining in the late-day sun, was looking at me, motionless, right foreleg frozen in mid-step. Moist black nose barely twitching, dark eyes focused, the creature appeared stunned at the bizarre scene sprawled before it. I craned my neck for a better view. This motion scared the deer. It turned and bounded away in one motion. On its flank I clearly saw a long, jagged scar, probably from a barbed-wire fence, that resembled the electric bolt on the helmets worn by the San Diego Chargers.

Something clicked in a slow mind. If I could find a buck after falling down, shooting one standing up should be a piece of cake. The rack would look good on a wall and the meat would come in handy during the depths of another cash-poor winter. That was the ticket. I'd come back to this spot for this particular deer this fall. The boys at the bar, after they finished commenting on my appearance and offering various suggestions about what I could do with my pennies, thought this was a terrific idea. "hell, you're already in full camo," they said in reference to my muddied visage. This set off a round of cackling, hacking and wheezing that seemed to last several days. Despite this encouragement, I knew I'd be back.

And I was for a couple of cool weeks in October and for ten miserable, sodden days in November. I never saw the buck. Sign was everywhere. Shiny, black pellets like immature Milk Duds lay scattered in piles along the serpentine trails on both sides of the little creek that was more ephemeral rivulet than honest flowing stream. And there were bunches of them in a small, sheltered area on top of the rise where wild berries grew in thick clumps. I found scrapes on birch and pine trunks where the buck had left his scent and gnawed on low-hanging boughs. There were places where his hooves had torn up the ground in what looked like a free-form, North Woods hockey game. His deep tracks turned the dirt alongside the creek into thick, gooey mud that smelled of gaseous rot, of decaying life. Not far from the lake, the creek widened into a clear pool maybe a foot deep by several feet in diameter. This was where he drank. The marks were distinct. Hooves spread wide as he bent down to the water, those prints were all around the pool. Why here I wondered? Less exposure to predators (mainly man, I imagined) than down at the lake? Whatever. This was a safe place tucked beneath the trees. Shelter. The area provided everything the deer would need. And I was obviously a minor and uncommon irritation or perhaps a passable form of entertainment.

I hunted hard those days. No, not hunted. I didn't know what that involved. The effort, concentration and commitment needed to even begin to think like a hunter eluded me, still does most of the time. I walked a lot learning the lay of this small piece of land. Not nearly as well as the deer, but much better than I ever thought possible. I spent long hours shivering in all the wrong places, though I did see plenty of grouse and the vanishing form of a wild cat, perhaps a lynx. But I never once saw the damned deer. All of the time I was convinced that he was nearby, watching, playing it close to the vest, waiting for me to move on.

The season closed and I almost called a halt to the

proceedings., but something kept driving me, wouldn't let me give up. Maybe it was the spirit of my friend. Who knew? That winter I did plenty of reading and learned a little, especially from a book called *The Still-Hunter* by Theodore S. Van Dyke. Originally published in 1882, a first cursory reading showed that Van Dyke knew a good deal more about hunting than I did, than I ever would. The guy was driven. That was perhaps my first lesson. If you want to embrace anything wild you have to be willing to jump in all the way, to spend the time, to endure the discomfort. One thing in particular leaped off the page at me: I'd been a loud buffoon clanking and crashing around in the woods. I'd never had a chance with this buck. The next summer I'd learn his country much better. I'd find places to hide, to conceal my unnatural form. And I'd work at being quiet. Very quiet.

From June through September I scouted that land hard, learning every dip, rise, moist spot, downed tree, clearing and clump of bushes. I saw the buck twice. Both times at dusk, the animal always sliding away with swift, silent motion. He was larger now. At once there in my sight, then gone. I was convinced that I saw the jagged scar each time. Without that buck, the hunt was a dead issue. Another deer wouldn't do.

When the season opened I spent every spare moment, and there were many back then, walking those woods or holding tight beneath a large poplar or birch waiting for the buck. During midday I paddled the canoe around the lake casting streamers for muskies, big ones, over twenty-five pounds. The fish slammed the patterns. The red glass rod finally exploded from this stress in a spray of splinters when one of the fish ran, stopped, then tore across the surface shaking its head in a gill-rattling display of power. I needed a new rod, anyway. By the end of the season Red Bass was frozen over and so was I. One evening after a hot shower in

Random Shots:
The Wanderings of a Montana Writer

my motel room – black-and-white TV, worn, chintz bedspread, "magic fingers" bed – I wandered up the hill to the tavern for a few drinks and a large, rare steak. I'd had enough. The buck had won. I'd stick to fish and grouse.

After dinner and a few more belts I struck up a conversation with an old boy who was always hunched over the bar working on shots of bar whiskey and a beer. He listened to my story of failure with little expression, sipping the booze and working on a long-necked Old Style. I managed to work in my successful musky exploits.

"Can't kill a damn buck stinkin' up the country the way you did," he said. Want that buck or a god-damned fish? Make your choice. You told me where he is and when he's going to be there," and he paused to fire up a Chesterfield. "Think the damn thing is stupid? You're up there banging around, probably along that little crick and burning wood in a smoky fire like some damned fool from Chicago. Make a lot of damn noise popping the tops to those beer cans, too, I'd imagine. Surprised the muskies didn't turn tail."

A long stare and then he went back to work on his drinks. I was dismissed, embarrassed, angered. I spent the winter, when I wasn't covering sports for the Beloit Daily News in the southern part of the state, thinking. Yeah, I'd think a lot in places like The Turtle Tap, The Zoo Gardens and Pinky's Pub. Next season things would be done right.

That summer I only visited the place twice to refamiliarize myself with the terrain and to see if I could spot the buck. I did on the second trip. He was standing on the rise above the creek in the fading, golden light of sunset. He was larger than ever. The scar had deepened, showing a rough, weathered brown surrounded by tan hair. He turned and looked at me. I said "This fall. This fall for sure. We both left.

On my way out to Red Bass Lake that fall I passed the sheriff's squad car pulled over on the gravel and brown grass along the side of the road. A man was slumped in the front seat, head bandaged. Blood had seeped through the layers of gauze. A county four-by-four was parked just behind, blue and red lights flashing. A handcuffed man was leaning against the Bronco. I stopped to see what was going on. The prisoner was my friend from the bar. Curious business here from the looks of things.

"What happened?" I asked.

"Jake shot the sheriff. He'll be all right, but he's real pissed right now. Give him plenty of room. I got his .357 away from him just in case. Jake's drunker than a skunk. Damn fool said he thought the light flashing off the squad car looked like horns," said the deputy as he headed over to the manacled hunter who was now sprawled on the ground. "Damn Jake used to be a hell of a hunter. One of the best in this country. Said he was going up to Red Bass to shoot some muskies or a big buck he knew about. I don't know which. He never makes sense anymore."

The deputy walked over to his wounded comrade, who was now stomping around and waving his arms while swearing creatively about hunters and where was his gun. He'd be okay. I looked at Jake. My pal from the bar. My mentor. The son-of-a-bitch was going to poach my turf. Couldn't trust anyone in this world. I climbed back into my truck and drove off wondering if this was a bad or a good omen. The rest of the ride to the buck's hold out was uneventful. The October sky was filling with dark clouds. There wasn't any wind. The forecast called for scattered showers later tonight. Nothing to sweat.

There was a perfect place to conceal myself just across and below the small pool. The breeze moved downhill, downstream late in the day. No chance of being winded when the buck came out of cover to feed and drink. I sat motionless, hidden in the brush, had been since mid-afternoon. My back and knees ached, but I focused on the

Random Shots:
The Wanderings of a Montana Writer

spot where I was trying to will the buck to appear forty yards above and through a gap in the birch and brush. He had to approach from there. My rifle was aimed in this direction, resting on my upraised knees and against my chest. All I had to do was sight and squeeze the trigger. Dusk approached and the light shaded down through gold to amber then pewter. Would he show? This time I knew that the answer was "Yes," but still had doubts about what I knew would be the inevitable sequence of this long-running deal.

Already looking through the scope at the gap, I saw the buck materialize. Empty sky one instant, then the animal's silhouette the next. I held my breath, aimed at the shoulder, exhaled slowly, and fired. The sound of the detonating round rocked the still forest. The buck dropped from view in the scope. I looked up and he was down. Motionless. Dead. The gunpowder smell was strong, pungent.

That was all there was to twenty-six months. This vision of the buck and his large rack. The sound of the rifle firing. The deer lying on the ground. The connection between my departed friend, the jar of pennies, falling in the mud and first seeing this buck, the talk with Jake at the bar, all of it, flashed through my mind, all of this noticed but not yet examined or appreciated. This, too, would come later. For now I had a deer to dress out.

BLUE LIGHT

Montana Crossroads Magazine – 1997

With the exception of one individual, everyone that I've spoken with regarding this story asks pretty much the same thing – "Did you really see the blue light that you described in the story?" The answer is "Yes," and it's not a lot of "bunk" as a lady friend once asked. I'm sure that there is some sort of rational, scientific explanation for the light described below. If there is, I don't want to hear it. I prefer the free-from mysteries and magic of the land whenever the powers that be allow me slight glimpses into the true nature of reality. I've spent many thousands of hours wandering about in remote places, especially on the Northern High Plains. I've spent hours sitting on a rock staring at the passing clouds and the ground beneath my feet that is often covered with prickly pear cactus and industrious red ants as I passed the time while my companion/best friend/wife Ginny, waited for the light to shift just right so she could perform her arcane photographic wonders. When you're parked beneath a hard sun and it's a windy 105 degrees you get broken down. This has happened often. Maybe all of these breakdowns have led to a form of submission to the land. Hell, I don't know, but possibly that's why I see this way-out-there blue light and a bunch of other things I have no intention of talking about. Keeping my life between the lines is a sporting proposition and I have no desire to spend my remaining days greased on lithium and weaving baskets in some state-funded facility. As for the one guy (aside from Ginny) who gets this story, the person who has

Random Shots:
The Wanderings of a Montana Writer

seen what I've seen – well, he's a long-time friend and a member of the Blackfeet People living on the Rez just south of the Alberta border east of The Rocky Mountain Front. Like me, he's pretty well nuts. Whenever we get together we just shake hands and laugh. We both know that the cheese slipped off our crackers many years ago. We get the joke and it's a damned good one.

THERE ARE THREE OF THEM alone out here looking like volcanoes that pushed up through the ground of the short grass prairie when no one was looking. Up this way by the Alberta border a hot wind shoves the browning grasses back and forth all day. Distant yellow fields of canola and fading emerald lakes of wheat ripple far south to Shelby and off west to peaks of the Rocky Mountain Front, snowfields blending with the miles of hazy, simmering air. A small pond below camp sparkles clear blue and sunlight flickers from its wave-broken surface, the water spring-fed and cool. Small rainbow trout leap from the surface chasing midges. Dragonflies cruise just above the water hunting down the same insects. In country that seems desolate, barren from a distance, life is everywhere. Yellow-and-white butterflies bounce around. So do grey-and-orange ones. Red-tailed hawks, Long-billed curlews, pelicans, mallards, and nighthawks dip and glide on hot patches of air or curl upwards riding the easy force of lazy whirlwinds. Sharp-tailed grouse kick up from moist draws. Spotted ground squirrels prance about like pets. Badgers growl from beneath the ground when their burrows are approached. Coyotes chatter and howl back and forth around evening. Later, a crescent moon hangs in the sky along with a rising Jupiter and some bold stars not afraid of the moon's brilliance. This land is not dead at all. It is alive in many ways.

The three buttes tower above the prairie, lower flanks covered with Blue Grama, Buffalo Grass and sage. Also, tall stems of Sweetgrass stand in isolated spots. Above this is dark grey almost black igneous rock, consisting of mostly feldspar, rock that rises steeply in ragged chunks and loose sheets for hundreds of feet, formed more than fifty million years ago, the surrounding, softer stone cut away by ice during the Bull Lake Ice Age. The buttes are like miniature island mountain ranges far out in nowhere.

Still the land is alive with a hum that sails beyond electric. The place is sacred to the Blackfeet and they fear for its vast spirit. In a way I know why. Why they feel so strongly about this place. Years ago I saw stick-like figures dancing on the northern horizon at sundown and later that night large trout leaped above the pond taking my fly before it ever hit the water. Wild, unexplainable doings. There is serious power here, not the false juice that comes from owning fancy cars, gaudy jewelry or a big house. The real thing.

Perhaps not for much longer. Rapacious mining interests from both Canada and this country want to level the hills and reduce the pulverized rock with a solution containing cyanide. The greedy bastards are after the gold that lies here in microscopic flakes. The mining industry doesn't give a damn about the heart of this country and what it means to the Blackfeet, people who have lived and worshipped here for centuries. Some of us who aren't tribal members love this place, too. Gold, money, power, conquest. The same perverted steps to the same old, sick dance. Level the Little Rockies. Plan to do the same along the headwaters of the Blackfoot. Destroy this country we're looking at. What's the difference? There's plenty more mountains just over the horizon. Who'd miss these three rising out where nobody really lives? Dead country to the mindless thieves. Except for the gold. That's all the fools can see. The Blackfeet believe, actually they know, that if these hills are cut down the spirits that live here will vanish. They'll fly far away. Imagine going to church, dropping on your knees and praying to a god that no longer exists for you. No all-powerful being to hear your pleas for mercy and forgiveness. Empty doesn't quite get it. No redemption this time around, kid. Try again in the next life, if you make it that far. Maybe the miners will be stopped. For now, there's always hope, but don't bet on it. The industry has lots of money and owns lots of people in all the wrong places. They'll probably get what they think they want.

We sit on the ground and look at the middle butte, watching it change in shape and dimension beneath the moving light of the sun, the grass and rock shining with brightness. Both of us look along the low rises flowing south from the butte. A thin line of blue light, pure blue, shimmers just above the land and begins to explode into bursts of charged clouds of this unreal color. We look at each other. Are we seeing the same thing? Of course. Crazy being crazy we always see the same things even if nobody else does. What's the damn difference. You must believe everything you see before the dream spins real. We turn back to the view from here. Bolts of the light shoot back and forth among these grassy knolls and to our left a darker more intense blue sizzles up the north slope of the butte before rolling over the crest like a swirling storm cloud blowing over mountain a peak. These edges of landscape are alive with the blue. Light fires back and forth between the hills and this lone mountain, wave after wave for hours that seem like seconds and last forever. The light just keeps flashing and then the grass at the tops of the hills shines copper and gold. Flickering beneath is the glow that pulses with a rhythm far beyond any jazz, farther along than any human beat. Time passes in a way and the blue slowly draws back into the earth as the sun begins to set, its light shading the country in soft oranges, reds and purples. Smaller bursts and bolts shoot from the ground and then the glow is gone. For now.

What the two of us experienced, we've never seen before. A shade of blue foreign to art. Unknown to photographers. Out of the reach of musicians. Beyond words. The land resonating with two humans who cannot explain what they saw but will always recognize the light whenever they see it again.

LIVING OUT A DREAM

American Cowboy – 1999

I've known David McCumber for a long time, ever since the first days of Big Sky Journal, a magazine he started. Since then we've become close friends sharing our love and obsession with writing books, Montana, chasing trout and the Chicago Cubs. David is a wonderful writer and has written X-Rated (about the Mitchell brothers and the San Francisco porn industry of the seventies), Playing off the Rail (a book about his fronting a nine-ball pool hustler for several months) and The Cowboy Way (where he worked as a ranch hand up near White Sulphur Springs on the Galt magnificent spread for a year. In 1996 I'd been divorced for a year. I'd sold my home in Whitefish and was wandering the road alone for many intense miles. Finally in August I landed in Livingston for no other reason than the fact that David lived here. At the time he was on the ranch researching his book, but when he heard I'd moved to town (how he found this out, I'll never know) he called and said, "I'm so glad you got out of Whitefish. That place was killing you. Livingston's going to be good for you and you'll be great for Livingston. See you soon." Well, at the time I had no idea what I was doing or where I was, but David's call made me feel, to slightly borrow from writer James Crumley, like I'd come home to a place I've never been. When I interviewed David for this story we were spending the day fishing a little creek on Bill Gault's place. The stream had rarely been worked. The miniature wonder flowed down out of the Belt Mountains and was loaded with rainbows, cutthroat, a rogue brookie or two, and some sizeable browns. We caught well over 100 fish

Random Shots:
The Wanderings of a Montana Writer

between us and enjoyed ourselves and laughed as two good friends do when they are in the middle of great Montana country.

IF YOU WERE A KID growing up in the fifties, at some point you wanted to be a cowboy. How could you not want to be one. Roy Rogers, Sky King and Penny, Gene Autry, pick a name. They were black-and-white matinee and television heroes whose images were as constant as was their shoot-from-the-hip honesty and devil-may-care derring-do.

Yeah, we all wanted to be cowboys, but in our forties?

Author David McCumber had the dream, too. Real bad. It stuck with him from childhood through early adulthood and raged on into those scary forties, but David did more than dream that dream. The guy went out and hired on as a hand up on Birch Creek Ranch in central Montana. Yeah, we all did want to be cowboys with all that romance and horseback freedom. Unfortunately that's all we've got, our fantasies and desires, but McCumber's here to tell us all about the real thing – the romance, of course and the beauty of the land, and the wild, ever-changing weather ... and the work, a whole hell of a lot of work. All day, every day. Now he's got the memories and he's written a book about the experience called *The Cowboy Way: Seasons of a Montana Ranch.*

"I think when you grow up as a kid in America and certainly in the time when I grew up, and particularly if you had some connection within your family with the West, I think it permeated you in a way," said McCumber as he took off his glasses and cleaned them, something he always did while talking, even when they were spotless. "I watched Roy Rogers and I read Zane Gray like you're supposed to, and I've always had a curiosity about ranching.

"As I got older, the curiosity grew stronger," laughed McCumber who grew up in western Nebraska. "There's magic to the openness and that kind of ground has always fascinated me."

The majority of people would probably look at anyone considering the idea of turning cowboy so late in the scheme of things, and then writing a book about the trip as being crazy, pretty well out of it. Birch Creek Ranch owner Bill Galt was no exception. Over the years in the course of managing hundreds of thousands of acres of land and keeping thousands of cattle headed pretty much in the same direction – feeding on protein-rich grasses, not straying too far down brushy creek beds or wandering up into the mountains or off to God-only-knows-where, and then finally to market, hopefully to be sold for a profit – Galt has seen his share of ranch hands. Lazy ones. Drunk ones. Dishonest ones. And sometimes the hard-working, trustworthy ones.

Why Galt and Birch Creek and not somewhere else? McCumber wrote to Galt because he knew his cousin Sid Gustafson (a veterinarian) and he knew about the ranch and the history of the place. Also it was only an hour-and-a-half north of Livingston, where he lived. "It just seemed like the perfect set-up, and so I wrote him a letter and he threw it away," said David. "I wrote him another letter and didn't know he'd thrown it away. He told me later that he had. I wrote him another letter and then I called him and apparently he (Galt) said to himself 'Well, if he wrote me a second letter and he called me, I guess I better give him a call.'"

So everything clicked when they first met, right? Not really. "Nope," Galt said when asked if he thought David would make it after the first time the two met. "He was persistent. I'll give him that. He called me a few times and wrote me some, so I finally agreed to meet him, but no, I didn't think he'd make it.

"I was afraid it was just another greenhorn and knowing he was a writer, I figured he was going to write just another 'green' book, something that didn't begin to understand ranching and was filled with typical 'green' preconceptions."

But as Galt said McCumber was persistent and one gets the impression that the rancher intuitively sensed something about the guy that made him take a chance. When asked what he knew about ranching David replied "I don't know shit," and Galt said "Well, that's okay, a lot of people that come here don't."

Eventually Galt gave David a shot at the work and just like he would anyone else. No special favors because you're a writer, buddy. You've got to pull your own weight or you're down the road.

"To be honest, I thought he was too old, a little long in the tooth," laughed Galt who also is in his forties, but somewhat more experienced. "I could see right off that he was up to the everyday mental challenge of the work and that he was honest, but I was concerned about the physical side of things." He wasn't alone. David had some doubts, also, especially after the first day as he writes in his book:

"I climbed into the bale retriever Fletch and Christian had parked outside the shed after feeding in the morning. It was the vehicle I had started this day in, or rather on top of. As Christian fired it up and started winding our way without benefit of lights back down to the county road, it seemed at least a week since that first hay bale. It had in fact been a little more then thirteen hours."

~ ~ ~

Even from the distance of more than a year and over one-hundred-thousand words, that first day still hammers at David.

"I mean it damn near killed me and I didn't know how

I was doing. All I knew was that I didn't know anything and I was having to learn everything step-by-step with the help of the other hands," said McCumber. "I was way behind everybody. I was older than everybody, and I thought he might think that I'm slowing his operation down. He might think this is just not worth it."

~ ~ ~

The history of Birch Creek runs the course of centuries. One of the bluffs on the property was used as a pishkun or buffalo jump, where hunters would stampede bison over a cliff to a broken-boned death, the remains used for food, shelter and clothing. The Crow and Blackfeet both had traditional hunting grounds in what is now Meagher County. Sioux, Pigean, Flathead, Nez Perce, Bannack and Gros Ventre all moved through this land. The hot springs near the North Fork of the Smith River not far from what is now the town of White Sulphur Springs were sacred to the Indians. In 1805 Lewis and Clark passed near what is now the ranch.

By the early 1920s much of what is presently Birch Creek Ranch was part of the vast Meagher County holdings of the Ringling family, of Ringling Brothers Circus fame. In the 1940s Wellington Rankin, a native of Missoula off to the southwest, and variously an attorney general, justice of the state Supreme Court and United States district attorney for Montana, purchased ranchland totally more than 66,000 acres. In 1951 he bought the 31,000-acre Lingshire ranch, then in 1954 the 71 Ranch, nearly 80,000 acres plus deeded Forest Service land. It was estimated that by 1960 he controlled a million acres of Montana, an area larger than Rhode Island and slightly smaller than Delaware. Rankin was the younger brother of Jeannette Rankin, who in 1916 became the first woman elected to the US Congress. She championed the women's suffrage movement and voted "no" for the country to enter WWI. This led to her defeat in the 1918 Congressional election. She was re-elected in 1940, and once again she voted "no" to enter a major war, this time WWII. The vote was 388-1.

Wellington married attorney Louise Replogle, who made headlines by raiding a Lewistown nightclub and charging the owner with operating slot machines illegally. She and Wellington prospered and when he died in 1966 at 81 he left her six hundred thousand acres. In 1967 Louise married Jack Galt, a cattle buyer and ranch manager. Galt had eight children from a previous marriage including Bill, who was known as an accomplished horseman by the age of 10. He worked for his father for $6.66 per day from well before dawn to well after dark. Bill labored on a traveling branding crew through July, then roamed the vast ranch holdings on horseback rounding up loose bulls and cows and doing whatever was needed. He rodeoed his last three years of high school and made the state finals in saddle bronc his senior year. Bill tried college but commuting from a ranch he and his brother Errol ran in Ingomar 300 miles away proved to be too much so he quit and worked at Ingomar full-time. Eventually Jack and Louise asked Bill to take over the Birch Creek and Lingshire (northwest of Birch Creek) operations and after a decade or so he assumed complete control of the operation from Bill Loney, a rancher who was somewhat of a legend for hard work hardiness. Loney was running a post and pole business plus a spread of his own up by Lingshire so he was ready to let Bill take over Birch Creek.

As David says in his book "...Bill waved his arm around to indicate the corrals and the barn. 'We built all this ourselves,' Bill said. 'The chute shed used to be the calving barn. We built the shop, the scale shed, the corrals, everything.' ... I watched the pride in the sweep of his hand and thought, now I understand a little bit of what I am dealing with here at Birch Creek."

~ ~ ~

It's 7 A.M. on a beautiful late-June morning, the kind that make pushing through the harsh, dark winters seem worthwhile. We push through the door at Dori's Cafe in White Sulphur Springs. The place is already full when David, Galt and I walk in. Everyone knows and respects Galt. He's earned it. He's a straight-shooting, no BS guy who runs one of the most successful ranches in Montana. "How's it goin', Bill?" "Hay in on the Meadow stretch, yet," and so on. Bill greets everyone with a smile, then orders a breakfast of coffee, orange juice, double side of bacon and whole wheat toast. David and I follow the procession with a number of men saying "Hello, David" or nodding and smiling to him. Following an hour-long breakfast with conversation that circles the cafe concerning what a good year this has turned out for grass after a terrible spring, the three of us hop in Galt's pickup and run ten minutes west down a dusty gravel road. The sky is deep blue and cloudless, barely 8:30 and already closing in on eighty degrees. We cross the Smith River which is running clear and cool. Hoppers are flying everywhere and David and I share a knowing glance. "Brown trout," but not right now.

We pull up to the shop and Galt heads over to get the crew organized for the day's work. David is soon lost somewhere inside with Galt so I look around and take a partial inventory of the equipment: four ATVs, three dirt bikes, a baler, two gatherers, two dump trucks, a pair of graders, two cats, four flatbeds, grain truck, two trucks of undetermined use, nine pickups loaded with everything from sprayers to chainsaws to hay to chain to fence-mending paraphernalia to stuff I can't begin to describe, several tractors, four snowmobiles and countless lawnmowers. All of this stuff is used hard and breaks down all the time. Keeping this equipment operational is a full-time task. While I'm writing all this down a whole bunch of other pickups pull up in dusty clouds driven by other hands and local ranchers. They leave a few minutes later in the dust.

~ ~ ~

During the first weeks of working at the ranch David was afraid he wasn't pulling his own weight and that for the sake of the other members of the crew, even the ranch itself, Galt would finally have to let him go.

"I remember two weeks after I started he called the shop where I was working that morning and he says, 'I am going to come by and we'll take a little bit of a drive around the ranch. Why don't you come with me,'" and David wipes his glasses again as he remembers that day. "I thought, oh shit, he's going to fire me. He's going to tell me just as nicely as he can, I'm sure, but he's going to tell me this isn't working.

"So we got in the truck and I was really nervous. I think he could tell that I was and he said, 'What's the matter.' And I said I was afraid he was going to have to let me go because I wasn't doing the job. And he said, 'Oh, no, not at all. You're doing great. You're a hustler. You don't know anything and I can tell that, but I can also tell that you don't mind work and it's all going to work out fine.'"

David sighs in the telling of this, looks up, smiles and says, "That was a huge relief."

~ ~ ~

Galt finally gets the crew lined out and they all disperse to their various assignments. I can't see either David or Bill, but I hear large metal tools clanging on the cement of the shop and the sound of the two talking and laughing. During the course of the year David spent on Birch Creek, he and Galt became friends. They haven't seen each other for awhile so I decide to look for trout in a small creek running nearby.

Looking out over the vast fields of grass, now emerald

in the midday sun, it was difficult to imagine running all of this or even working here. Moving cattle from here to there, keeping the machinery running, pulling calves in March – often the worst weather of the year with rain, sleet, wind and blizzards, branding countless cattle each year and rounding up the many strays that have wandered off into the forest, down the brushy coulees and creek drainages and over the far ridge.

That's what Galt does. That's his life and in a large way it became David's. He learned ranching the tough way – mucking out stalls and equipment; repairing fence in brutal cold, wicked heat and amid swarms of mean-spirited mosquitoes. And he learned how to irrigate; and to some extent, how to repair machinery, though he never did shake the good-natured nickname of "Mr. Goodwrench" that Galt had for him. He learned that staying with something hour after hour, day after day is what ranch work and most of life is all about. In his year at Birch Creek David learned a lot.

"After a month I saw that he was a good worker. He wanted to work and it just went uphill from there. The best thing was his work ethic, that he liked what he was doing and that he was honest," again Galt stresses the importance of honesty in a worker on his ranch. "People around here assumed that David was just an observer on the ranch. Even today they don't believe he was actually working.

"Well, they're wrong," Galt said with vehemence. "He was every bit the good worker, the ranch hand. David literally became a rancher from the ground up. He lost his preconceptions about ranching."

David and his wife, Sarah Greene, are gone from Livingston for now. They're off researching another book. Another dream, I guess you could say. They are circumnavigating the Lower 48 States in a 1959 Ford Edsel Ranger and the last I heard they were looking for a replacement fuel pump for the old rig somewhere in Texas.

Random Shots:
The Wanderings of a Montana Writer

They'll find it and they'll make it, and just thinking about this latest adventure recalls to mind something that David said about ranch work just before he hit the road in the Edsel. Something that should apply to all of us.

"So, a lot of what you learn is to clean up your own messes and you pay attention to what you're doing, pay attention to what everybody else is doing," he said. "You help wherever you can and you help other people and that's pretty much it."

STOCK TANK DELUSIONS

Santa Fean – 2002

I was studying in the creative writing program at Beloit College in Wisconsin in 1971. The place was fast track then if you had Bob "I left my heart in Amarillo" Ray for your faculty advisor. Just to pass one of courses you had to bang out about 40,000 words. If the stuff managed to have any style and coherency, so much the better. After class on warm afternoons he and I would sit on his patio talking writing, drinking tequila and having contests to see who could kill the most flies. Not exactly what you see in the super-accurate movies about the writing life, but that's how it was back then in Beloit. The school was crazy. Perhaps 900 students on campus loaded on LSD. Bands like Cream, Zappa, Mose Allison and the Airplane passing through and so on. At the conclusion of the winter trimester a friend and I drove down to the Grand Canyon in my bright-yellow, convertible Scout. She was eager to meet up with her boyfriend who was also in the writing routine at Beloit, but was taking a break and working for the Park Service. After a three-day run we reached Bright Angel Lodge. My friends had their reunion and I had a few beers. The next morning we drove down a two-track for 17 miles to the head of Bass Trail. The canyon country knocked me out – the size of the place, the riotous shadings of the rock, the enormous, roaring silence. This was before millions of people descended on the country and before California pollution choked the canyon. We spent a couple of days at the bottom along the Colorado River, then my friends decided to make the 12-mile hike back to the South

Random Shots:
The Wanderings of a Montana Writer

Rim. I told them I was going to hang out for a couple of more days down beneath the immense walls and cliffs by myself. Nearly two weeks later I returned to the real world. I'd spent the time down in that eternal place wandering the Tonto trail that ran along the cliffs 1,000 feet above my camp located on a sandy beach, eating peyote, sipping some Jack Daniels, reading Faulkner (*Light in August, Mosquitoes* and *The Hamlet*) and catching carp on doughballs with a bamboo fly rod (God forgive me). I'd thought ahead and left a six-pack of Pabst in an old cattle watering tank that was steadily replenished with icy, clear water by a windmill standing on a small hill nearby at the top of the trail. Never has beer tasted so good. That stint in the canyon opened my eyes some and this story, written 30 years later, is a result of that adventure.

DAMN HOT. LATE APRIL. LOW NINETIES. I'd been wandering around the red sand flat a 1,000 feet below the South Rim of the Canyon during the morning then struggled back up the trail in the growing heat. Heading down the trail at dawn the sunrise was a good one. Every shade of red, yellow, orange and blue I could image flashed across thin reefs of clouds, the light running hot then fading as it moved along the clouds. At the edge of the plateau I looked down hundreds of feet, down through the next serious cut in the rock that spans millions of years of linear time, down into a dry wash of scrub and jumbled boulders. I stared into that for a long time and watched as dark purple shadows slid across the ground and finally vanished beneath the climbing sun.

Eventually I turned back and started the short, steep climb to my camp. The sun wasn't cutting me any breaks as I walked the last few hundred yards to a stock tank where

I'd parked my old Suburban beneath some pines. My feet kicked up puffs of grey- and ochre-colored dust. I kicked a few desiccated pine cones ahead of me. This place was only a few hours away from the tourista madness of Bright Angel Lodge, but no one ever came here. Too far away. No guided pack trips. No curio shops. No restaurants. And the big tour buses from LA and Vegas would high-center before they lurched too far into this isolated country. The two-track leading in soon degenerates into a free-form exercise in dodge-the-rocks, watch out for the jack rabbits. The stock tank where I set up camp was full of cool, clean water that was replenished by the efforts of an old, rusting windmill. A luxury in this parched land. All the water I would ever need and no cattle. Never had seen one in all the times I'd been here. Not an Angus or a Hereford or, sadly, a long-horn. Loved those Spanish-blooded beasts. At the tank I reached down through the water pulled a cooler from the water and fished around for a can of Pabst buried in the ice. I took a long pull of the beer and then another before looking around.

The sky was light blue burning to white-silver as the sun hammered away. Nothing moved. No wind. No sound. I was alone. The intense light of midday turned the small pines a dusty green and the soil simmered, waves of radiating heat distorting the air making spectral images of the landscape. Well above a small rise not so far away, a pair of vultures circled, enormous dihedral wings curled slightly to take advantage of the thermals. The birds rose higher and higher slicing the sky. Black ghosts against the sharp horizon. I looked away from them and down at my sweat-soaked shirt. My jeans and tennis shoes were covered with the colorful dust from down below.

A fantastic place. The kind of land I could disappear in forever.

I didn't work anymore. I'd Jim Beamed my way out of

Random Shots:
The Wanderings of a Montana Writer

a good job with a small daily up north in Montana, but money wasn't an issue. Every time I considered this financial blessing, Blood, Sweat and Tears' cover of "God Bless the Child" ran through my head. David Clayton Thomas deep, rich voice singing about rich relations and such. Yeah they gave me money to stay lost, way out of sight. I'd blown a "career," and was considered an embarrassment to my clan. Get lost sport. Stay out of sight. Every month enough family cash found its way into my account to allow me to wander the high, dry country of Utah, Nevada, New Mexico and the Kaibab Plateau here in Arizona. I still wrote a story every so often for one of the fly fishing magazines, but that was because I was born a writer, and even if I didn't write I was always looking at things the way we do. Like an x-ray technician on acid. Always seeing things most others didn't, like that blue light flickering across the tops of the trees and shooting electric connections to a pile of crazy rocks not so far away on that rise where the vultures flew. And on and on.

No job. Not too many worries. I'd given up on being a productive member of society a bunch of mistakes ago. Enjoyed the hell out of the people I met on the road. Like the guy at the Exxon yesterday who poured in 40 gallons of Premium Plus for about $600. Took so long we killed off a pack of smokes and a six pack in the process. He was a Cubs fan and liked to fish so it was easy time. Then I drove on down an empty, sunset highway like I'd never been here before and wasn't really here now. A crazy life, but, then, all of it seemed a little nuts when I covered the cops up in Shelby. The constant wind driving all of us over the edge. Ranchers found just driving their Massey Fergusons in endless circles out in wheat fields the size of New Hampshire, or people betting who could eat the most pickled pigs feet in five minutes at The Mint Bar. And I was supposed to write about this. Yeah, whiskey has its moments, but there were a few too many up that way. I finally couldn't take it anymore and the managing editor couldn't either. That was a few years back and now I was here.

Over on the ridge the vultures were gliding low across the rise, banking sharply and coming in lower over a spot near a lone juniper. I finished my beer, secured another and went off to see what the big deal was.

What seemed a 100 yards was more like a half mile. The clarity of the natural situation here had tricked me, but I got there. The birds rose up at my approach, the air moving across their feathers sounding like gentle wind slipping through the trees. At first I couldn't see anything because of the intense light. Then I spotted the body not far from the juniper. I'd seen a few corpses doing the police reporting deal, so this one wasn't something new. And whoever this person had once been, had been here for some time. The dry climate, the heat, the wind and, no doubt, scavengers had cleaned things up. Mainly bones and some ragged, torn clothes. Jeans, shirt, tennis shoes, and a bunch of beer cans scattered around. Schmidt. Used to drink Schmidt, but that was a few years back. Bitter tasting after a couple of cans. Some brown hair still clung to the skull. Beneath one hand was a book. The cover bleached and when I pulled it from beneath the bones the pages crumbled. I could barely make out the title. *Blood Sport*. A little-known classic by Robert F. Jones. I'd had a few drinks with the guy once in Casper and he was alright. A little crazy, a touch surly and a hell of a story teller. We got along for those few hours at least. Never seen him since. Whoever this body had once been ... well, hell, he could have been me. Dying out on the high flats of the southwest full of cheap beer and Bob Jones. I could see it. There'd most likely be a pint of Beam in there somewhere, though if I was involved.

I thought about reporting the body to the police when I

Random Shots:
The Wanderings of a Montana Writer

returned to town somewhere, but decided not to. Dead is dead, and I did not want to interrupt the important course of my life by dealing with the authorities.

I turned away and started back to the stock tank. Halfway there an image of the dead man, perfectly formed but without substance, liquid clear, zipped through me like his body went through mine in an instant with the slightest ripple of feeling, like a very mild shock. Odd I thought and aimed for the cooler.

I set a cold beer on a low, weathered wooden shed that protected the water output for the tank, took off my clothes and stepped over the edge of the galvanized aluminum tank, managing to catch my foot on the edge and splash head-first into water that was maybe 60 degrees. Damn near stopped my heart. I stood up in a chaotic spray and let the sun dry me as I worked on the Pabst. Naked to the world.

Then the vultures blasted in at tree top level moving at a good clip. They dipped towards me. I ducked and could feel the rush of hot air rushing across their two-toned black wings as they roared overhead. The pair dipped down lower, maybe six feet above the ground, before soaring up the rise where the body lay. I reached over the edge for another beer. When I turned back they were gone.

The afternoon was hotter now, the air dead still. Cooking. Lifeless.

I wondered what I'd be doing tomorrow.

FLY-FISHING WITH THE LOST PATROL

Art of Angling Journal – 2003

Since 1998 Ginny and I have been traveling up to the North Country of the Yukon and Northwest Territories researching a book to be published (in autumn 2004) by Countrysport Press called <u>Arctic Aurora</u>, a novel I'm working on called <u>Paradise Lay North,</u> and also a book about the Lost Patrol. At the time I'm writing this I'm without an agent. My last one retired. Some friends have suggested that I'm responsible for this. To me during these calm days agents appear as a gate-keeper waste of time. I doubt this opinion will change. As a writer friend, the late William Hjortsberg, once said to me "Changing agents is like rearranging deck furniture." I like that and he's probably right, but not having an agent is like, to borrow vaguely from Fire Sign Theater, "being nowhere at all." Writing is an insane business (and I'm being generous here). You pull ideas and then books out of thin air, bring them to life, find publishers for them, and then endure snide comments from nitwit critics, most of whom don't have a tenth of the talent, passion or stamina that is required to complete a project. I see that I'm raving once again, so back to the following story. Passion doesn't get it when it comes to how I feel for that vast, insanely free land up north. The landscape is in my blood, in my soul. I'll be sitting in front of the keyboard working on yet another inane fishing article for someone when images of the Yukon or the Territories come flashing out of nowhere. I

Random Shots:
The Wanderings of a Montana Writer
feel the place in my stomach and my heart. Writing about
this land works as a weak substitute for being there.

~ ~ ~

**"All money in dispatch bag and bank, clothes, etc.,
I leave to my dearly beloved mother, Mrs. John
Fitzgerald, Halifax. God bless all."**
          - F.J. Fitzgerald, R.N.W.P – March 24, 1911

L IFE IS ANYTHING BUT COLD or barren on this
sunny, early-September afternoon in the 21st century.
I'm standing in a shallow riffle of the Blackstone River not
far from the Dempster Highway, a rough dirt and rock road
that slices through the heart of the Yukon as it winds its way
from east of Dawson City hundreds of miles north to Inuvik
in the Northwest Territories well above the Arctic Circle.
The road is a wild ride through paradise, through some of
the last truly fine country anywhere. The tundra, brush,
birch and pine trees and mosses are glowing with an intense
autumn radiance that flares briefly before the onset of the
long, dark winter. Purples, oranges. crimsons, yellows,
every color imaginable, shimmer beneath an intense sun
and a clear blue sky. The air smells of approaching cold, the
moving water and the trees, Moose stand shoulder deep in
lakes and ponds munching aquatic plants, huge masses of
green vegetation hanging from their jaws, water streaming
down. Grizzly bears forage on nearby slopes in a late-season
frenzy, the large animals crashing through the willow and
alder. The bears devour berries, leaves and stems. They
aren't discriminate. There is no time for such luxuries.
Grayling evolved over hundreds of thousands of years
swimming in the truly ice-cold waters that tumbled and
crashed at the bases of the mile-high or more ice sheets that
covered much of North America periodically until about
10,000 years ago. The ice will return, and humans will be

forced to move south into more and more cramped quarters, but the grayling will survive in this fierce, fluctuation boundary between ice and green land. The fish's large, sail-like dorsal fin is no doubt an adaptation that helped them maneuver in the harsh currents of the snow and ice melt of the glaciers. This fins serves the grayling well today in this river that flows with speed and power, sapphire elegance. I cast a small dry fly to a seam of current less than 40 feet away and a large grayling arcs above the surface, distinctive dorsal fin extended fully with turquoise spots fluorescing clearly, then crashes down on the pattern. I reach back with the rod and the fish zips and zings in the river, jumps once, then gives up the fight. I bring it to me. Twenty inches and over three-pounds of perfection. Silver purple flanks, turquoise spots, white-tipped fins, all of this intensified as the colors fluoresce driven by the fish's anger and fear. I drop down in the water, twist the hook free and point the grayling towards deeper water. It's power returns quickly and it disappears in seconds.

I stand up and follow the course of the Blackstone with my eyes as it rushes and glides beneath overhanging pines and along its bed of colorful rock and gravel. Then I look up at the mountains rising to the east. Dark pines cover the lower slopes, but a thousand feet above the valley floor the ridges and cirques are treeless, covered only with shrubs, and mosses that flicker in wavering intensities as a light band of clouds plays with the sun. I stare at the purple-grey rock of those mountains and then at the Blackstone and I wonder what it must have been like for Fitzgerald and his men over 90 years ago when no one was around to help and it was so very cold and eerily dark as only the perpetual night of an arctic winter can be. And I remembered a poem by Robert W. Service, the most honest and real voice of this country, a man who lived and wrote of the Yukon at the time of The Lost Patrol. This one is called *The Land God Forgot:*

Random Shots:
The Wanderings of a Montana Writer

The lonely sunsets flare forlorn
Down valleys dreadly desolate;
The lordly mountains soar in scorn
As still as death, as stern as fate.

The lonely sunsets flame and die;
The giant valleys gulp the night;
The monster mountains scrape the sky
Where eager stars are diamond bright.

So gaunt against the gibbous moon,
Piercing the silence velvet-piled,
A lone wolf howls his ancient rune-
The fell arch-spirit of the wild

O outcast land! O leper land!
Let the lone wolf-cry all express
The hate insensate of thy hand,
Thy heart's abysmal loneliness.

Service is truly one of the clarion voices of the North Country and this poem rings starkly real to me as I stand here in the middle of a vast wilderness that dwarfs anything I have ever experienced in Montana. This is like being on another planet with all my conceptions of how reality operates not just suspended but shattered. Anything is possible in this land. I don't think this. I know it. Perhaps Fitzgerald and his men were plagued by something as simple and destructive as voodoo. Not the weird stuff with snakes, candles, manic drumming and crazed zombies raising hell at midnight in some third world jungle, but rather those inexplicable, seemingly-connected, series of events that lead to often unfathomable outcomes. That's the species of voodoo I'm talking about. There have been many instances of this difficult to quantify force in my more than 30 years on the road, both good and bad.

Last year on one of our drives to the north country to work on a book, my companion and I were rolling down a back road in northern Alberta on our way to the Yukon when our 1983 Suburban's engine suddenly quit running. I edge the car over to the side of the road fighting the now defunct power steering. When we stop I look over to my friend and say "Now what?" or something less delicate along those lines. At her suggestion I go out and raise the hood in the universal signal of abject defeat with no hope of rescue and little hope of redemption. I trudge back to the car and sit down, thinking that we will be here for a bit. In less than two minutes orange flashing light ricochets off the rearview mirror. Looking behind we see a tow truck. A what? And out here?

The driver hops down from the cab and says "Good morning. Looks like you two need help. I was on my way into the station when I saw you raise the hood."

Hell, it seems like we always need some kind of help. And by the way "What station?" I look around and see nothing but miles and miles of pine trees, swamp and bugs.

Our savior tries to start the Suburban. No luck. He fiddles under the hood and says the fuel pump is probably shot. Within 15 minutes he's towed us to the station that is a couple of miles down the road hiding in the trees. The mechanic, a cheerful, grease-covered guy, comes out and fiddles his own tune with the Suburban's engine, looks up at us and says "Fuel pump's shot," and smiles. "Nice thing about these old Suburban's (ours was an '83) is that parts are easy to locate, eh. You'll have to wait a bit though, maybe an hour, so go next door and have a cup of coffee. I'll ring over when it's ready, eh."

Forty-five minutes later we are running down the road bound for Grand Prairie. The entire incident took less than

Random Shots:
The Wanderings of a Montana Writer

90 minutes and $100 dollars out of our lives. What were the chances of our breaking down under such fortuitous circumstances? Slim and none more than 500 miles above the Canadian-US border. And to have the repair done so quickly. Even in our hometown of Livingston the whole deal would have consumed at least a couple of days and much more money.

That's good voodoo.

Bad voodoo is when we're driving to an isolated camp we have on the southern flanks of the Bears Paw Mountains in north central Montana and a sharp rock slices the sidewall with a nasty eight-inch gash of our left rear tire, and then a few miles later running and praying our way into Havre, the nearest town, to buy a replacement, a cousin of the first rock does in our spare in a similarly ugly fashion and no one comes by for two days, the nearest ranch being 40 miles away across broken, parched country filled with rattlesnakes and surly arachnids. In all the years of coming her I'd never had a single flat before. The tires we were running on are called Toyo. Rancher friends of mine recommended them because of their toughness and thick sidewalls that all but eliminate sidewall gashes, in theory anyway. So, two flat tires on rancher-endorsed Toyos was unexpected. So we camp in the middle of a mosquito-ridden sage flat in 110 degree heat and try not to go crazy, until long, very long, hours later a cowboy hauling a trailer holding a brace of quarter horses pulls up around 6 A.M. The truck is banged up and the engine rattles and coughs loudly without the aid of a muffler. Sweet music from our perspective in the early morning, dry heat. He asks with a good-natured wise-ass smile "You two havin' a good time over there?" and takes us to salvation, which in this case is a tire dealer, motel room and some delivered pizza.

That's bad voodoo.

So I'm in the middle of the Blackstone River catching

grayling and wondering if The Lost Patrol was nailed by that old black magic or did Fitzgerald and his men make a series of minor and not-so-minor mistakes that added up to failure of the most dire variety. I've experienced, read and heard about so many instances of this voodoo, the word "luck" doesn't quite get the essence of the phenomenon for me, that I believe the power exists. Why voodoo happens in a certain place at a certain time is beyond my comprehension. Maybe as Spalding Gray says in his video *Swimming to Cambodia* who knows why evil happens where it does. Perhaps it's just swirling around our planet and drops down on a whim or at will. Good enough for me. And possibly this is what doomed The Lost Patrol.

The thing is, ever since I first learned of The Lost Patrol some years ago, Fitzgerald, his men and their horrible fate I've wondered about this. And fishing for these grayling in this remarkably beautiful river at a spot where Fitzgerald and his men would have traveled more than 90 years ago had they made their way across the mountains I'm looking at makes me consider this question. I find it difficult to believe that a man as experienced as Fitzgerald could have screwed up so badly. He was a respected, competent Mountie with many years of trekking through the harsh wilderness of what is now The Yukon and Northwest Territories. A number of his exploits were so difficult that it is beyond me how he accomplished them. He was an excellent officer of exceptional discipline and possessing abundant organizational skills, great stamina and high principles. How would, how could, such a man lead such a disastrous mission, one that lesser men had made six times previously? And the word "lesser" is a relative term in this rough country. Mere survival translates easily to tough and resourceful.

Consider Fitzgerald's first posting in the far north, Herschel Island in the Arctic Ocean, about 80 miles

Random Shots:
The Wanderings of a Montana Writer

northwest of the mouth of the Mackenzie River. This post was to be an example of the importance of law and order even in one of the most remote regions on earth. Fitzgerald and the Mounties were up there to show that no matter what the cost , the laws of Canada would be enforced and the native population protected, in this case from the crews of the whaling ships that made Herschel their northernmost home port. The men on these ships were rough, hard-drinking types who introduced the highly susceptible Inuits to alcohol which ravaged the Indians as did the venereal disease and smallpox the crew members carried.

There is something appealing to my imagination when I consider then Sergeant Fitzgerald along with Constable Sutherland and Interpreter Thompson establishing law on this desolate, mossy-covered, rocky island that was constantly awash in gale-driven waves and battered by storms of the fiercest magnitude. It was the least inviting post in the entire Canadian Dominion. In these latitudes for two entire months the sun never rises above the horizon. The closest this island comes to daylight from the middle of November through the middle of January is an eerie twilight where the stars still shine and the northern lights flicker weirdly across the sky. There is no fresh water on the island, so blocks of ice were cut from a small lake in October to supply drinking water. In the summer this lake is unfit for use because it is clouded with sediment and choked with aquatic weeds. The barracks consisted of rude structures constructed of scavenged timber from the whaling ships and driftwood. This frame was covered with sod and the walls lined with canvas. Ventilation was made by punching holes in the roof. Imagine being confined in these huts in the middle of a raging blizzard that continued for long dark days with the temperature more than 40 below zero with only a smoky wood fire for heat and a crude oil lamp for light to read and fill out journals by. Yet within a year

Fitzgerald and his tiny contingent had restored order to the island concerning the whaling crews and the natives. He had improved his quarters to extent that the post now boasted a log headquarters complete with billiard room.

The point of this example is that Fitzgerald was a strong, determined and obviously self-sufficient individual. For a man of this caliber to disappear and eventually perish on a dogsled mail run sent shock waves through the land that are felt even in modern times.

So considering all of this, was The Lost Patrol victimized by bad judgment or by voodoo or by both?

~ ~ ~

The story of The Lost Patrol goes far beyond myth and legend in the Yukon and Northwest Territories. What happened to these four men could happen to anyone who lives in this country. Trappers, semi-truck drivers making the haul up the Dempster Highway in the middle of winter, gold miners, loggers or just someone driving from Dawson City to visit family or friends in the Territorial Capital of Whitehorse 300 miles to the east. Even a small mistake in this place can translate into death. For that matter, no mistakes is no guarantee of survival. As Service says in his poem *"As still as death, as stern as fate..."*

And the Royal Northwest Mounted Police were figures that commanded the utmost respect from men who lived hard, rough, brutal lives. Many of them were outlaws or murderers of the cruelest sort. Robbery and death over huge fortunes in gold nuggets and dust were common before the Mounties asserted themselves. A handful of these men in their red tunics could and did restore order to a gold-boom town like Dawson City filled with 10,000 rowdy, drunken miners, saloon operators, hustlers and whores. Less than two-dozen Mounties established relative calm and lawfulness from Dawson City all the way north above the Arctic Circle at the whaling port on windswept, barren Herschel Island. To cross a member of the RNWMP meant imprisonment or often death. They were the law of the land and all who lived in this region clearly understood this fact.

Sam Steele, a Mountie during the more than 125 years ago summed up the absolute and supreme powers of the Corps in his book *Forty Years In Canada:*

"We had the detestable prohibitory liquor law to enforce, an insult to free people. Our powers under it were so great, in fact, so outrageous, that no self-respecting member of the corps, unless directly ordered, cared to exert them to the full extent. We were expected, on the slightest grounds of suspicion, to enter any habitation without a warrant, at any hour of the day or night, and search for intoxicants; no privacy need be respected."

With essentially carte blanche concerning law enforcement granted as a result of parliament's fanatic concern about liquor consumption, the Mounties were able to tame, as this is a relative term even today, this frontier, a land that is still a wild outpost far from modern civilization.

So, when four men led by Inspector Ftizgerald vanished without a trace the news of this stunned the residents of the Yukon and Northwest Territories in 1911. And even today the mention of The Lost Patrol resonates with those who live up here. What happened to those men nearly a century ago, could happen to anyone in the North Country in an instant today. Death is a natural and accepted companion in the North. The tale of Fitzgerald and his men is not looked upon as romantic or even cautionary. The impact on contemporary residents of the dire fate of that long ago patrol is as real now as it was so many years past.

~ ~ ~

Fitzgerald had no way of knowing how many miles it is to Fort McPherson from far out here in the middle of the brutal weather that is the anthem of winter above the Arctic Circle. (Much of what follows I discovered through several days research at the wonderful Dawson City Museum. The rest is informed conjecture based on a lifetime of poor decisions, bad judgment and my own peculiar brand of voodoo.) I've never been as disoriented or so hopelessly lost as he and his men must have been during that winter march over 90 years ago. There have been times when I was unsure of where I was for several hours and found myself, for example, on a high, vertiginous ridge looking down at a mountain cirque lake where I had planned to camp. But situations such as this occurred for me in the relatively halcyon weather of summer or early autumn and not in the heart of a savage arctic winter. The Lost Patrol's condition must have been at once terrifying and maddening. Is the shelter and warmth of the fort just a few miles distant, perhaps around that sweeping bend to the north? Inspector Francis "Frank" J. Fitzgerald of the Royal Northwest Mounted Police was likely beyond the point of being concerned about the bitter cold. After a withering battle against minus 64 degree temperatures, blizzards, fierce winds, starvation, desperation that comes from being totally lost in country so untamed, so unexplored as to seem alien, he and his men had trudged through these last days beneath dense stands of trees, through dead brush and across snow encrusted sweeps of shattered rock more than likely as men who understood that they were doomed to this ice-bound hell for eternity. His mind was no doubt numbed, staggered. His hands and feet were frozen stumps, the skin turned a ragged red and black from extreme frostbite. The wind howled down the steep slopes of the mountains above him. Barren peaks flashed in and out of dark grey-silver clouds, plumes of ice crystals streamed from the summits

Random Shots:
The Wanderings of a Montana Writer

like ghosts for hundreds of yards as the gale screams both above him in an almost subliminal wail and into his chest as the wind cuts through the trees in an unwashed roar. There have been times when I've been working vast wheat fields reduced to rough stubble in late November, trudging these wide-open tracts on the northern high plains looking for late-season sharp-tailed grouse when a sudden winter storm roars down from the arctic, blasts across the nearby Alberta border and cuts through my wax-cotton coat, wool sweater, flannel shirt and silk long-underwear like a knife blade of the purest ice. From nearly sweaty-warm to frozen hypothermic in mere minutes out in this exposed situation is brutal, but I have the warmth of my Suburban, visible less than a mile away, to count on, and beyond that a warm meal and motel room in a nearby town. Even with all of this modern opulence, imagining how Fitzgerald and his men must have felt when they were trapped in the middle of a serious Yukon winter is no big stretch for me. I've been there a little more than once. The air of the North Country surely smelled of polar cold and nothing else. Waves of snow swirled through the forest and across the ice-bound Peel River, or formed tight spirals that tear into the trees scattering pine needles and branches. Again, I've experienced this at times when cross-country skiing along the eastern edge of Glacier National Park as winter storms broke down from the Canadian north country with unrestrained and unbelievably cold ferocity. Trees snapped in the icy wind and diminutive tornados whipped between gaps in the forest and along sheer rock faces. Caribou, moose, wolverine, eagle, all of them are probably vanished from sight for The Lost Patrol like they never lived in the arctic, ever. There are less than four hours daylight at this time of year, and that is only a dull illumination like that of dusk edged by a soft silver glow to the south. Billions of stars, a planet or two and the northern lights burned above him in the always-night sky. The aurora spun and whipped in the solar wind, pinks, oranges, greens and delicate blues lit the landscape in the subtlest of shades. The stars shone as they had for billions of years through all of this with an intensity that was bright enough to cast shadows from the trees. The dark shapes thrown by the pines danced grimly about him driven by the wind. They moved as the tree limbs outside my window move now in the windy winter darkness here in Livingston, Montana. He probably tried to rise from his hands and knees but was too weak from starvation to do so. His pain was constant and extreme. I've read enough accounts on dying by cold and hunger to know this. Those two are his awful companions now. He may have crawled across the ground to the body of Chief Constable Sam Carter. Carter's responsibility was to guide Inspector Francis Fitzgerald and his men through the ragged mountains and barren winter tundra of The Yukon and Northwest Territories. He had failed. He was dead as are two others – Constables George Francis Kinney and Richard O'Hara Taylor. The sled dogs have all been killed and eaten in a futile attempt at survival. Even the sled's leather harnesses have been gnawed for sustenance. Now only the Inspector remained.

Fitzgerald probably hooked his arms beneath Carter's armpits and dragged the corpse inches at a time away from the river bank and the long-dead fire. After what seems hours he gave up, exhausted, out of breath and dizzy from hunger, loneliness and the surety of his impending death. He arranged Carter's body length-wise at the base of a large fir tree, feet pointing to the Peel, arms crossed upon his chest. He tore the remaining blanket in half and covered the man with the this. He may have tried to push down Carter's eyelids but the body was already frozen solid in the intense cold. The dead man's eyes stared up at him. Perhaps retrieved a ragged, scorched handkerchief from a pocket and draped it carefully over Carter's face in a small act of dignity and respect for the dead man. If he was anything like most of us, Fitzgerald sobbed in the gale, the emotion sending ripping pain through his frost-burned lungs. And I bet he looked back upstream along the wide banks of the Peel and wondered 'How far? How far?,' then turned back to Carter and whispered through cracked and blackened lips "Ye go with God. Along and fair well." Imagining still further, I see Fitzgerald pulling himself back to the blackened fire ring now largely covered over with gale-swept snow, righting himself into a sitting position, knees pulled to his chest. Fitzgerald then stretched what remained of his bare hands, long emaciated fingers extended out, over what had once been a modest blaze. He rubbed those hands together over imagined flames and felt the almost sacred warmth that comes from a life beyond desperation, a place where the body barely lives in this world and perhaps the soul is already moving to another.

His was a trip other men had made before him, six times between 1904-1910. The others had set out in winter like he had bound for Dawson City nearly 500 miles to south to deliver reports, dispatches and mail. They'd all made the arduous trek successfully, sometimes cold, hungry and frostbitten, but they'd made the run. Those patrols completed their missions and then those men were able to enjoy the warmth, food and nightlife that the gold rush city of Dawson had to offer. But Fitzgerald's patrol was different. Everything seemed to go from wrong to bad to worse and the Inspector, who was a skilled far north campaigner, was no doubt unable to understand the nature of his failure nor was he likely capable of accepting his end. His expedition, he and his men and their final fate would be known forever as The Lost Patrol. I see him leaning closer to the fire now sparkling in his mind and saying to those dancing flames "Where did I go wrong? How did I fail? How did I fail?"

~ ~ ~

Much of human life is dictated by the surroundings we find ourselves in whether that is the dense tangle of people moving about in cities like New York and Cairo, or the agrarian lifestyle of an Iowa farmer or a small village in the Amazon jungle. Big cities equal fast pace. Farm life is slower and in tune with the rhythms of the land and planting cycles. Life in the jungle is subsistence orientated and the tribal members are closely united to share the work. Nowhere is this more evident than in the Yukon and Northwest Territories. I live in Montana, a vast land of mountain ranges, dense pine forests, wild rivers, enormous lakes and reservoirs, the wide open expanses of the northern high plains with its sage flats, coulees and bluffs and always changing, frequently fierce weather. The people are friendly and open, but life tied to the land makes them shrewd judges of character. Honesty and straightforwardness count for much. There are times when I'm way out in this openness that the nature of our awesome aloneness hammers down with such an intensity that fear shows up. In the fall while I'm walking up a brush-choked draw hunting sharp-tailed grouse and I crest a rise and look out upon miles of rolling prairie and salmon-colored buttes topped with nothing but an enormous blue sky with maybe a trio of turkey vultures riding the thermals far above me that I am struck by the magnitude of how insignificant my life and the planet I live on really is – small planet, small solar system on the edge of a small galaxy whizzing through eternity. A frightening realization until after a few days away from all things civilized and electronic I gradually ease back into a more natural rhythm and subconsciously submit to the land. Then the immensity of Montana and the freedom it offers begins to make sense and I slide into a sense of peace and even wonder at the scale of the place.

Random Shots:
The Wanderings of a Montana Writer

Sitting around a fire late at night listening to coyotes do their jazz riff howlings among each other as a full-tilt moon rises above the land while miniature cyclones of sparks swirl above my small blaze, I look to the night sky and the billions of stars and galaxies. The numbers of them numbs my brain. They seem to drop down from the darkness and surround me. Meteors fizzle by overhead trailing a wake of silver-blue sparks. Northern Lights glow instrument dash green on the northern horizon. The coyotes chatter away discussing the evening's activities. This is another world far from the manipulative, plastic television, computer, automobile-driven reality of the world we all know. The land out here above and surrounding my fire is a much grander, more powerful place. There's space to move, think, roam. I never thought anyplace would surpass this.

I was wrong.

The first time I went to the Northwest Territories I was unprepared for the boreal forest that began a few hours north of Grand Prairie, Alberta. I figured this concentration of trees would be similar to that of the western US Not even close. Hour and after hour hundreds of miles of birch and pine swept off in all directions. Cruising at 70 mph in the Suburban, Ginny and I would glide through the wide corridor of the Mackenzie Highway seeing only trees and an enclosed world of limited horizons. When we did top a rise the forest stretched forever in all directions. Never ending. Clouds drifted above the forest pulling shadows with them. Much of this country was located in swamp-like taiga similar to that found in Siberia. This is a place where streams and rivers barely moved, the current was undetectable as the water from snowmelt and rain collects in what amounts to a massive sponge. Slowly gravity asserts itself and all of this water works its way towards the Mackenzie River drainage, or other rivers, and finds its way to oceans like the Pacific and Arctic. By the time this water escapes the taiga rivers, races and crashes through carved rock corridors and plunges over towering falls. But not here in the heart of the boreal forest. Motion, what there is of it, is subtle in the extreme. And 50 feet from the road was a lost world of density and wildness. Biting insects the size of half-dollars and called moose flies roared at us from all directions. Their bites took chunks of flesh from our arms and faces. Fierce country. There was no wind. Only the sound of our car's cooling engine interrupted the total silence. By the time we reached the Territories the landscape seethed and flashed energy. The sky was a charged, glowing blue that vibrated and danced. When we reached Great Slave Lake, one of the largest and deepest in the world, we looked upon an inland sea that again rolled on forever. Waves crashed upon ragged reefs offshore before giving way to a dark freshwater wilderness that heaved and rolled to its own pace. The outlet of Great Slave was The Mackenzie River and the river was six miles wide. Immense country. Beyond anything I've experienced in Montana and this was only the beginning. The land stretched for a thousand miles north to the Arctic Ocean. Mountain ranges, uncharted rivers, lake trout weighing over 70 pounds and living more than 100 years, thousands of grizzlies and polar bears, woodland bison, waves of caribou whose numbers are measured in the hundreds of thousands and more and more. Now I'd thought I'd seen it all.

I was still wrong.

Driving along the Klondike Highway in the Yukon heading west from Watson Lake, bound for the gold rush driven Dawson City we encountered the Liard and Yukon Rivers flowing with a swiftness and power that dwarfed anything I'd encountered in the West. Water powered over gigantic midstream boulders the size of condominiums. Standing waves rose eight, ten feet or more. The rivers

Random Shots:
The Wanderings of a Montana Writer

flowed with such velocity and force that they created a wind that rustled the birch leaves in a downstream direction. The scale of the land was huge. Mountain ranges piled up upon one another in all directions. An enormous geological fault called The Tintina Trench ripped the land apart for hundreds of miles. Lesser rivers streamed down isolated valleys cloaked in virgin forest. The sky was right on top of us, the clouds scudding what seemed only a few feet above our heads. The land was immediate and possessing a scale beyond anything I'd experienced. The rivers were filled with grayling and in some cases salmon making their spawning runs up from the Pacific Ocean. Farther north Arctic Char colored blaze orange and deep purple swam upstream from the Beaufort Sea in autumn. Arctic terns zipped by. Others species we'd never seen perched in trees or hunted insects along the water. When we turned up the rock and gravel road known as The Dempster Highway all of this was amped up still another notch. Moose, grizzly and caribou were everywhere grazing in the arctic tundra, wandering hillsides or standing near the road as we clattered by in either a cloud of dust or a sea of mud. The farther we went above the Arctic Circle the grander the scheme of the land. Vistas continued to expand taking our pedestrian conception of linear time with it. This was all new and crystal clear real. Along well-used game trails piles of rock left my native Dene First Nation People hunters marked forks in the paths or possibly prime areas of game concentrations. Up on a long, wide ridge the trees were dwarf in size and heaved at odd angles by the movements of the perma frost a few feet below the surface. These shiftings and heavings through the years had established a chaotic order in the forest, a varied but consistent rhythm. Farther north mountain ranges became treeless, rolling off both east and west as far as we could see, the distant peaks hidden by dark bands of boiling storm clouds. The wind came in from the north and smelled of the cold and faintly of the distant sea. The rivers powered through first timbered valley floors and then as they coursed more to the north the water pushed across gravel flats still partially covered in ice even in late August with the tundra lining these streams like a natural Persian carpet. And the sky glowed in blues, silvers, golds and whites in hues that seemed otherworldly and alien. In the brief late-summer night when we camped just off The Dempster near rivers called Olgilvie or Peel we'd look up to see the Northern Lights blazing in unfamiliar colors. We imagined we could hear this aurora sizzle and snap in the brief dark. Sounds of large animals tracking through the forest fired our febrile imaginations. A wolf howled. In the morning we saw a timber wolf gliding on the mist not many yards from where we slept, the animal never giving us a glance but well aware of our presence.

And this story never ends. This wild, undisciplined often harsh country is many times the size of Montana. Much of it has not been explored or ever seen by human eyes. And this is the 21st century. Imagine what Fitzgerald and his men experienced almost a century ago and in the middle of an arctic winter. No roads. No people. Nothing but the land. This is the country that those men were forced to deal with and in many ways it was the genesis for the adventurous adult lives they lived. Maybe the natural wildness of this land was always the source of the voodoo.

~ ~ ~

Prior to the disaster that befell The Lost Patrol in the winter of 1910-11, The Royal North-West Mounted Police had run six successful patrols either beginning in Dawson City in the Yukon Territory to the south and traveling north-northwest to the Hudson's Bay trading post at Ft McPherson in the Northwest Territories or in the reverse direction. All of these expeditions followed relatively the same route with minor variations that were dictated by the weather or the chance of finding a more expedient course of travel. In fact, Fitzgerald returned to his Herschel Island assignment, where his duty was to maintain order and decency at the whaling port between the sailors and the native Inuits, with the second patrol led by Constable Harry G. Mapley and guided by natives Sam Smith and Louis Cardinal. The group went by way of Mayo to the east of the accepted route so that they could follow the length of The Wind River. The patrol took 56 days to reach Ft. McPherson, the longest of any in the 17-year history of the patrols. Temperatures dropped so fiercely that men had to wait out the weather for up to four days at a time. Along the way the men shot five caribou and three moose. In addition they purchased 300 pounds of moose meat from Indians they encountered. It is quite possible that Fitzgerald surviving the extreme cold and this groups hunting success coupled with the meat purchased from the Inuits influenced his planning for The Lost Patrol and directly led to the men's deaths. He may have figured that this second patrol handled weather that was as rough as it could get and may have also felt that being able to shoot and trade for game would see his men through the worst of times.

The first patrol encountered similar success, and was also led by Mapley. This initial patrol went northeast until it crossed the Blackstone River just south of where I caught grayling some 100 miles north up The Dempster Highway. From there the men turned east to reach trapper John Martin's cabin, a well-known source of shelter in a land of few dwellings, where they escaped from the cold for the night. Enough cannot be made of the extreme weather this far north in the winter. When temperatures reach minus 60 and the wind blows at over 40 mph the wind-chill reaches minus 150 and flesh can freeze in less than 30 seconds. Breathing through one's mouth can allow the icy air to crack teeth. Even the sled dogs with their thick, matted fur coats were not immune to the danger. Their paws would frequently become clogged with snow and ice that would wear through the skin creating raw wounds that rendered the animals useless. The only incident of note on this patrol was the injury to Inuit guide Little Pete who was replaced at the Blackstone Indian camp by Jacob Njootli. In his report, Mapley may have also contributed to The Lost Patrol's demise when he wrote that the Mounties would have been better off without civilians meaning Inuit guides. Fitzgerald relied on Sam Carter instead of on men who had lived in the rugged mountains and valleys all their lives. Years of experience coupled with knowledge passed on by tribal elders is required to navigate the labyrinth of valleys and mountain ranges than can all began to look the same when a man is lost and approaching panic in this country. Carter's inability to recognize crucial landmarks was instrumental in delaying The Lost Patrol, forcing the men to use up diminishing food supplies.

Carter made his only trip along the route in 1906-07 when he transferred duty stations from Dawson City to Herschel Island. Perhaps key here is that Carter went from south to north and not north to south as Fitzgerald's patrol would do three years later. Landmarks viewed from one direction can look entirely different when viewed from an angle reversed 180 degrees. The men on the Dawson City to Ft. McPherson patrols also had the advantage of a horse and sled to break trail for the first 50 miles. Any time saved under winter conditions can mean the difference between life and death. Fitzgerald did not have this luxury. Based on his experience with this patrol Carter was able to convince Fitzgerald of his abilities to guide the men to Dawson City, Carter's miscalculation concerning the location of Forrest Creek which gave way to the pass over the Wernecke Mountains and down into the Blackstone River drainage was critical. The third patrol's commander A.E. Forrest made these observations concerning this area of the trek in his diary:

"31st Dec. 1906, left camp at 8:30; traveled to head of creek and crossed over the divide into a creek (later named Forrest Creek) running into the Little Wind River; these divides are very low."

"1st January, '07, left camp at 7:30; traveled down the creek to the Little Wind River, and down the river for about two miles and camped."

"2nd, left camp at 8:00 a.m.; continued on down the Little Wind; had a hard time on the glaciers today, the ice being so smooth and the wind so high that it was almost impossible for men and dogs to travel."

"3rd, left camp at 8:30; made mouth of Little Wind River, about 25 miles and camped."

Diaries from the three other patrols seemed to indicate the value if not necessity of having a native guide. Whenever these groups of men ran low on food the native guide was able to head out in even the fiercest weather and shoot several caribou. Fitzgerald's men did not encounter any animals along the way. This is analogous to me working many square miles of the high plains in Montana hunting for my sharp-tailed grouse. Perhaps this is the first time in this part of the state and I am hunting without the aid of my Springer Spaniel. Tramping through the thigh-high native grasses that appear to offer excellent cover for the birds for three long, empty days I fail to flush a single bird. A few weeks later I return with a friend who has worked this country before and we both have our dogs with us. With my friend's experience, his knowing where small springs perk through the dry ground and where clumps of berries grow, coupled with the keen noses of our dogs we limit out each day and flush countless other grouse. Knowledge of the terrain is essential. Lifeless, barren land to Fitzgerald and his men may have actually contained sufficient caribou and moose to ensure their survival.

The rescue/recovery patrol headed by Corporal W. J. D. Dempster, the highway's namesake encountered problems before eventually finding The Lost Patrol on March 24.

"We were now on the slope facing Trail River, and it was getting dusky and hazy, making the outline of the hills very indistinct...dropped down over a bad hill into a stream running in a general northeast direction, but very crooked. After traveling this stream for a couple hours we found that we were on Trail River, but had got on to it much higher than we should have."

Even Dempster's patrol had problems and they were moving through the country with the expanded daylight and warmer temperatures of approaching spring. Again, all of this country looks similar in a confusingly different sort of way. 'That valley and river look familiar to me, but was that escarpment to the left there before?' Fitzgerald may have wondered. "Is this the right turn or is it the next stream ahead?" Mapmakers have consistently erred in locating Forrest Creek and the Little Wind River. Some maps show Forrest Creek as being part of the Little Wind River. Others have Forrest Creek coming into the Little Wind from the north when it actually enters from the west. Even small confusions in such a convoluted landscape can have extreme consequences.

Anthropologist Vilhjalmur Steffansson who was camped along Coal Creek south of the Arctic Ocean had this to say when he was informed of Fitzgerald's death:

"It is always easy to see when a tragedy has happened how it could have been avoided, but it has always seemed to me that so long as you are traveling in country supplied with game, you are safer to start with a rifle and resolution to find food (but without a pound of food on your sled) than you would be in starting with a sled heavily loaded with food and no provisions made for getting more when the sled load is used up."

In other words, prepare for the worst in the North Country and plan on total self-reliance. To Steffansson the mindset of any expedition was of paramount importance. Without the determination to tough it out and rely on one's outdoor skills, any venture out into this country would be hazardous.

What is clear to me after my research and a good deal of reasonably coherent thought, is that Fitzgerald's fatal error was in choosing the inexperienced Carter as his guide instead of a native who was far more familiar with the country between McPherson and Dawson City, and who also was better able to find and track game. Not taking more food than the bare minimum required for a trip that ran true to form on a tight schedule was another major error. Those fatal mistakes led to wrong turns, lost time, insufficient food supplies, hunger and disorientation. Maybe all of this wasn't bad voodoo, just bad judgment. Or maybe the two or one in the same thing.

I think of all of this as I make one more cast along a bright riffle. A large grayling pounces on my fly then arcs above the water in a spray of silver, turquoise and the faintest of indigo. The mountains that Fitzgerald never crossed so long ago provide a sternly beautiful background for the fleeing fish.

~ ~ ~

Staggering blind through the storm whirl,
Stumbling mad through the snow,
Frozen stiff in the ice-pack
Brittle and bent like a bow;
Featureless, formless, forsaken,
Scented by wolves in their flight
Left for the wind to make music
Through ribs that are glittering white;
Gnawing the black crust of failure,
Searching the pit of despair,
Crooking the toe in the trigger
Trying to patter a prayer;

~ ~ ~

Service could well have had The Lost Patrol in mind
when he penned this stanza from The Law of the Yukon.

SECTION TWO

The Environment

BIG SKY LAWYER

ABA Barrister – 1988

This one profiles my long-time friend Jon Heberling. When things turn to baseball, he's a Cardinals' fan, but I've been able to get past this obvious shortcoming. Jon has been there through thick and thin concerning my life. He's also the godfather of my daughter, Rachel. In terms of the law and protecting the environment he's as good as anybody. In the mid-eighties the Flathead Forest released its management plan with the intent of upping its timber cutting (or harvest as the agency puts it) from around 100 million board feet (mbf) per year to over 250 million. By the new millennium the forest, including what little old-growth that remained, would have been decimated. I called Jon and asked what could be done to prevent this. That was the beginning of our friendship and years of hard work appealing the plan. Few people understand the time and effort needed to reign in the Forest Service. There were six of us, led by Jon, fighting an enormous bureaucracy controlled by timber corporations. When all was said and done we had more than 40,000 hours of donated time invested in the project. Maps were interpreted, thousands of pages of documents were dissected, experts interviewed, countless Freedom of Information Act requests had been filed, court hearings held and many strategy sessions were conducted. Along the way some of our phones were tapped, death threats were cast in our direction, private investigators explored our heady pasts, logging trucks ran us off roads and a few shots were launched. But, when we were finished with the Flathead National Forest, less than

93

Random Shots:
The Wanderings of a Montana Writer

10 million board feet were being sold on the forest, much of it never cut. This level is remained relatively constant to date. The fine country is hanging in there, and now Whitefish is a tourist Mecca rivaling Aspen and Vail. We all regret this and wonder if maybe letting the whole place get clearcut would have been a better idea, but that's another story. These days Jon has all but retired but still assists with taking on another large corporation and the asbestosis horrors the entity has visited on the logging and mining community of Libby west of Whitefish. Nothing ever seems to change on the environmental front, nothing ever seems to get better, but guys like Heberling always take their best shots no matter what.

MONTANA IS SPARSELY POPULATED, and with the exception of "population centers" like the Flathead Valley, people are few and far between. The area abounds in spectacular mountains ranges, wild forests, and pure lakes and streams. Glacier National Park, the Bob Marshall Wilderness complex, and the wilderness region along the North Fork of the Flathead River near the Canadian border provide the best grizzly bear habitat in the lower 48 states. Large numbers of bald eagles make an annual migration to McDonald Creek (*note: This no longer holds true. The Montana Dept. of Fish, Wildlife and Parks introduced mysis shrimp into the system. The shrimp out-competed with salmon for food. The salmon population disappeared, and now the eagles look elsewhere for fish.*) to feast on spawning Kokanee salmon in the fall. Grey wolves have made a comeback in the region and there is some speculation that caribou may travel through the area. Native trout species such as westslope cutthroat and bull trout (a species that travels inland waters over a hundred miles to spawn, and reaches weights of more than 20 pounds) live here.

But all of this natural beauty is under attack.

Northwest Montana is logging country and until recently little attention was given to the value of recreation and the wilderness experience. Few had ever questioned the dominant value of timber cutting. The logging community is adamant in its claim of its right to cut the forests without restrictions. Oil and gas interests view the geologic formation known as the "overthrust belt" as a potential source of petrochemicals. Sub-dividers are cashing in on a growing market for real estate in pristine mountain surroundings.

With all of this development came a similar boom in conservation ethic. As more and more people experienced the unspoiled aspects of the West, a rapid shift in public opinion concerning how these resources should be used is taking place.

The main problem is that the Forest Service has been slow to shift its stance in this change in the winds of public opinion. Foresters resent input from the private sector that suggests that they are not performing their duties properly. As a result, decisions affecting the forests and waters of the West are often at odds with the desires and current needs of a community.

Enter Jon Heberling.

A 42-year-old lawyer who practices in the northwest corner of Montana in Kalispell, a town of 12,000. Heberling has compiled an impressive 13-0 record in environmental litigation over the past decade. Impressive all the more considering the lengths he must go to in researching a case. There is no decent law library in Kalispell, so Heberling must either drive 120 miles to Missoula or order documents through the mail from the state law library 230 miles away in the state capital of Helena.

Most of his cases are now handled regionally through

administrative proceedings. "The Forest Service now tries to avoid court because it doesn't want any precedent-setting rulings," said Heberling.

Heberling is among the best in the country when it comes to environmental law, and his number of cases continues to grow.

"I've been involved in six cases concerning logging and no one is cutting any trees yet," he said.

It takes a fairly rugged individualist to survive the climate and often the loneliness of the Montana landscape, but some attorneys have been willing to take the chance. For young lawyers interested in taking this plunge, Heberling offers a bit of advice – don't come expecting to handle complicated or time-consuming cases. "Most lawyers around here are pretty much obligated to do local kind of work – real estate closings, tax returns. It's scaled-down law." There isn't a great deal of competition, either. There are 100 lawyers in the 55,000-resident Flathead Valley or one in 550. The national average is one in 360, according to the American Bar Association. There are parts of the state where the lawyer-to-resident ration is one to almost 24,000.

Heberling isn't the only lawyer taking on environmental issues in the Flathead Valley, but he is the most visible. He is currently working on a lengthy appeal of the Flathead Forest use plan, and its outcome will have significant impact on future forest plan appeals around the country. His work in the struggle was the subject of a timber planning seminar, sponsored by the American Bar Association's Section of Natural Resources Law. In the appeal Heberling is requesting that the Forest Service follow its own guidelines in protecting endangered species, indicator species and related habitat, along with recognizing other uses of the forest besides timber cutting. Winning this type of case takes meticulous preparation, long hours and perseverance.

"We have a chance to preserve something here," said Heberling. " The last of the big-time splendors, and I think this has been a chance to pursue the ideals of the Sixties in a slightly altered form. I've retained my idealism from the Sixties, but it has shifted from a political perspective to one that is more aligned with the idea that humans are entitled to a clean, healthful environment."

The number of attorneys making a living strictly from environmental practice is small. Heberling maintains a comfortable lifestyle by handling enough personal injury and commercial litigation to "keep the boat afloat. His firm, McGarvey, Heberling, Sullivan & McGarvey, specializes in trial practice.

"He's the big reason I came up here in the first place," said partner Roger Sullivan. "I'd done some environmental work for the National Wildlife Federation and I was well aware of his reputation and level of involvement in the state of Montana.

"He's made a conscious decision to dedicate a very substantial amount of time to environmental work. His other trial work, essentially, allows him to do this pro bono."

In his first environmental case in 1976, Heberling represented The Flathead Coalition, which appealed the Flathead National Forest Environmental Impact Statement concerning oil and gas leases. Heberling argued that, in effect, oil companies were being given a blank check in the forest without due consideration of consequences, including the destruction of wildlife habitat and degradation of air and water quality. The Region One Forester, that issues appellate rulings within the Forest Service system, agreed with Heberling's reasoning and found the environmental impact statement was inadequate.

"People come to me who have been wronged horribly

by some corporation...and to right that wrong is very satisfying," said Heberling. "It's very rewarding to see government agencies and the public take a harder look at the values of the area and see things change."

In another case Heberling represented the Montana Wilderness Association in the appeal of a proposed timber sale on the Canadian border on the west side of Glacier Park. The plan was to put roads in a wild area at a $1 million taxpayer expense. He wrote an eloquent appeal urging the court to maintain the area's natural state. The Forest Service ultimately dropped its sale plan and later proposed the area for wilderness.

The son of a former district court judge, Heberling received his bachelor of arts degree at Duke University before graduating from Bolt Hall at the University of California, Berkeley in 1971.

"I guess my interest in law began when I found out as a child that if I said 'I want to be a lawyer,' good things would happen," he said.

An interest in student activism and the "golden age" of rock music in San Francisco drew Heberling to the Bay area. As a law student he worked as a research assistant for the Legal Aid Society of Alameda County, handling bail hearings for people arrested in the streets, litigating student rights in high schools, and assisting in a $28 million welfare entitlement case. Unsure of how he wanted to use his law degree and not all that happy with "America's direction," he left for an extended stay in Europe, living the life of an "academic bum."

At the time, student loans could be used at European universities. In 1972 he received a Master's Diploma in Comparative Legal Studies at Cambridge University in England. His thesis – "A Comparative Study of Plea Bargaining in England and America – was published in the *Anglo-American Law Review*. In 1973 he was a doctoral candidate at the University of Aix-en-Provence in France.

There people who are drawn to the active life of big cities, and there are others who feel hemmed in by concrete walls. A native of Moline, Illinois, Heberling remembers what it was like growing up in a small Midwestern town and seeing acres of open land. The more he traveled in Europe, the more he wondered how things were going back home. Heberling decided it was time to find out. The move to Montana came in 1974 when he decided to try his hand at practicing law.

"Returning from Europe I had a chance to be a blond, Spanish-speaking lawyer in rural California or to try Montana," he said. "I'm from a rural background and didn't want to practice in a big city, so I chose here. He also remembered a backpacking trip he had taken years earlier in Glacier Park and thought Montana would give him the breathing room he needed. He also quickly learned that there was something called old-time Montana hardball – big business versus people's interests.

A classic example occurred in 1982 when he represented 127 homeowners on the eastern edge of the mining town of Butte where the Anaconda Company had proposed placing a large toxic waste dump. Heberling questioned the company's planned dumping process, which would increase the level of air pollution around Butte. He pointed out in court that the respiratory cancer rate in Butte was already 80 percent higher than the rate in the rest of the country.

The cancer rate wasn't higher because they were smoking cigarettes in Butte," he said. The town's reliance on mining for its industry had taken its toll in dangerously increasing the respiratory cancer rate. To raise it any higher would be akin to committing corporate murder. After a three-week trial with multiple expert witnesses, the district judge signed all findings in favor of the Anaconda

Company. Heberling appealed. The Montana Supreme Court reversed, finding that the company lacked a sufficient environmental impact statement for the proposed toxic waste dump. In an effort to settle the case, the Anaconda Company agreed to conveyor dumping, which would reduce air pollution by 75 percent.

Working alone – something you must td when there aren't many other specialists to rely on – Heberling logged 3,000 hours on the Butte case. "Now I get the clients involved. I have them doing document searches, witness interviews. You can't do it all by yourself. I've learned."

For an environmental lawyer in Montana there are basically two kinds of cases – either you fight to keep the land as is, or you represent those companies that want to expand its use. Heberling feels most comfortable helping to preserve the land. Ask him for more anecdotes and he's eager to respond.

His favorite, he'll tell you, is the case of a farmer's fight against Montana Power Company. The case says a lot about Heberling's approach to law. He digs for information others seemed to have overlooked. He calls it "the classic case of an honest, old farmer against the mighty power company."

In 1939 Montana Power completed Kerr Dam at the south end of Flathead Lake (the largest naturally-occurring freshwater lake west of the Mississippi), thus raising the water level six feet. This, in turn, raised the water table in the lower valley at the north end of the lake by over five feet. That put 100 acres of land under water and damaged another 350 acres on the Jess Blasdel farm located two miles from the lake. The case had been pending for 18 years when Heberling stepped in.

"Montana Power maintained that the water on the land was due to increased rainfall since 1940," said Heberling. " This would mean that Kerr Dam did little if anything to destroy the property in dispute. Under questioning the power company's expert agreed with Heberling's discovery that there had been a peak rain period from 1915 to 1920. Given that testimony, Heberling argued, it would be likely that the Blasdel farm and nearby property would have been under water at some time during the peak rain period. "in addition to hydrologic proof," Heberling said, "we found a 93-year-old lady who used to ride her horse along the farm road. She said 'Oh, no, there wasn't any water there back then. My sister got married at the grange hall in 1916 and people parked cars on a part of the farm that is now under water." The jury ruled against Montana Power and the company was required to pay a judgment of $409,000, the largest in the history of Flathead County. On appeal, the Montana Supreme Court affirmed the decision.

It's that love of the land that keeps Heberling in Montana. With his success rate he could probably write his own ticket to any number of larger firms, but he seems tied to the land that he fights so hard to protect.

An avid cross-country skier, Heberling injured his back and has since slowed down his outdoor activities. He's now in the process of examining his spiritual growth. "I'm interested in psychic factors and development of intuition in the law. Trial lawyers talk about intuition a lot – the ability to read witnesses, read people. I believe it's basically an issue of exchanging energies between people and developing an understanding of people's energies."

He used a little bit of that intuition in a case with its own unique twist. This was when he represented farmers whose land adjoined property that developers wanted to use for 225 townhouses, with a golf course and a 240-slip marina, all located next to a 2,300-acre federal wildlife preserve.

"It was the craziest subdivision I'd ever heard of," said Heberling. " In this fragile, unstable wildlife area they were going to float townhouses on cement buoys."

But he had a hunch and he began asking around the

neighborhood. He figured with a wildlife preserve next door, maybe the wildlife wasn't exactly staying in its own backyard, He discovered that during this controversy somebody tore down an eagle's nest and the birds relocated on the developers' property. A neighbor kept a telescope focused on the nest for months, making hourly entries in a journal. Heberling was able to use this journal in his argument that the property was really a refuge for endangered eagles and that the court should not allow construction in the area. The marina permit was denied and the townhouses were shifted to nearby hills.

Sitting across from Heberling can be an unsettling experience. During the course of a conversation he makes judicious use of protracted periods of silence. Gaps that eventually propel an individual into saying more than he'd planned or to examine his motives for being in the office in the first place. Discussions are punctuated with raised eyebrows and subtle expressions of humor that seem to say "Don't you see how ridiculous their position is? Look at the irony of the situation."

Perhaps the most complicated case of Heberling's career centers around his current work concerning appeals of the 1986 Flathead National Forest Plan. This enormous document, along with similar ones throughout the country, are supposed to provide integrated management direction for each resource in the forest. The plans are to be in compliance with the National Forest Management Act of 1976, the National Environmental Policy Act of 1969 and the Endangered Species Act of 1973. A preferred alternative of action, based on an analysis of a given forest's resources, along with past and future management directions, is issued after a lengthy process that includes computer programs and models, surveys and public hearings. The Flathead Plan was the first issued by Region One and drew 39 appeals. Heberling represents Resources Limited, The

Audubon Society and The Swan View Coalition, three groups whose appeals are detailed and comprehensive. The Flathead Plan was the subject of an ABA seminar in Portland, Oregon last year. A large number of Forest Service attorneys attended. to hear Heberling's presentation.

"The plan may be the first one litigated, and I think people are watching both because of the wonderful recreational activities here and because it is the first plan out of Region One," said Heberling. " I think there is a lot of interest because so much of the forest borders Glacier National Park in the US

"What bothers me about the plan is that the Forest Service proposes to destroy fisheries and compromise wildlife habitat, all at a loss to taxpayers (Timber sales return just sixty cents on the dollar according to a 1984 study by The Wilderness Society). The recreation industry already overshadows timber in the area. The Forest Service's own figures show this."

While Heberling is confident about the outcome (oral arguments are yet to be scheduled), he is leaving nothing to chance. He has marshaled experts and concerned individuals into a work force that has conducted projects ranging from studying the effectiveness of road closures in critical grizzly habitat, to analyzing land types on steep logging sites near critical fish habitat, to calculating amounts of old growth timber remaining in the forest.

"When you work with Jon, you work until you drop or until you learn to say 'No,'" said James Connor, chairman of the Flathead Group of the Sierra Club.

"There's no question the guy is brilliant," said Kalispell attorney Jim Vidal. "He is very thorough and his attention to detail is unmatched."

"There are not too many people who could integrate all of the details involved in the plan appeal into a cohesive argument," said Sullivan. "This plan is a major undertaking, but he is always well prepared. In fact, amazingly well prepared. He has a very sharp intellect and it's fun to be around someone like that."

Does Heberling ever stop working long enough to really enjoy Montana?

"Most of my goals are spiritual, I guess – to gain a deeper appreciation of the balance of human energies and environmental needs," he said. The next 50 years will see an unparalleled boom in wilderness interest. There is almost none left in Europe and Japan. Already people are traveling great distances just to come here.

"There will be problems handing the millions of people. The national parks may become largely controlled 'view from the asphalt' experiences, with adjacent national forests managed more for recreational hiking and camping.

"I would much rather see the forest managed more for recreation rather than continue the dominance of roads and clearcuts. Most of the old-growth, large-saw timber has been taken," he said "Recreation management would provide a more healthy environment and economy."

You hear all the time in Montana that nobody moves here to get rich. They come and stay here because of the land and their love for it.

Jon Heberling is proof of that.

PARADISE LOST

Fly Rod & Reel – 1991

Sometime in the dead of winter in 1990 I received a call from Tom Rosenbauer at Orvis asking me if I'd like to come to Chico Lodge in Montana's Paradise Valley in early May. He wanted me to join Silvio Calabi (then editor and publisher of Fly Rod & Reel) and writer Robert F. Jones to both mingle with the participants at the company's annual guides and outfitters rendezvous and to give a presentation/talk on the angler's environment. I said of course, and it was one of the best decisions I ever made. I got lots of free stuff from Orvis (Uncle Orvis has since wisely disinherited me), managed to get to know Silvio a little bit, and began a friendship with the now late Bob Jones that I'll treasure the rest of my life. The night before all of this madness began, I pulled up in the depths a May blizzard. I was muddied, cold and splattered with turkey blood following a hunt down in Tongue River country. A large Meriam's turkey lay chilled and stiff in the back of the truck. Bob answered my knock on the door, introduced himself, acknowledged the dead bird with a smile, built us each tall drinks, and guided me to a chair in the living room of the cabin we were to stay in. That was the beginning of our close, unique relationship. During the days the four of us fished the area's spring creeks for rainbows and brown trout. In the evenings we mingled with the attendees, ate wonderful dinners then retired to the lounge where we, over the course of four days, cleaned the place out of whiskey and most of the vodka. A tip here. Never tell a trio of writers that drinks are on the house.

Random Shots:
The Wanderings of a Montana Writer

This will prove a costly mistake on several levels. During this time we discussed the state of the natural world. One evening after dinner Silvio suggested that we all contribute to a special section in the now departed FR&R for April 1991 that he would call "The Angler's Environment." Bob and I thought that this was a great idea. Silvio's been known to have a few. What follows is my contribution to what is now an annual and much-needed feature in the magazine.

THANKS TO CORPORATE GREED, archaic government policy and public indifference, Montana's world-famous trout fishing could be history in 10 years. Every single major trout stream in the state is threatened, damaged or being destroyed by a murderous row of problems.

The Beaverhead needs water. The Bighorn is gridlocked. The Clark Fork is choking on heavy metals. The Swan is being logged into oblivion. And on and on. From the Big Hole to the Madison to the Missouri, the outlook appears bleak for rivers and trout. At least at first glance.

So what do we do? Turns out there really is value in "fighting the good fight," and there is slight room out here in "The Last Best Place" for cautious optimism.

"Sometimes I have trouble believing the amount of progress we've made in the past couple of years," Jon Heberling, a Montana attorney who devotes much of his time to environmental litigation. "You can't ever let up and I'd like to think we're winning, but even if we weren't, I would be willing to fight for the last six trees on a hill somewhere."

National, regional and local conservation groups have made the destruction of Montana a national issue, one that politicians and businessmen must now deal with. Changes benefiting the state's prime waters are slowly taking place. In some cases the fishing is better now than it has been for decades.

So why all this jive about no more trout by AD 2000?

Here are the ugly answers about water rights, overcrowding, pollution and clearcutting gathered from a miasma of troubles clouding the peaks and prairies.

The Beaverhead is a river of legend, of big fish. And it is a most difficult stream to work skillfully. Brush banks protecting large trout lies appear and vanish in an instant as the current zips your raft along, but then everything clicks for the fly fisher and a big brown takes the fly. Successfully fighting such trout in the fast current is an accomplishment, too. That one special fish can turn into permanent memory, but these trout are disappearing, fast.

Drought is a fact of life in the West. To protect ranches, irrigation rights were granted and dams built to store water in huge reservoirs. The interests of anglers, outfitters and fish come in dead last. Big fish numbers and total biomass are down over 50 percent in the Beaverhead and low flows are why; storing water in the Clark Canyon Reservoir comes first. Dick Oswald of the Dept. of Fish, Wildlife and Parks had to plead for 35 cubic feet per second in the winter of 1989-90. Oswald said it takes at least 140 cfs just to maintain the status quo with the trout. More and more of the fish taken by anglers are big-headed and narrow-bodied, sings that the population is stressed.

"This is a river on its knees and its not alone around here," said Bob Butler, an outfitter in Twin Bridges. "The only way we can change things is to exert outside pressure. To get those who live outside Montana to write and call. The ones in charge of water flows don't listen to state residents."

Compounding the problem, ranchers pull vast quantities of water from the river in high summer when trout need cool, steady flows to survive. But so do crops, and

Random Shots:
The Wanderings of a Montana Writer

it is difficult to criticize someone whose livelihood depends on this water. The feed he's growing in the meadow you just floated by keeps his cattle alive through the winter. And most of us still eat beef, at least once in awhile, don't we?

Hard as this is for us to comprehend, a lot of people don't care about trout or whether they live or die. "They'll always be plenty of fish in that little creek over the draw, and besides "Did you ever get a look at those folks in those rafts? One hundred damn degrees in the shade and they're out there in rubber waders and covered with all those useless gadgets. Nice talking with you, though, but I've got to get back to work now."

Ranching is a respected way of life and there aren't any quick solutions to the water-usage dilemma.

After someone lobs a big rock in the pool I'm fishing, someone else gives me the finger as they float by, and other neoprene-clad souls call me a bunch of dirty names. I begin to wonder if maybe synchronized swimming would be a better use of my energies than fishing on the Bighorn or other rivers, for that matter.

In Montana, fly-fishing has reached plague proportions on some waters. One September day over 100 vehicles and trailers were in the Afterbay parking lot on the Bighorn: dozens of boats were visible in the first half-mile of water, myriad fly lines whizzing back and forth. Through the day we jockeyed for position, avoided collisions and, in general, experienced a contentious outing. I've observed similar scenes of mayhem on the Madison, Missouri and even the out-of-the-way Smith. There are few or no restrictions on most Montana rivers concerning the numbers of boats and anglers on a given section daily. The situation is out of control.

"I defy anyone to say they're not catching big fish, lots of them on the Bighorn," said Dave Kumlein of Montana Troutfitters in Bozeman. "There are plenty of ways to avoid crowds, like leaving very early in the morning or fish off-season."

How about fishing at 3 A.M. or in mid-January, Dave? Sounds doable and like a hell of a lot of fun, and maybe you can even hustle a few sports for these times in one of your slick brochures or on your glitzy website. Most of the trout that I took on my last trip to the Bighorn had flies in their jaws or hooking sores and/or scars from previous encounters with anglers. One fish was trying to pass a hook-and-leader, an ugly sight. Hey Dave, is this what you mean by "quality angling?"

Realistically, the solutions are to raise fees so high that the "average" person cannot afford a guide and to institute a permit system as used in hunting around Montana, or make reservations months or even years in advance. Guys like Dave will be happy to take your order. Each year more water is being bought up and closed off in order to make a private experience for a chosen few.

"I'd be in favor of limiting the number of people on a river. I think we have to do something in order to preserve the experience," said Bill Bryan of Off the Beaten Path, a business that designs trips in the Rockies. "We must realize that there's more to floating a river than just catching fish. The aesthetics are important." Bryan said that some guides now hand out cards to anglers on the Bighorn that list rules of etiquette to try and improve life on the river. The owner of the Royal Bighorn Lodge is trying to establish a scenic corridor along the river to help preserve its character.

So even with all of us clamoring for big trout, there is a little room for hope. We only have to look to the Bighorn and the beginnings of positive change by those who stand to benefit the most – those who make their living from the river.

Montana is known as the Treasure State for good reason. Mining for gold, silver and copper is why most people came here in the first place, and it still generates big bucks. Unfortunately mining also creates tons upon tons of toxic heavy-metal waste in the form of tailings. Undisturbed, these refuse piles do no harm; they merely look and smell bad. But when hard rain falls on this stuff, lethal amounts of metals wash into streams. In the summer of 1989 it happened on the upper Clark Fork, one of the finest fly-fishing stretches in the state. The river had from 1,500 to 2,000 browns per mile, but because adjacent settling ponds couldn't hold the runoff and Atlantic Richfield hadn't yet put in a diversion dam, most of them died. The river has suffered at least seven similar disasters since 1981.

The Clark Fork heads not far below the city of Butte and its famous Berkeley Pit., a hole in the ground a mile wide and 1,000 feet deep resulting from over 100 years of mining. An estimated 185 million cubic yards of tailings litter the countryside for miles in all directions. This is the largest Superfund site in the country, but the river still runs red, orange, yellow and brown with toxic waste during periods of heavy weather. Millions have been spent in studies, but not one yard of waste has been removed.

The Clark Fork is not an isolated situation. Mining has harmed the fishery in Lake Creek, a tributary of the Kootenai River, and his nailed portions of the Blackfoot, Missouri and many smaller streams and feeder creeks. Cleaning up this killing legacy will take billions, but that money just isn't around. The future for many of these waters is dismal.

If there's one problem in Montana that the rest of the country is aware of, it's the clearcutting of our forests. In western Montana, up until recently, the timber industry was unchallenged in its right to cut as many trees in any way, anywhere it wanted. What was once mile upon mile of pristine forest protecting hundreds of watersheds that were home to native species like cutthroat, grayling and bull trout, are now checkerboards of scattered disaster. On the Flathead Forest every major cutthroat or bull trout spawning stream is threatened by cutting schedules in the Forest Plan. Similar fates await the Kootenai, Lolo, Lewis and Clark, basically wherever one looks.

Clearcutting is now mostly done on steep, erodible slopes (all of the easy pickings are pretty much gone). This means that thousands of miles of logging roads, on hundreds of thousands of clearcut acres deliver many tons of sediment to our streams every spring runoff and after heavy rains. Trout eggs suffocate in the muck and native populations are severely decreased. But this is one problem that is changing rapidly for the better. Appeals by conservation groups, grass-roots and national, and overwhelming criticism of massive logging on private holdings of companies such as Plum Creek Timber have reduced the cut dramatically. In the Flathead, where cuts of over 150 million board feet (mbf) were once a way of life, 36.8 mbf were sold in 1989 and 34.3 in 1990.

Change is also occurring within the Forest Service, where Jeff DeBonis, then a timber manager for the agency in Oregon, started the Association of Forest Service Employees (AFSE). This was done to draw internal attention to what DeBonis and others saw as management policy heavily skewed in favor of industry at the expense of forests. DeBonis and the original members faced tremendous pressure and thinly-veiled threats to their careers when starting up the group, but they steadfastly refused to be intimidated, and AFSE is now firmly established and forcing the Forest Service to re-examine its goals.

On private holdings, however, cut-and-run continues largely unchecked. Montana under pro industry/pro development governor Stan Stephens is reluctant to slap hands. A recent disaster on Plum Creek land severely affected spawning bull trout. Montana levied a fine of only $6,000. The state official who investigated the situation now works for Plum Creek.

Protecting habitat on National Forest land on one side of a stream does little good if the riparian zone is ripped apart on private land on the other side. What's needed is a state forestry practices act with some teeth in it. Public pressure is the only hope.

Positive change is happening all over Montana, but with agonizing slowness. Groups like the Alliance for the Wild Rockies, a coalition of grassroots conservation groups, are battling long odds on small budgets. Forest plans are being reworked; industry is beginning to examine its timbering methods; and proposed mining operations no longer receive rubber-stamp approval. Much has to be done and many streams have been destroyed beyond redemption for at least several lifetimes.

"The only reason government agencies and big business have changed is because people make the costs of doing business as usual too costly," said Heberling. "When you force the Forest Service to do a proper Environmental Impact Statement or make it clear to a company that it will be accountable for its actions, then things will be done right. That's just good economics.

"But turn your back and you lose in an instant everything you've struggled years for. Hard work and vigilance are required."

LOGGING & TROUT:
THE CASE FOR JIM CREEK

Fly Fisherman – 1991

In the early seventies I spent much of my time living in a cabin on the shores of Holland Lake at the foot of the Swan Mountain 25 miles north of Seeley Lake. The structure was owned by the parents of a woman I was quite close to. Thirty years ago the Swan Valley had few residents, the streams were full of native trout. Grizzlies, deer and elk roamed all over the place. Across the valley are the Mission Mountains, a beautiful area of jagged peaks, incredible stands of old-growth pine, and pure lakes and streams. The Jim Lakes area butted up and into these mountains. There were at least a dozen of them, some only a few acres, some larger. They all held wild westslope cutthroat. I used to run up there on summer and early autumn days and spend hours hiking, fishing and shooting grouse. Sometimes I'd backpack to the higher lakes and spend a night or two. Along the way up- and-in I'd often see moose feeding while they stood chest-deep near shorelines. And I'd spot grizzlies working along the ridges far above me. Marmots whistled to each other, the shrill sound echoing off the rock and ice. Then in the eighties Plum Creek Timber raped the forest. They left nothing but denuded, eroding slopes, silt-clogged creeks and savaged lakes. When I wrote the following story the company took a lot of heat, to say the least. They invited my editor, John Randolph, out from Harrisburg, Pennsylvania to try and hypnotize him with their BS and new "environmental

113

ethic." *I went along, too. He didn't buy a word of this nonsense. He's from a logging family and knows the game. I'll always respect John for backing me up. One thing sticks in my mind about that day. As we were driving in a Plum Creek van up to the scene of devastation, the company's vice-president of operations in the area reread this article. Next he turned to me and said "You really did a number on us. We had our attorneys look at this with thoughts of legal action, but they said it was bullet-proof. I don't like what you wrote, but I respect the hell out of you for having the guts to do this one all on your own and to get it right." Then he offered me his hand. That was the highest compliment I've ever received for my environmental work.*

DRIVING ALONG THE ROADS of the Jim Creek drainage of the Swan River Valley in northwest Montana is a gut-wrenching, ugly experience these days, not just because of the bumps, potholes and ruts. What was once a beautiful northern Rockies forest that drifted wonderfully silent and green up to the sharp peaks, sheer cliffs, and blue-white snowfields of the Mission Mountains, is now acre upon acre of brutal clearcut, all done in the last few years. The clean waters of this system, including the West Fork of Jim Creek, are now often clouded with silt, and the colorful streambed gravels are choking in the stuff that comes washing down from the logging roads and scarred land with the spring runoff and with each rain.

Clear-cutting and road building in the area by Plum Creek Timber Company have led to a decline in spawning success of native bull trout.

Plum Creek, Burlington Northern's timber operation in the Northwest, is cutting all of its merchantable forest in a cut-and-run program fueled by fear of a possible leveraged buyout and by corporate avarice.

"This is not a sustained-yield program," said Bill Parson, director of Plum Creek operations for the Rocky Mountain Region during a press tour in the area during the fall of 1989. "We are not on a sustained-yield program. We have never said we were on a sustained-yield program, and we have never been on a sustained yield program.

"Let's get to the heart of it," said Parson. "Sure it's extensively logged, but what is wrong with that?"

The excessive logging in the Swan Valley and its effects on trout (in this case bull trout and to a lesser extent, westslope cutthroat) provide a microcosmic view of a much larger problem – logging economics and how they are affecting watersheds, and trout fisheries across the Northwest. As fierce environmental-economic battles rage over how private timber companies and national forest managers treat the land, the cutting on private land continues at a rate unprecedented in history, and trout fisheries are one of the casualties. This is the story of Jim Creek in a small corner of Montana, but it is also the story of the Northwest today.

Bull trout are one of the largest freshwater salmonids in the world and are closely related to lake and brook trout and arctic char. They occasionally exceed 20 pounds, and the average weight of those caught in northwest Montana is about eight pounds. When they make their fall spawning run out of Flathead Lake up the Middle and North Forks of the Flathead River, they may swim as many as 150 miles to reach their natal waters in British Columbia. Unfortunately, in northwest Montana, country that holds some of the continent's finest bull-trout water, every major spawning tributary is threatened by logging according to a 1987 study endorsed by the American Fisheries Society.

Bull trout tried to spawn in Jim Creek last year, but the emerging fish embryos suffocated and rotted in the strangling, quarter-inch or smaller fine sediments now in the stream as a result of improper logging practices. A recent study by the Montana Dept. of Fish, Wildlife and Parks (MDFWP) revealed a nearly 100-percent mortality rate in embryos, caused by sedimentation that deprived the eggs and embryos of life-sustaining oxygen. The study was prompted by complaints in 1988 from a local resident who noticed unusual turbidity in the portion of Jim Creek that runs through his property. Biologists believe that there was a water-quality violation of Montana laws in Jim Creek caused by Plum Creek logging operations in the valuable bull-trout spawning tributary of the Swan River. They brought the case to the attention of the Montana Water Quality Bureau.

Initially the Water Quality Bureau claimed that no violations were found on Plum Creek property, but the study, along with results from studies compiled by the Forest Service and the bureau, indicated departures from Best Management Practices (BMP), designed to protect water quality standards in Jim Creek. (Larry Brown, who initially investigated the matter for the bureau, has since left the agency and now works for Plum Creek). The study documented the near-total mortality rate in the drainage's spawning recruitment. Trout eggs did poorly in the fine sediments produced by the improper logging activities. Not only are they threatened in Jim Creek, but in hundreds of other streams and rivers that are experiencing or about to experience a similar fate in the Northwest due to these negligent cutting practices on private and public lands.

Plum Creek originally signed off on the MDWFP study but changed its position and hired a consultant to review the results. Using the state's own data, and without visiting the logging site to take measurements of his own, the consultant disputed Montana's findings, ranging from population analysis to substrate (gravel) sampling.

Scott Rumsey, the MDFWP fisheries biologist heading

up the study said, "We drew some conclusions some people may not have wanted to see, and we did take a few samples that indicated that maybe two percent of the embryos would survive, but few if any of these survivors will live long enough to spawn themselves. In retrospect we may have overestimated the damage done to the stream; we did find some successful reproduction this fall. But there was a definite adverse impact on the reproductive capability of Jim Creek. Plum Creek hired fisheries-sedimentation consultant Bill Platts to review our data., and he concludes there was no damage. Our study techniques are based on established scientific methods, some of which he has endorsed throughout his professional career, and we'll stand by them."

Region I fisheries manager Jim Vashro supports the work done by his department and adds, "All through the Swans, Plum Creek has greatly accelerated its harvest of timber. They're going higher and harder than ever. Some clearcuts go right to the Mission Mountain Wilderness boundary. No doubt the fisheries are being impacted in other drainages, but it is difficult for us to say to what degree. We can't afford to monitor on a drainage-by-drainage basis."

Bull trout only spawn in a half-dozen or so streams in the Swan River drainage. What are the chances for the fish's survival in the future? Rumsey said of the Swan River bull trout, "We're doing redd counts as an index. The bull trout seem to be holding their own, but we can't predict the future. Four tributaries carry 90 percent of the spawning in the Swan watershed, and right now two have logging on them, and Plum Creek has land on one of the unlogged streams and apparently has plans to log. There has been talk about a land swap, perhaps by the Nature Conservancy, to protect that tributary."

Logging in the Swan drainage is being blamed by many

in the area for the demise of what was once a quality fishery, but that's another story.

Commenting on the effects of Plum Creek's corporate logging in northwestern Montana, John Osborne, publisher of *Transitions,* a monthly compilation of articles dealing with environmental problems in the Northwest, said, "Plum Creek Timber Company is liquidating its forests to finance debt, exporting raw logs mostly to Japan for premium returns. Having overcut its corporate lands, Plum Creek Timber Company is now bidding against smaller mills for public timber from the national forests – and bringing economic and social turmoil to the inland Northwest. Two-thirds of the company's profits come from the sale of raw, unmilled logs, a large proportion of which is shipped across the Pacific to Japan. The corporation pays no income tax on these sales.

US Representative Pat Williams (D-Montana), in a thinly veiled reference to Plum Creek made before the US Senate Subcommittee on International Finance and Monetary Affairs on November 7, 1989, said, "Recently, a major timber company in the United States was split off, sold. It sold under a limited partnership, although it has public stock. It has taken on an enormous debt, as have many other companies to prevent their being bought out. It now needs to finance that debt...It sells to the Orient raw logs off of its private holdings at enormous prices...It then moves east, primarily into Montana, buys up and harvests everything it can in forests in Montana on federal land."

Plum Creek expects its harvest rate to stabilize at 450 million board feet by the middle of this decade, but with its current annual net growth of 210 million board feet, you do not have to be a rocket scientist to figure out the future of the Northwest's forests. And when Plum Creek is done stripping its own lands, lands given to the parent company, Burlington Northern Railroad, by the US government as an incentive to build railroads across the continent in the nineteenth century, critics say the company will put pressure on the Forest Service to make available increasingly large amounts of timber from the national forests, much of it sold at below-cost prices by forest managers.

"Our facilities have an adequate timber supply," said Charles P. Grenier, Plum Creek's vice president for the Rocky Mountain Region, in a May 28, 1989 article in *The Missoulian*. "That presumes the Forest Service and state will put up all their planned volume."

If you don't think that Plum Creek is serious about turning its rapacious attentions to our national forests, consider these recent company expansion projects.

Building a new 55-million-board-foot sawmill in Kalispell, Montana to replace an outdated 25 mbf plant.

Adding 8 million square feet of milling capacity to its medium-density fiberboard plant in Columbia Falls, Montana.

Building a new lumber remanufacturing plant near Spokane, Washington to make laminated posts for export and domestic markets.

Constructing a new sawmill in northern Idaho or eastern Washington where the company has no sawmill. This mill will produce about 45 mbf of lumber annually for export to Japan.

This hardly sounds like a business worried about where it will find its next tree when its own lands have been completely cut. And because of the size of Plum Creek and the large amounts of capital it has to use for bidding on timber, smaller mills in the Northwest are slowly being squeezed out of business. These mills are shutting down because they don't have the cash flow to bid against Plum Creek and other giants in the industry suck as Weyerhaeuser, Champion and Maxxam Inc., which took over Pacific Lumber Co. in 1985 financed with $754 million in junk bonds.

"An article about the construction boom in Turkey recently caught my eye," said Congressman Peter Defazio (D-Oregon) in an issue of *The Runoff.* "Turkey, having devastated its own forests, is importing logs from the Pacific Northwest. Consider, for a moment, the absurdity of the situation. Oregon mills are closing for lack of logs. The cries of 'timber shortage' are reaching a crescendo. Yet, instead of acting in our self-interest, like every other industrialized nation, we continue to allow a few giant corporations to ship the future of our forests overseas. It's stupid; it's bad policy; and it's got to stop."

In one situation paper prepared by officials of the Flathead National Forest, which contains portions of the Swan River drainage, the agency predicted "major shortfalls" of timber and the closure of at least one mill in the Flathead Valley. The agency has promised to meet timber-sale goals, but no one knows how.

In 1989 less than 35 mbf of timber were harvested on the Flathead as opposed to a goal of 100 mbf. And according to an internal Forest Service memo discussing timber strategy, the "Secretary of Agriculture (is) not letting up on the Forest Service's assigned timber targets. RO (Regional Office) strategy is to get enough NEPA (National Environmental Policy Act) documents through the process to meet intent ... Districts have projected 81 mbf."

What this translates into is the fact that Flathead Forest officials realize that they will be unable to complete documents analyzing potential environmental damage from timber cutting fast enough to satisfy current environmental appeals and future appeals brought by conservation organizations including Five Valleys Audubon Society, Resources Limited and the Swan View Coalition, to meet assigned timber harvest quotas of between 100 and 105 mbf. In turn, the amount of timber available for harvest will be greatly diminished. In fact, on the Flathead the level may have been less than 20 mbf in 1990.

The bottom line here for fly fishers and for the trout and other fauna that live on the Northwest's forests is that their habitat is under tremendous pressure to be harvested by giant corporations like Plum Creek. The Forest Service and national legislators will yield to this influence if an equal or greater amount of force is not forthcoming from those, such as anglers, who want to save the forests and streams from destruction. Legislation is cropping up on Capitol Hill with frightening frequency that would gut the appeals process and weaken wilderness-release language, further accelerating the clearcutting.

While many bull trout (and westslope cutthroat trout) spawn on streams flowing through private holdings, if these acres are destroyed by excessive timber harvesting, there may be no future populations of fish moving back downstream to provide sport for fly fishers on public waters.

In an effort to draw attention to the devastation, musicians Bob Weir of the Grateful Dead, and John Oates of Hall & Oates, along with local, regional and national environmental leaders, mountain biked over 200 miles of logging roads in the Swan Valley during August 1990. I spoke with Weir during this time. He looked at the mountains and trees around us, then summed up the timber industry's attitude towards our forests.

"They're monsters – heartless, soulless monsters, and it's hard not to be smitten a little bit when you see a clearcut. The loggers say that there are plenty of trees, that there will always be plenty of trees. Someone said that about the buffalo, too."

LOGGING THREATENS ROCK CREEK

Fly Fisherman – 1992

Rock Creek will always be one of my favorite trout streams – the rugged, timbered mountains it flows through, the sheep that come down from the high country each autumn, the seemingly endless variety of riffles, runs, deep pools, dark glides against undercut banks, challenging fishing for everything from cutthroat to brook to rainbow to brown to bull trout and, of course, the mountain whitefish. Rock Creek is only 30 minutes east of Missoula. Back in the days when I was sort of studying creative writing (after being asked to leave Beloit College in Wisconsin in 1971 for reasons as spurious as poor attendance, poor grades, drinking too much and doing a lot of acid) at the University of Montana, Rock Creek is where I first began to learn how to read water with the help of two fine friends – Glenn West who owned Streamside Anglers back when it was just a little, funky shop for serious fly fishers, and the late Harmon Henkin who was one of the most knowledgeable anglers and kindest men I ever met. And it was on this incredible water that I began to slowly discover how to consistently take trout of 15 inches and larger. Over the past 30-some years Rock Creek has been threatened by housing development, over-fishing, mining and, as always, logging. This is the first of two stories I did for John Randolph at Fly Fisherman on Rock Creek. The second follows in a few pages. John has always held the environment above all

123

else, especially when it comes to fish. The idea of destroying this magnificent watershed for a few bucks enraged both of us. Always will. And for those brain-dead souls out there blaming environmentalists for all of the damage caused by forest fires in recent years, consider this. Seventy percent of National Forest lands that have burned by wildfire are range and non-timber woodlands. On Bureau of Land Management holdings the figure is 95 percent. At the same time the Forest Service wastes close to $80 million annually preparing timber sales that are never bid on by those fun-loving souls in the industry. Give me a break.

IF **SOMEONE SAID TO YOU** that they knew of a developer who planned to put a 12,000-home subdivision along the headwaters of your favorite stream, what would be your reaction?

Joy and happiness?

Not likely.

Anger and despair would be more likely.

Unfortunately (and this is becoming a common word in articles about Western fisheries), such a sad situation in slightly-altered terms is about to take place on Rock Creek, one of the best fishing streams west of the Continental Divide in Montana.

Current management plans for the Lolo and Deer Lodge National Forests call for removing about 60 million board feet (mbf) of timber along the headwater tributaries of this beautiful drainage.. Much of the cut will take place in roadless (until now) country covered in dense stands of pine.

A modest home uses 5,000 board feet and a little division of sixty million equals the 12,000 homes I mentioned.

A large portion of this action, mainly in the form of clearcutting, is scheduled for the Ross Fork, West Fork, Middle Fork and East Fork of Rock Creek, all prime streams in themselves. Many smaller creeks will experience similar fates. Most of this land is steep mountain slope with a small layer of topsoil that is just deep enough to support the root structures of conifers, small bushes and grasses. Log in this terrain and large amounts of soil will wash away during spring runoff or heavy rains, eventually winding up in the watershed.

"Rock Creek is a litmus ecologically for the Rocky Mountains' ability to produce and sustain life," said John Adza who guides on the stream. "If we diminish Rock Creek, we diminish where we stand on the environment. Jeopardizing this water would be like throwing away the ecological handbook."

What effects will all this logging have on the rainbows, browns, cutthroats and other salmonids that swim here? They won't be good. Even an increase of just 30 percent in sediment loads can translate into mortality rates of over 60 percent in emerging fry. In other words, Rock Creek as a quality fishery would cease to exist, at least for several decades. According to studies done on similar drainages in northwest Montana, large amounts of logging, particularly clearcutting on steep slopes reduce affected tributaries to marginal fisheries and the main river suffers significant damage to its fish populations.

The Forest Service counters with some very strong words about protecting Rock Creek, including these from Orville Daniels, supervisor of the Lolo National Forest, during a telephone conversation we had.

"*Fly Fisherman's* values and my values concerning Rock Creek are identical. We don't want to take any risks with Rock Creek. We just won't do it," said Daniels. "We are fully concerned and committed to preserving the water quality of Rock Creek. There is flat out no question in my mind that we are trying carefully to manage Rock Creek to preserve that stream as the quality fishery that it is."

We have all heard things like this before, and then seen a favorite stream cut to oblivion, so I asked Daniels if he would be willing to knock back the volume to be cut if his agency's data indicated that the current planned level would damage Rock Creek.

"If it turns out that the level we have set right now would hurt Rock Creek's water quality, we will absolutely scale back the amount of timber to be cut," he said. "You can quote me on this and hold me to what I have said. Rock Creek will not be harmed."

In talks with another member of the Forest Service, a slightly less optimistic picture appears. In response to mounting criticism of the proposed cuts, the Lolo and Deerlodge forests announced in July that they have suspended all timber sales after 1992, including those in Rock Creek. The Forest Service says it plans to take a new look at Rock Creek and will this include the hiring of an outside expert who will look at the various competing interests on the stream. Among these are fly fishing, floating, grazing, timber cutting, mining and hiking.

While this sounds good, the volume of timber logged during 1992 will be in the millions of board feet, a level that might in itself have serious effects on Rock Creek trout populations.

"Anytime we enter into that country we are required to study the impacts, but we are kind of heading into uncharted territory," said Tom Heintz of the Deer Lodge Ranger District. "Most of the harvesting will be even-aged (clearcut) management."

The Alliance for the Wild Rockies, a coalition of determined environmental groups in the Northwest, would like the Forest Service to do a cumulative Environmental

Impact Statement (EIS) for Rock Creek. In a letter to supervisors of both the Lolo and Deer Lodge national forests the group states:

"We were astonished to learn that there is no single EIS planned to consider the cumulative effects of these disturbances on either Rock Creek or the equally important adjoining roadless wildlands known as Quiggs Peak, Stony Mountain and South Sapphire roadless areas.

"We assume you know this is not a good way to plan management activities especially in such a critical area. We therefore submit the attached request for an expanded EIS on these sales that will consider the cumulative effects of your management activities in the Rock Creek drainage for at least the next ten years."

What is being asked for is a study that will examine the drainage as a complete system rather than a series of individual habitats. The main reason for this is basically that logging in one drainage, or several, may not harm Rock Creek. The watershed may be able to flush away the choking sediments in a few streams, but when tributary after tributary is heavily clearcut, the thousands of tons of sediment will probably prove too much for Rock Creek's waters to handle. Stream braiding will then occur, disrupting established streambeds and places of shelter used by trout to escape predation. Key spawning gravels will be buried. Water temperatures will rise. Oxygen levels will decline, as well as the size and numbers of catchable trout. The situation has happened and is happening in rivers and creeks throughout the Northwest because of extensive logging.

What was requested by the Alliance was an evaluation and full disclosure of the total effects of past (and there has been plenty), present, and the "reasonably foreseeable future" roading, logging, mining and grazing on the fisheries of Rock Creek and all affected tributaries. This would include stream crossings, the ability of culverts to allow fish to pass, sedimentation problems, and impacts on streambed and bank conditions. These seem to be reasonable requests, but in a letter signed by both forest supervisors, the following admission was offered:

"We are concerned that many meaningful tradeoffs would be diluted by the complexity of the analysis and the magnitude of information ...We are committed to and have been systematically addressing the inter-relationships of activities in Rock Creek. However, your concern that we have not clearly conveyed how we are tracking the interrelationships is well-taken."

Daniels added in our conversation that "The complexity I am referring to in that letter deals with the entire system from elk habitat both in the bottoms and up on the ridges to water quality. But let me explain that the water quality analysis for the entire system is manageable. We are willing to work with anyone on this and we understand that we have to have ongoing studies on the effects of any activities up in those headwaters. I am fully concerned about water quality, and as I said before, I will go on record as saying that no harm will come to Rock Creek's fishery."

When I asked Heintz if any minimum widths for riparian zones had been determined yet, he said, "This will vary from area to area and it may be desirable to go in and pull out the old timber in these zones, most likely with cable so we don't muck around in there too much and do some damage."

Riparian zones are those streamside buffers of diverse forest that provide shelter for wildlife (including bankside sanctuary for trout) and help to slow and partially halt the entry of sediment and large amounts of water during runoff or rain. They are natural protectors that can help ameliorate a multitude of sins caused by clearcutting. Most experts on the subject agree that the minimum width of these zones should be at least 100 feet and 200 would be safer. Many sales in Montana have allowed widths of 20 feet (or less) along with numerous stream crossings for heavy equipment.

One of the interesting and alarming aspects of the Rock Creek situation is how little information is circling in public. Had it not been for a tip from a friend, I never would have known about the scope of the cutting planned for the area. The same is true for most of us. Nothing about the cut has appeared in western Montana newspapers or on TV or radio. Even members of Trout Unlimited who signed off on the letter to the Lolo and Deer Lodge national forest supervisors seemed stunned by the degree of clearcutting that was scheduled.

"Yes, I am quite surprised at this," said Bob Whalen, president of the Missoula Chapter of TU. "The Forest Service seemed to be willing to go along with helping to preserve the fishery. I really feel like there should be some sort of cumulative analysis, that we should derive some document that addresses the whole situation, instead of relying on individual environmental assessments for each sale."

Threats to Rock Creek are not new as Carol and Paul Brouha's article "Rock Creek Winds Again (FFM, June 1984) attests. In 1984, Rock Creek was facing the invasion of hordes of anglers eager to try their hand at fishing a stream labeled "blue ribbon" by the state in many of its slick travel brochures. At the same time, adequate management guidelines and regulations were not yet in place to handle the increased pressure, and the resource suffered accordingly. This has been remedied to some extent, and the fishing (and the fish) are recovering.

For the past few years the Forest Service has been unable to get out the cut assigned by agency management in Washington, D.C. The amount of timber coming out of

Random Shots:
The Wanderings of a Montana Writer

Region One has been well under what was ordered. When I spoke with Paul Brouha several months ago, he suggested that there are a couple of possible reasons that Rock Creek is facing this current threat.

"As you know, John Mumma is under tremendous pressure to get out the cut in his region (Region One) and this has not happened," said Brouha, who is now executive director of the American Fisheries Society. Mumma did not want to get into those roadless areas and he left them (unprotected) because he thought the wilderness bill would pass instead of being vetoed by Reagan (just prior to the 1988 election). He hoped it was going to go away." (*In late 1991 District I Regional Forester John Mumma retired after 35 years of service. Some environmentalists allege that he was forced out of the agency because he was not allowing enough cutting on the national forests within his region*).

The wilderness bill that Brouha speaks of was hammered out by Montana's congressional delegation after years of political infighting among just about anyone who had ever breathed a lungful of Big Sky air. Passed by Congress, the measure was then vetoed by President Reagan, some suggest just in time to help then challenger Conrad Burns defeat incumbent Democratic Senator John Melcher, who had pushed for the passage of the wildlands measure.

Part of the timber, the 11 to 12 mbf scheduled to be taken from the Lolo Forest portion of the Rock Creek cut, came about, at least indirectly, as a result of the Lolo Accord> This is an attempt by some, but not all, members of the environmental and business communities to legislate "localized" wilderness agreements. Accords such as the Lolo and the Kootenai to the west are generating as much heat and controversy as the wilderness bills ever did.

So things are becoming spirited in Montana's forests

130

once again, and the streams and the fish will suffer if we don't do something soon. Steve Kelly, president of Friends of the Wild Swan, a member of the Alliance for the Wild Rockies, sums things up.

"As conservationists, we must realize that the fight to protect our native forests will last a lifetime, and beyond. Our children and their children, will fight for wildlands protection. Our job is to leave them something worth fighting for."

And maybe the Forest Service is beginning to move in a more ecologically-sound management direction. When I talk with people like Orville Daniels, I can almost dare to hope that this is so. I don't think you can log 60 million board feet of timber out of that country without serious damage to the fishery and everything else, but let's give Daniels a chance to make good on his words. While we're doing this, let's also make sure we keep a sharp eye on what takes place at Rock Creek.

RUBBER TROUT: THE CASE FOR PRIVATE STEWARDSHIP

Free Perspectives – 1993

In 1993 I attended a conference of writers and economic analysts sponsored by the Foundation for Research on Economics and Environment (FREE) held at the plush digs of Big Sky Resort near the Gallatin River in southwestern Montana. All of us met for long hours over a period of several days. We were ensconced in plush surroundings, wined and dined, treated like we were quite important. We discussed and debated the future directions of managing our wild public lands. At the time I thought that all of this was heady, cutting edge stuff. Several months later I came to realize how wrong I was. What took place at that conference was frightening. We weren't contributing to a "new paradigm" as FREE chairman John Baden, PhD often told us. We were being oh-so- subtly brain-washed. The food and booze, the high-class resort (which by the way is located in the drainage of the first stream I ever fished in Montana back in the sixties when all of this hideously and venally developed land was unpopulated sage flats, foothills, mountain, antelope and trout) and the never-ending discussions broke us down into accepting the party line, at least for a while. Consider this excerpt taken from convert Don Snow's article titled "Lords of Yesterday:" If public lands can't be improved to commercial standards of stewardship and sustainability, at private cost, then they should be removed from commerce. If they can be so improved, then the person who's willing to make the investment should be given lifetime tenure." If you don't pick up on the horrifying nature of this statement, keep rereading and thinking about those words until you do. This is scary as hell. These guys raise millions of dollars for political candidates that buy into this exclusionary hustle. And there are dozens of groups just like them all over the place. The FREE seminar scheduled for the month after the one I attended was to host judges from around the country. FREE had already enlisted a number of attorneys at another conference held before we assembled. I bought into the con briefly and still can't believe that I wrote the following bit of fascist drivel. And I made five-hundred bucks as a reward. I now look at all of my FREE experience as a cautionary and illuminating tale.

FOR THOSE WHO FLY-FISH, the distinction between wild trout and those that are raised artificially in hatcheries is dramatic and obvious. Trout that are bred and reared in the wild are healthier, stronger and more colorful than their anemic, drab hatchery cousins.

For fly-fishers wild fish are what the game is all about. They represent a feral creature that is the product of thousands of generations of natural selection. They are tremendous game fish that provide a many-leveled challenge for the serious sportsman, and they are found in some of the most spectacular, unspoiled country in the world.

On the other hand, hatchery-reared fish, or "rubber trout" as Robert H. Smith refers to them in his wonderful book, *Native Trout of North America*, present all the challenge of department store gold fish. Once hooked, most of them fight with all the intensity of a tennis shoe. Succinctly put, hatchery fish are an anathema to fly fishing.

The notion of rubber trout came up at a FREE conference years ago at Big Sky, Montana, "A New Paradigm for Western Environmental Policy." One of the participants, an economist, suggested that fish and game departments could bioengineer trout in state and federal hatcheries that would replenish or replace depleted trout and salmon stocks in rivers and lakes throughout the country, and further, that anglers would not notice any difference in the quality of fishing. I immediately and emotionally (after all, we're talking fly fishing here) objecting, citing many of the reasons given above. I offer a better solution.

In my corner of northwestern Montana, bull trout, *Salvelinus confluentus,* have been declared off-limits to anglers because of the species' record low numbers. Bull trout are a direct relative of the brook trout with one major difference. Bull trout can exceed 20 pounds. They are superb predators that live in only the cleanest, coldest waters running through our country's wild forests. On a fly rod they are heart-stopping sport as they surge across deep runs in powerful rivers. That pour out of glacier-carved mountains.

A number of environmental groups have requested that the bull trout be listed as an endangered species. At first glance this may seem to be a simple and effective proposal. Looking deeper, two problems appear that go to the heart of the matter concerning game management and the trout themselves.

First of all, if bull trout are declared endangered, they are immediately taken into the federal hatchery system. A number of fisheries biologists I have spoken with concerning this said that bringing the fish under this form of management would render the question of wild versus hatchery bull trout moot. Also, hatcheries are extremely expensive to construct, staff, and maintain, especially in light of the inferior product they turn out. To restore just this one species in one relatively small area of the country would cost hundreds of thousands of dollars per year with no guarantee of success. Hatchery trout are not adapted to survival in wild conditions, which brings me to my second point.

Wild bull trout (or any salmonid species) embody all of the characteristics that fly-fishers treasure in gamefish, and fly-fishers are willing to spend large sums of money in travel, lodging, equipment, and guide fees to pursue wild fish. They will not pay serious money to cast for rubber trout at Billy Bob's Trout Pond and Knickknack Emporium.

Considering this, the solution is obvious. Instead of using taxpayer money to raise an unacceptable product, why not turn over habitat control to private interests? Those with prime streams flowing through their property would be encouraged to preserve and/or restore riparian corridors through the incentive of sportsman dollars. Many fly-fishers would be willing to pay $100 or more per day to catch a ten- or twenty-pound trout, though I'm not one of them.

Those that use public lands, such as private timber companies, would be encouraged to maintain these drainages through conscientious logging practices. The advantages to the companies are obvious. Public good will translates into less resistance to future sales, and this more sustainable form of cutting would provide a suitable timber base for the future. Indeed, the Plum Creek Timber company in the Northwest has already adopted an environmental logging variation of this theme, creating at least a modest shift in public sentiment.

This approach can be applied to millions of acres of public and private lands containing catchable populations of rainbow, brook, brown and cutthroat trout, not to mention salmon rivers or smallmouth bass watersheds. Trout and other gamefish are but one small example of how taking government out of the recreation business may reap benefits for many of us, not to mention the fish themselves.

The possibilities are multitudinous, and a definite improvement over spending taxpayer dollars on rubber trout.

TROUT AND MINING

Fly Fisherman – 1993

There is nothing as devastating as a hard-rock mine or that of an open-pit coal mine where the land is concerned. These enormous scars on the planet's surface never heal. In Montana they are all over the place. The coal mines near Decker in the southeastern part of Montana use equipment that is built on a scale that dwarfs conventional earth-moving equipment. Some of my favorite country is out on the coulee and bluff lands that roll off to the horizon not far from the Decker mines. I wrote a novel about the mining and this country called Hunted in Paradise in an attempt to make others aware of what this form of mineral extraction does to the landscape. The following story is the first of several I did for magazines such as Fly Fisherman (another follows shortly) and the late, great Kinesis. It's about the 1872 Mining Law, and despite outrage and concerted efforts by people across the country, this abomination remains unchanged to date. I realize that anyone reading this section of my articles on the environment straight through will more than likely become overwhelmed with the information and the never-ending threats to the environment. I'd like to say that I'm sorry for this, but I'm not. What is truly overwhelming and depressing is driving around the West and on north through Alberta and seeing mine after mine, clearcuts everywhere resembling some massive, earthly skin disease, and all of the related destruction. If relentlessly banging on people's heads is what it takes to get even one soul truly outraged, then that's what I'll do. Good country is my sanity and

Random Shots:
The Wanderings of a Montana Writer
salvation. Those that destroy it are my enemies.

THEY DON'T CALL MONTANA THE TREASURE
STATE for nothing . Millions of tons of precious metals
have been dug, blasted, and filtered from the ground and
nearby streams. Enough gold has been mined to sink a large
freighter. Much more of the same holds true for silver and
copper. And rarer metals of equal or greater value are now
coming into their own in the eyes of mining company
executives and investors on world markets.

Propelled by the 1872 Mining Act, an act many feel is
nothing more than a federal giveaway program, speculation
in precious metals is undergoing renewed interest.
Everywhere you look these days some mining operation has
its eyes on a mother lode of staggering value. Millions of
dollars' worth of silver ore may be extracted from beneath
the Cabinet Mountains Wilderness by the Noranda Mineral
Corporation. Gold fever is rising again in the headwaters of
the Blackfoot River at the Seven-Up Pete Joint Venture east
of Lincoln. Gold exploration is in the works in a joint
venture by the Canadian firm Manhattan Minerals and
Ernest K. Lehmann Associates of Minneapolis.

So what does all this have to do with trout and fly
fishing? In Montana, and other parts of the mineral-rich
West, nearly everything in some river drainages.

Sloppy disposal of tailings, settling pond failure,
leaching of cyanide into the aquifer, soil erosion – any one
of these can spell disaster for trout populations not just for
a year or two but for decades. Look what has happened
around Butte, once the nation's largest copper-mining
location. Nearby streams are so full of heavy metals that
trout find survival there difficult or impossible. This area
and on west to Anaconda is the nation's largest
Environmental Protection Agency Super Fund site.

Does this renewed interest in mining in Montana mean yet another nail in the coffin of the state's classy trout fishery?

At first glance, quite possibly yes, but there are strong indications, both in and outside of the mining industry, that positive change and serious commitment to our wild resources may avert disaster.

The best place to start (and the most alarming from the standpoint of a fly fisher) is with the controversial 1872 Mining Law that was passed in part to help fuel the homesteading drive in the West that had its genesis in the 1862 Homestead Act. The 1872 law allows individuals to purchase mining claims on federal lands at a price of only $2.50 per acre for placer claims (normally located along stream bottoms) and $5 per acre for lode claims. Purchase prices have not changed since the law's inception.

Where mining claims occur, mineral development, under the 1872 law, is considered the best and most appropriate use of the land. Some estimates place the amount of land sold at greater than 20 million acres. According to the Department of the Interior, the federal treasury misses out on $880 million annually from lost royalties and lost land value, not to mention costs of environmental damage and its cleanup. The US Bureau of Mines estimates that 12,000 miles of streams have contaminated water from past mining activity, not including adjacent habitat destruction by placer mining.

According to former Secretary of the Interior Stewart Udall, "The most important piece of unfinished business on the nation's resource agenda is the complete replacement of the Mining Law of 1872."

Udall has a right to be concerned. Consider the following abuses listed in an article by Montana Dept. of Fish, Wildlife and Parks pollution control biologist Glenn Phillips. He is the new president of the American Fisheries

Random Shots:
The Wanderings of a Montana Writer

Society Western Division. In the March-April issue of *Fisheries* Titled "The 1872 Mining Law: Reforming a Dinosaur," he mentions the following:

One western Montana miner is capitalizing on his patented placer claim (purchased at $2.50 per acre) by selling summer home sites along a trout stream. Others are maintaining claim sites as private hunting camps in prime elk country. In Oregon, a portion of the Oregon Dunes Recreation Area was successfully patented for a total price of $1,950 with the new owners now trying to trade or sell the property back to the Forest Service and the Bureau of Land Management (BLM) at an asking price of $12 million. And a 1989 Government Accounting Office report lists values of lands given away for the going patented price at anywhere from $200 to $200,000 per acre.

Sounds like a great deal. Where do we sign up?

Outrage over the 1872 Mining Law is reflected in a poll released in 1992 by the Northern Plains Resource Council. By a 12-to-1 margin, Montana residents wanted to update the patented provision of this archaic legislation. Sixty percent of those surveyed agreed that the law needs revision because it does not require royalty payments to states or the federal government, and because patented fees have remained unchanged for more than 100 years. Over three-fourths of those polled agreed that hard-rock mining should be at least as strictly regulated as coal mining. Seventy-five percent opposed mining that permanently damaged other important natural resource values. The 1872 law gives mining companies the "right to mine" on public lands, regardless of potential environmental damage. Finally, 78 percent opposed exemptions that let mining companies degrade the water quality in Montana's pristine streams. Several companies have asked for exemptions in recent years.

According to EPA findings, the hard-rock mining

industry creates between one billion and four billion tons of solid waste each year. Almost no hard-rock mining sites are currently required to be restored to pre-mining condition, except where state laws require it. Groundwater impacts are frequently ignored by the BLM. The Mineral Policy Center estimates that the cost of cleaning up historical hard-rock mining sites is somewhere between $20 billion and $50 billion.

Sounds gloomy at best. Factor in comments by the head of the US Bureau of Mines' T.S. Ary in a 1992 speech before a group of miners, loggers, ranchers, farmers, and other advocates of developing federal lands gathered in Denver, and the future looks grim.

"I don't believe in endangered species. I think the only ones are sitting here in this room," said Ary. Because the gathering was titled "National Wilderness Conference," Ary mistakenly assumed he was going to be addressing environmentalists. When he found out otherwise, he commented, "I thought I was going to come out and be a sacrificial lamb for a bunch of nuts."

"There are lots of degrading things to the environment – logging, grazing, etc. – that will heal themselves over time, but mining scars will be with us long after the earth is a cinderball and there is no sun," said Gary LaFontaine, who lives in Deer Lodge close to the country's largest Super Fund site. ARCO (Atlantic Richfield) has been charged with the cleanup, but they refuse to pay, saying that they were encouraged by state laws, but they were in charge of the state legislature back then. To say things are a mess is an understatement."

The situation in many cases is as bad as it has been detailed above, but there are small rays of light shining here and there that give fly fishers and everyone else who cares about the land some cause for optimism.

Legislation (HR 2614) was proposed to amend the 1872

law by Representative Peter DeFazio (D-OR) that would retain the self-initiated claim system but would remove patenting. Other key provisions of the bill include: requiring miners to pay a five-percent royalty on gross income from mineral production, resulting in approximately $200 million that could be used to help restore damaged streams; residential occupancy on mining claims would be prohibited; reclamation and bonding would be required on all mining claims at a level that would restore the land to the same productive uses that existed prior to mining; federal land-use agencies would be required to create strict reclamation standards and would be given discretion to weigh proposed mining activities against other resource values and, if necessary, deny mining; and miners would be subject to civil and criminal penalties for violations of the revised act, and there would also be provisions for citizen lawsuits. The American Fisheries Society made specific recommendations to protect streams during hearings on the Defazio Bill.

Sounds great, doesn't it? Unfortunately there was a very strong core of resistance in both houses led by Montana's pro-business, anti-environment former Congressman Ron Marlenee. (Although Marlenee was not re-elected in November, he still represents many mining interests in the region). Whenever any proposal to change or eliminate the 1872 Mining Act surfaced, Marlene rose to the challenge like a rainbow to a salmon fly during the height of the hatch.

Marlenee has been quoted as saying that modifications in the mining law may be necessary, "but the law should not be gutted. It has well-served the public's need for more than a century."

Whether the 1872 Mining Law is ever changed or not, there are other bright moments in the situation. The Pegasus Gold Corporation's Beale Mountain Mine stands as a good example of what can be accomplished when the mining industry places strong value not only on the minerals beneath the land, but the land itself.

The mine sits almost on the Continental Divide at about 8,000 feet above sea level in the Pioneer Mountains west of Butte. The region contains the Mount Haggin Game Range and critical winter habitat for elk, deer, moose and bear. The mine's main source of water comes from German Gulch, which holds a viable population of pure-strain westslope cutthroat trout.

The company tried an approach almost unheard of in the industry. It held numerous meetings with sportsman and environmental groups, conferred regularly with government agencies and held a series of public meetings. Acting on all of this input, Pegasus designed what is currently a state-of-the-art mine that protects the environment.

Montana native Carson Rife took control of the project with the simple dictum that if any part of the activity would harm the environment, that work would not be implemented. The major problem facing Rife was the possibility of having cyanide used in the leaching process escape through the leach pad and into the groundwater. The pad was constructed using water-proof compacted clay with a heavy plastic liner on top. In order to avoid an accidental spill into German Gulch, the company made the costly decision to truck the ore uphill away from the stream. This is the reverse of the more fuel-efficient process of having loaded trucks coast downhill and then expend less fuel going back uphill empty.

During construction of the pad a bulldozer accidentally tore the liner. Instead of patching the tear, the company replaced the entire item at a cost of $400,000. In order to minimize impacts from the mine on area wildlife, an electrified fence was built prior to mine construction to keep animals from wandering onto the site. A net to keep out migrating waterfowl was placed over the holding pond where the cyanide solution was stored.

An added side benefit at Beale resulted from the construction of a fish weir made necessary because of rehabilitation taking place on Silver Bow Creek. The weir stopped the migration of other species of trout that might hybridize with the cutthroat, thus ensuring genetic purity of the species in German Gulch.

"It's about the best in the state for wildlife mitigation," said Jim Jensen of the Montana Environmental Information Center in a 1991 article for *Trilogy* magazine by Mike Lapinski. "Beale Mountain is a good example that what's good for the environment can also be good for business."

"We take the view that environmental protection is good business, and are proud that our efforts have been recognized," said Eric Williams of Pegasus. "...there are times when regulation can be onerous industry while offering little or no protection of the environment. We have found this to be more of a function of requirements set at the bureaucratic level, which do not coincide with what is required statutorily.

"That said, I must stress Pegasus believes in prudent, reasonable regulation which allows responsible development of our natural resources and ensures environmental protection."

From a historical perspective there have been some pretty serious problems related to mining, but Pegasus has done some pretty neat things at Beale," said Ray Tillman of Montana Resources and an active member of the George Grant Chapter of Trout Unlimited in Butte. "The industry is aware of public concern and that a bad operation can give it a black eye."

From all of this it is obvious that the situation concerning mining and trout in Montana is in a state of flux.

There are still many mining operations (particularly smaller placer setups) that are seriously degrading the environment and destroying trout populations. But there are also examples like Pegasus at its Beale Mine that can point the way to the future, where possibly, just possibly, historically one of the state's most environmentally destructive industries can exist, perhaps even thrive, along with the trout and fly fishers, and all the rest of us.

As Beck Garland of the Big Blackfoot Chapter of Trout Unlimited said concerning mining in her part of the state:

"If you have a healthy river valley from the top of the basin to the bottom of the basin, you have a healthy living and business climate, and that's the reason we're all here in the first place."

REEL DEEP
IN RADIOACTIVE
RAINBOWS

Wild Forest Review – 1993

Earlier in the book I discussed (dissected?) the Free conference that I attended at Big Sky, Montana. Well, it wasn't all bad. My friend Steve Bodio was there and we stayed up late at night talking and gently sipping Jack Daniels. Steve is one of hell of a writer and a damn good guy, so this was time well spent. And I met Jeffrey St. Clair, who joined us for those evening sessions. At the time, Jeff was the editor of "Wild Forest Review," a cutting-edge magazine that examined environmental issues and excoriated in a wickedly subtle way those who were perpetrating the wrongs. He went on to co-found Counterpunch.org an even better and wicked effort. He asked me for an off-the-wall story about the fishing environment and I gave him the one that follows this. Jeff has one of the finest, sharpest and intuitive minds I have ever had the pleasure of being around. This morning before writing this intro I did a search on the web for Jeffrey and came across his email address. I sent him a brief missive filling him in on my doings since last we'd spoken. He immediately responded enthusiastically, asking if I had any stuff he could use on his website. I do, and this site is must reading for anyone who is tired and disgusted with the homogenized junk the mainstream media is force-feeding us. Jeff and the late co-founder

Random Shots:
The Wanderings of a Montana Writer

Alexander Cockburn have done a number of books together including Al Gore: A Users Manual, Whiteout: CIA, Drugs and the Press, *and* The Politics of Anti-Semitism. *Jeff is one of the real good guys in the struggle against all of the madness swirling around our heads these days. As I sit here writing this, I'm wondering why it took me so long to get back in touch with him. What can I say other than I am often distracted by a red-haired companion.*

NOTHING COULD BE MORE SERENE than the little one-acre gem we are working this warm September evening. Huge marauding rainbows, some over two-feet long and thick like rounds of bologna, slash and blast Woolly bugger streamers as they are stripped quickly to shore. The trout are everywhere. All over the place. Swirling, boiling, making large wakes like Trident submarines as they chase terrified minnows and hapless insects trapped in the meniscus. There are some wall hangers riding down with a vengeance on every cast we make. Unbelievable. Fly fishing at its finest here in God's country.

But when we shift our glances from the water and the cruising rainbows, a different view emerges, looming moonlike, awesome, disorienting. There are no trees here unless you count some scrub willow hanging on for dear life alongside a blackened streambed sporting a warm trickle of dead-brown-orange, algae-choked water. Even knapweed and thistle are scarce. There are no distant ranges of ragged mountain peaks wandering off into the west like still-life ocean waves. Dikes of white, grey and tan rock tower above us, The ground surrounding the pond is made up of the same rubble, terrain that during the height of a bright day reflects the sun's light back into our eyes as a crystal-clear, blinding blaze. Wide tire tracks marked by severe indentations indicate the recent passage of a herd of giant earth-moving machinery. Several of their number are parked on a pile of tailings nearby. In their rusted, dusty condition they resemble a grazing band of enormous, surreal elephants. Orange plastic flags flap in the evening breeze from atop hundreds of survey stakes marking the future course of moving water through this stark landscape.

Admittedly this is a vision of angling paradise, made all the more sylvan by the thunderings and whizzings of cars, obese motorhomes and heavy trucks flying along Interstate 90 just over our shoulders. A large green sign heralding the appearance of Warm Springs is clearly visible. The gigantic stone stack that is the signatory visual landmark of the smelter town of Anaconda (soon to be home to a Jack Nicklaus-designed golf course built atop the blackest of the tailings; a golfing treat for sure) looms in the southwest a few miles away. The thing glows soft orange in the fading sunlight.

Fly fishers are a twisted lot who will strike off at the drop of a rumor. They will head anywhere, anytime of the year, spending what money they have chasing trout – big or little. Size is unimportant here. Getting the hell on the road and running down fish tales is the game.

So where is "here" you might ask? My friends from "back East" are wondering what they've gotten themselves into. This concern simultaneously manifests and ameliorates itself in Boodles gin martinis served in empty Pabst cans that have their tops can-opened off. Perfect containers for the task. A few Spanish olives, the threat of vermouth along with plenty of ice turns the trick as do some excellent Cuban cigars smuggled in from somewhere, somehow. Rich smoke from Havana slips off on the evening zephyr. The gin disappears with the grace and ease that comes from years of fishing long and hard in strange places.

Random Shots:
The Wanderings of a Montana Writer

Looking around at the desolate, bombed-out surroundings makes us laugh. Trophy-fishing right here on Mars, Montana. The good life in full regalia, and we knew we'd earned it. We'd paid our dues on countless famous trout waters around the world. Often with nothing more to show for our efforts than sunburn, blown rotator cuffs, temporarily-damaged expectations and busted synapses.

Damn right we'd ride this fishing for all it was worth. So what if "here" happened to be the Anaconda Settling Pond system smack dead-center in the heart of the largest Superfund site in the country. From roughly northeast of Deer Lodge (home of the state prison) all the way over the rise and into Butte (home of Evil Knievel) piles of toxic tailings lay strewn along the Upper Clark Fork River Basin. Millions of tons of crushed, blasted and pulverized rock loaded with heavy metals in lethal proportions are scattered beneath the dying late-summer sun, the result of a century of mining for copper and silver and a bit of gold. This is the region that earned Montana the proud nickname "The Treasure State."

Yes. This is it. The glory hole in the middle of rock-hard nowhere. Adding to the weirdness are a half-dozen other ponds and lakes, all much larger than our little corner of paradise. They are filled with browns and rainbows that sometimes exceed ten pounds. These big boys can be extremely difficult to catch, even by the superbly skilled among our esoteric clan.

"Holt, you're a sick man," said Boston George.

"He's much worse than that," said Baton Rouge Kevin, downing his cocktail upright. "Only a lunatic would fish here."

"I don't see you clowns piling into the Rent-A-Wreck to go somewhere else," I said. "And look over there, on that road by Pond Number Three. Christ! There are plates from Illinois, Texas and one demented soul from New

Hampshire. We are not alone!"

"Live Free or Die!" we offered reverently to the angling gods watching from above.

We downed another round of crystal yum-yums (a.k.a. white loudmouths). There is still some time to tag a few more trout, so we check knots and hook points, finish off our Boodles and then slip and slide over the rocks to the level tailing banks to try our hand once again.

Most of the tailings at this site came from the Berkeley Pit at Butte back from when the Anaconda Company had a stranglehold on the state (reptilian metaphor gagging the Big Sky). The company left a hole in the ground a mile wide and more than a 1,000 feet deep. An estimated 185 million cubic yards of tailings are scattered about the area. Killing compounds containing copper, zinc, and cadmium are mixed in the rock, patiently waiting for periodic deluges from rollicking thunderstorms. Then this unexpected burst of water rushes over the baked rock taking toxic levels of heavy metals downstream into the Clark Fork, killing the wild browns with emotionless efficiency. Past runoffs have knocked off hundreds, even thousands, of browns, trout carcasses of a couple of pounds or more littering the brushy banks. A lovely sight.

More than a billion dollars is needed to clean up the mess, but ARCO, the company now in charge of the site, is balking at the cost. When the region will ever be rendered completely "safe" for living things is an open question. Musings for a dead planet?

But for now all of that is just a minor detail in the scheme of our fishing and future big-trout aspirations. Most of these toxic wastes have sunk to the bottom of the lakes and ponds. A thick mat of aquatic plants nourish insects that feed these fat trout. The word is out about this place and its big fish. Hard-core fly fishers from everywhere travel to this bizarre system in hopes of connecting with that one enormous trout of a lifetime. Some do. Others lack our angling sophistication (or is it the Boodles?) to fool the rainbows and the discerning browns. All the same, merely looking at monster fish swimming at your feet is fascinating in a frustrating way.

But I wonder: Is this where trout fishing is headed? Off into man-made, other-worldly landscapes of plunder and destruction followed by bizarre attempts at putting the whole thing back together again in some lunatic vision of nature?

Imagine fishing for Atlantic salmon in a renewed Love Canal, a place where abandoned housing developments, neighborhoods where children got very sick years ago, stand silent watch over fly fishers clad in thousands of dollars of high-tech gear chase fish in manufactured surroundings. Or how about chasing golden trout in the Berkeley Pit itself? What a tourist attraction for Butte and what a curious angling adventure for some: catching the most glorious of all salmonids at the bottom of a hole three football fields deep, surrounded by layered walls shaded corrosive green, rusting red and decaying orange.

The stuff of dreams for those who love trout and good water, wherever it is to be found. From Alaska to New Zealand to Tasmania to Butte, Montana. There's a certain rhythm to this. Or is it once again the Boodles? And what's more? There are other toxic systems already in place that support burgeoning sport fisheries. Consider the PCB-laden Great Lakes with their walleye, salmon and steelhead. Or how about the stripes fighting the scum and filth of the Hudson as they strive to reach ancestral spawning grounds? The vision is rapidly becoming reality. I'm excited.

The olive-and-green bugger I'm working is hammered in a frenzied boil of living metal and dark water, tearing me back to the business at hand. The fish leaps across the still surface as is its genetic heritage, before I wrestle it to shallow water near the steep embankment. Rocks, gravel and sand avalanche in a small, dry stream into the pond as I slide to the fish like a spastic skier, fly rod held high, flashing darkly in the light of a summer's evening star show. The trout is gorgeous as it fins angrily at the end of my line. Twenty inches or so, flashing iridescent reds, black spots and quicksilvers. A hooked jaw indicates a male, and he races from view upon release, swimming hell-bent for the weeds down deep.

My friends are catching fish, too. They are laughing crazily. The very last of the day's light gently illuminates the rock around me. The sound of interstate traffic is now familiar background noise fading to white. Very strange fishing, jiving away at the Superfund Bar and Grill. We must be mad. We must be all out of our heads. That must be it.

MOVING MOUNTAINS IN MONTANA

Fly Fisherman – 1994

This article is about a proposed mine in the headwaters of the Blackfoot River, the setting for Maclean's novella "A River Runs Through It." I've fished this river for decades. The stream is beautiful, filled with wild charm like a refined lady. The possible destruction of this watershed led me to write the novel called Where Paradise Lay *about the river. A couple of summers back Ginny and I stayed in a motel in nearby Lincoln set beneath Ponderosa that reached for the sky and were centuries old. Deer casually wandered the streets. In the restaurants, cafes, grocery store, laundry and the bars everyone was happy and friendly. I fished tiny tributaries for little cutthroat that were native and pure. Towards evening I worked the deep runs and pools and long washes that danced over colorful gravels for rainbows and more cutts that approached a few pounds. Coyotes barked in the timbered hills. A moose wandered by. Ducks burst up from still waters by shore. I was in heaven and I knew it. When I researched this story I spoke with the mine manager and his geologist at the company's office in town, a town that would be devastated if the mine were ever put into operation. I'd made the two-hour drive down from my home in the Flathead Valley. On his desk and on a nearby table were copies of some of my articles and a few of my books. He had a large yellow legal pad filled with notes. He was ready for me and there was an uncomfortable buzz*

Random Shots:
The Wanderings of a Montana Writer

in the room that made me quickly realize that the logging industry was sweetness and light compared to the mining boys. The manager asked if I had a degree in geology because my previous articles were "quite accurate." I said "No," that I've read a number of books and papers on the subject. We talked for an hour, then we went to eat. It was high noon. The manager said he'd buy me lunch if that wasn't against my ethics. He said this in a polite tone that was anything but polite. I said that since he was being generous I'd take a beer and a shot of Jim Beam, and we went from there which went on to an extensive tour of the proposed mine. (For now the project is on hold, but once gold prices rise through the roof, as they surely will again, what happens is anyone's guess). As in any environmental story, I pulled a few punches for the sake of maintaining the illusion of impartiality. That how these things work. When all of this was over I headed up the Swan Valley and decided to spend the night along a small mountain stream at the base of the Mission Mountains. I needed to plunge my hands and face in the cold, clean water, and I needed some time in the woods to distance myself from my day at the proposed mine site.

TRYING TO STOP THE MINING of a gold deposit with the potential worth of billions of dollars is like trying to slow down a steamroller by placing cartons of eggs in front of it. The eggs get scrambled along with anything else that gets in the way of the outfit as it lumbers inexorably down its inevitable road of huge profits and altered landscapes.

Such is the case with the Seven-Up Pete Joint Venture, located a few miles outside of the small community of Lincoln, Montana about 80 miles north-northeast of Missoula. Phelps Dodge (the majority owner in the project at 75.25 percent) and Canyon Resources are currently engaged in preliminary exploration of the reserves located in the headwaters of the Blackfoot River just above its confluence with the Landers Fork in the McDonald Mountain area. Both the main Blackfoot River and the Landers Fork are home to native populations of cutthroat trout and dwindling numbers of bull trout, a species that often exceeds ten pounds. Other portions of the drainage contain brown, rainbow and brook trout along with sizeable numbers of indigenous mountain whitefish and forage fish.

To get a general idea of the scope of this project, these initial activities have already cost the two companies more than $30. Since 1986, 491 drill holes totally approximately 364,000 feet have been sunk. A decision of whether to proceed or not will be made by early 1994 at the latest.

According to the companies' Conceptual Plan of Operations, during the 15-year or so life of the open-pit, cyanide-heap, leach-process mine, more than 600 million tons of rock will be dug up and moved to a nearby location. This is the equivalent of 10,000 freight trains hauling 100 fully-loaded cars. On the average, only .03 ounces (less than $12 worth at current prices) of gold per ton are expected to be recovered. Modern technology and gold prices of at least $375 per ounce makes this miniscule amount of ore profitable, despite tremendous costs in equipment, engineering and labor. This includes moving portions of Highway 200 about 1,000 feet closer to the Blackfoot River. Piles of tailings from the leaching process will tower more than 600 feet above the road.

"Frankly, we will be altering the landscape," said project manager John Marsden. "Essentially, we will be moving the hill from one spot to another. By relocating the highway we will be compacting the operation and protecting the valley. There is a selfish reason, too. While this will help save some other land in the area, we will also be minimizing our costs. I see this as a win-win situation."

Marsden claims that the new road will pass through the 1,000-year flood plain only in a couple of locations and not come near the 100-year plain. Flood plains are areas that would be covered by flood water during the maximum high-flow of a river anticipated during a certain span of time.

"We are going to eat the cost of the EIS (Environmental Impact Statement) instead of an EA (Environmental Assessment)," said Marsden. "The EIS is more costly and time-consuming than the EA. "And we're not going to try to piggyback our findings in the area on the back of the McDonald site. Also, we recognize that the 1872 Mining Law needs to be made fair and equitable, that changes are coming.

This is a world-class gold deposit. The question is can it be mined and processed profitably, and can it be permitted. We believe the answer is yes."

Those who enjoy the beauty of the valley, including the Ponderosa pine covered butte about to be mined, may disagree with Marsden concerning his "win-win" assessment. But it's hard not to like the guy or senior project geologist Jim Volderberg. As employees of the mining company, they are quite obviously excited about the project. They both even like to fly fish, play pool, and drink beer. Regular guys. Spend enough time with these two, and a person, even a stone-cold fly fisher, could begin to believe in the mammoth project. Almost.

As I said to Marsden during a recent tour of the area, "If I had my way, I would like to see that this mine is never built, but there is simply too much money involved to stop this if you decide to proceed. That being the case, I would like to see that your company is held to the absolute highest environmental standards and safeguards available. That's what I hope to accomplish with any stories I do on this mine."

The manager said, "Fair enough," and added, "We can't afford to be poor stewards of the land we are mining, especially considering the possibility of obtaining future permits to mine gold in Montana."

While the mine is huge in scope, the process is relatively simple. The rock is drilled and blasted. Then the ore is hauled either directly to a lined leach pad engineered for crushed ore, or to a crushing facility and then to a pad designed for crushed ore. Dilute cyanide solution is then applied to the ore to dissolve precious minerals, in this case mostly gold.

While at the site, Volberding showed me a chunk of gold-bearing rock. It looked like a piece of concrete speckled with smaller pieces of stone. The gold is not visible to the eye: it is measured in dimensions of microns. Until recently it was not technically possible to extract such deposits profitably. The geologist said that the gold perked up into the rock millions of years ago as a result of a now-extinct geologic feature similar to Yellowstone National Park's Mammoth Hot Springs.

"To a geologist this is an exciting find, and this is the only place that is exposed," said Volberding. We were standing on a pine-covered, grassy slope several hundred feet above the valley. The Blackfoot River twisted and curved along the edge of timbered mountains rolling to the south. Off that way is the site of the Seven-Up Pete gold deposit that according to the manager is a "tar baby" that sucks up man-hours and money. A much more difficult and costly area to mine. Gold prices will have to go much higher before the companies consider working the location, perhaps to more than $600 per ounce.

Putting aside the fact that the open-pit mine will dramatically alter the landscape and damage the aesthetics of the place, the greatest concern to fisheries biologists, environmentalists, local residents, and fly fishers is the possibility of a cyanide leak from one of the leach pads. Cyanide, even in dilute levels, kills fish and other life forms by inhibiting their ability to absorb oxygen. Trout have been identified as the most sensitive fish to chronic or acute cyanide poisoning. Concentrations as low as ten parts per billion free cyanide can rapidly and permanently affect the swimming ability of salmonids. Invertebrates are even more sensitive. A leak could decimate the Blackfoot River, which has been on the rebound largely through the efforts of groups like Trout Unlimited and the state Dept. of Fish, Wildlife and Parks.

Cyanide solutions used in the mining process can also leak into groundwater resources. Once in the groundwater, there is no known method of cleaning up the aquifer short of pumping the water to the surface for treatment, an extremely costly process. The cyanide ponds attract wildlife, and at least 10,000 deaths of animals at these sites have been documented, according to the National Wildlife Federation. According to the DuPont Corporation, the mining industry used about 105 million pounds of cyanide in 1991.

Spills of cyanide are not rare occurrences, According to the Dept. of State Lands, three out of five active heap leach operations registered in Montana in 1989 received water-quality violations due to illegal discharges of cyanide solution.

The leach pads at this operation will have composite pad liner systems of compacted soil and a geomembrane liner consisting of two compressed six-inch layers of clay. All of this will be overlaid with a PVC liner of sufficient thickness to withstand the pressure from 600 feet of rock.

"The lining is a good design," said Marsden. "We will also hire a third party to monitor quality control during construction."

The overall system according to Marsden is designed to

handle a 100-year maximum event, which is 2.9 inches of rain in a 24-hour period. This includes runoff generated from melted snowpack containing as much as 11 inches of water during the storm.

"We've got to be damn sure we can contain all of that solution," said Marsden. We're trying to give the maximum impacts of this project to everyone. We're not trying to sneak anything by."

Other problems could be changes in the flow of the groundwater, and Marsden said they are drilling extensively to map this underground system with the intentions of designing the mine so that no damage is done in this area. He expects to exceed the standards of the Beale Mountain mine near Anaconda, an operation touted as state-of-the-art when it come to the environment..

As many as 390 employees will work the site, creating a potential overload disaster for the small town of Lincoln. Marsden said that some workers may live in Helena, an hour away, to help mitigate some of the impacts on services and facilities like law enforcement, water and schools.

We don't want this to be a shanty town; that would be real bad news," said Marsden. "We're looking at all of the amenities and also at employee distribution. We certainly don't expect Lincoln to shoulder the huge influx of people. Our approach is that this is not a 'boom-and-bust' operation.

The companies plan to reclaim the tailings pile, expected to be a small mountain in itself. Native grasses, shrubs, and trees will be planted on slopes contoured to blend in with the surroundings. Pit slopes will be stabilized, and all equipment and facilities will be dismantled when the mine shuts down.

The project sounds pretty good, but Phelps Dodge has a past track record of neglect, abuse and environmental violations. Its operations in the Southwest have been cited and fined frequently for discharges into nearby water systems, and some of its smelters are considered among the dirtiest in the country. According to a Mining Report Card prepared by the Mineral Policy Center, the company's greatest problem concerning management practices "is not expertise, but commitment...Phelps Dodge's defensive approach to seeking permits pays financial dividends in the short run, but its basic assumption – that regulators' expectations are merely a nuisance for the lawyers to handle – has led to serious long-term problems."

The Center goes on to say, "The company frequently takes obstinate stances with environmental regulatory agencies, and negotiates relentlessly to do the least amount of work possible for permit approvals. The company's attitude has reportedly improved in the last year or so, perhaps heralding a thaw in its historically icy approach to regulatory relations."

Concerning reclamation, the Center states, "The Phelps Dodge Corporation receives its lowest grade in this category. The company's southwestern operations fail even the most minimal standards of reclamation...Reclamation activities have taken place at some Arizona properties, but the record here is relatively unimpressive. Each time, initiative came from a regulatory agency, not the company itself."

Recently Phelps Dodge has done a good job at an operation in the Northwest. The Sherwood mine in Washington "seems to be the exception to the rule," states the report. "Reclamation of this former uranium mine was prepared prior to its 1979 startup, owing in a large part to the requirements of state and federal regulators. Thirteen years later, reclamation seems to be proceeding smoothly and efficiently."

Other comments in the report include: "...management style is notoriously secretive. In instances where community residents have expressed concern, the company has not been especially open or welcoming...Since the company's operations tend to dominate their small communities, outspoken objections to company positions are unheard of. The test in these communities is whether Phelps Dodge of its own volition reaches out to include community residents in a constructive partnership. At the Chino (New Mexico) mine, for example, they suffered numerous leaks and wastewater discharges during 1988, yet failed to proactively inform nearby townspeople of the situation or request their comment."

Marsden obviously takes issue with these assessments, saying that his company has been very active in this area and has shut down some smelters.

"We can't honestly say every one of our mines is up to snuff, but we are making significant change. We've been at the forefront of the industry in technology that replaces processes that waste energy or pollute."

Maybe so, but this last statement is a little like saying the South African government is at the forefront of trying to eliminate apartheid.

Another problem is the fact that federal land is not involved. Private and state land is, meaning that the primary regulatory agency will be the Montana Dept. of State Lands. Based on past mining abuses overseen by the department, this is a lot like having the fox guard the hen coop.

"This will be a huge undertaking," said Bruce Farling of the Clark Fork Coalition, an environmental watchdog group founded to protect the drainage. "I would like to see them held to even stricter guidelines than those at Beale Mountain. Every precaution must be taken to protect the river."

The Big Blackfoot Chapter of Trout Unlimited passed a resolution that stated in part, "...the Big Blackfoot Chapter publicly states its grave concern about the potential impacts that the Seven-Up Pete Joint Venture may have on the Blackfoot River...to assure that the company can conclusively prove that the technology it will employ during and after the proposed mining operation will result in complete containment of cyanide and all other pollutants...and be it further resolved, that, through the regulatory process and all means available, the chapter will call for the total reclamation of all sites disturbed during the mining operation including the requirement that Phelps Dodge provide sufficient bond prior to the commencement of further exploration of mining to support all reclamation costs."

This would be wonderful, except trying to have them refill an open pit seems about as likely as stopping the mining in the first place.

From the windy ridge at the proposed mine site, the view up and down the valley is beautiful. Timbered mountains running in all directions. It is hard to comprehend that the ground I'm standing on will, most likely, in the future, be a huge hole more than a 1,000 feet deep and that this butte will be a pile of rock lying next to the highway just a short distance from here.

I ask myself: Twenty years from now will there still be trout swimming in the river running so peacefully below me?

OH CANADA! DOES THE GREAT WHITE NORTH DESERVE IT'S GREEN REPUTATION

E – The Environmental Magazine – 2004

When I moved from Whitefish to Livingston years ago I made the conscious decision to switch from what passed for factual writing and reporting to working on fiction. I've written a number of short stories that have been published, and several novels, including Blown Away Under The Big Sky and Plain Crazy in Paradise. I turned my back on writing about environmental issues because I was both discouraged and burned out. A couple of years ago I decided to return to the environmental wars. For two years I bombarded Jim Motavalli, the editor of E – The Environmental Magazine, with article proposals that ranged from the damage cause by irrigation drawdown to the horrors of upscale, exclusionary development communities in the West. He passed on all of these. Then I sent him a story idea about my experiences in Canada where that country's residents constantly took issue with my country's environmental policies and its commitment to wild lands. I endured nasty, snide remarks from Calgary to Dawson City. After seeing the way Alberta and British Columbia were being ravaged by the extraction industries in the form of enormous clearcuts, open-pit mines, seismic-exploration roads, etc., I decided that I'd

Random Shots:
The Wanderings of a Montana Writer

*had enough of these "north of the border" putdowns. Jim
called one day and said he wanted the story. I'd worn him
down, I thought. Turned out he would wear me down. For
the next year I interviewed, or tried to interview, as many
Canadian sources as possible. I did extensive research on
the scope of the destruction both in Canada and the US The
following story is the final product of all this work that
included a number of revisions suggested by Jim in order
to make the thing strong and tight. I still believe that fiction
has a more profound and long-lasting influence on
readers, but I also realize that I'd made a mistake in
walking away from my magazine environmental work.
Onward and upward, I guess.*

THE WIDELY HELD NOTION that Canada is taking
excellent care of its wild, pristine lands far better than
the gluttonous citizens in the United States is nothing more
than a misperception approaching myth. Americans, or
Yanks as they are often called up north, are frequently
verbally assailed by Canadians with the misplaced,
disingenuous and perhaps naïve notion that all US citizens
are swine when it comes to caring for and preserving quality
country. Canadians, in contrast, are valiant, conscientious
souls who have no blood on their hands. This stance is at
best spurious and possibly created to hide the obvious fact
that the western provinces of Alberta, British Columbia, the
Northwest Territories and the Yukon are being plundered
at an astonishing rate.

While having a couple of drinks in a bar called The Pit
in Dawson City, Yukon last summer a Canadian came up to
me and asked where I was from. When I told him he said,
"You damn Yanks don't give a damn about your own land.
You log it and strip-mine it all to hell. Then you come up
here to enjoy our country." Over the years I've heard many

comments along those lines.

True, there are individuals in Canada who have devoted their lives to preserving the land and there are, as most of us know all too well, greedy bastards tearing apart the last remaining shreds of unspoiled country in the US But fair is fair, and the bottom line is that Canadians should take stock of their own environmental situation before gleefully casting aspersions America's way.

Forty years of being an inveterate road bum, traveling back roads on a skinny budget, fishing malarial bogs, inadvertently canoeing class X whitewater, hiking non-existent trails bound for nowhere and unavoidably staying on top of environmental issues in Canada has provided an ongoing opportunity to see disturbing change in a land of incredible splendor and abundance—one peopled with some truly remarkable, generous and creative individuals. In the last five years these destructive shifts in direction have been seismic, both metaphorically and literally.

From Fort Nelson in northern British Columbia to Rocky Mountain House in central Alberta to the vast Tintina Trench region in the southern Yukon and over east to Yellowknife on Great Slave Lake in the Northwest Territories, the landscape is under siege. The extraction industries are running the show, tearing, blasting, sucking and cutting every diamond, gold nugget, drop of oil, chunk of coal and stick of timber they can access. If it's of value, these industries intend to have it. What's going down in western Canada puts the devastation being visited on states like Montana, Wyoming and West Virginia look in a more balanced perspective. What are obviously horrendous clearcuts or devastating open-pit coalmines in the US West are everyday situations in Canada, too. Both countries are mining their natural resources at an alarming rate.

"We want Earth to speed up, our forests don't grow fast enough for us," said David Suzuki several years ago in an interview in the Hamilton Spectator. Suzuki, a Canadian has long been outspoken in his opposition to the Western world's enormous appetite for resources. "We have to realize that humans are not the most important species on the planet."

Canadian provincial campgrounds are filled to the brim with late-model pickups tricked out with all the options and pulling expensive fifth wheelers and pricey speedboats and ATVs and jet skis. The Cypress Hills along the Alberta-Saskatchewan border, the setting for Wallace Stegner's book *Wolf Willow*, are now so overrun as to resemble a scene from *National Lampoon's Vacation*. Housing developments in cities like Calgary and Edmonton stretch for miles with thousands of quarter-million-dollar homes. All of this comes not only from the jobs provided by these corporations but also from royalties paid by the industry based on the amount of a given mineral extracted from a province. In Alberta, this figure exceeds $6 billion annually just for coal. The money is flowing in direct proportion with the abundance of the oil coming from countless wells hammered into the Canadian countryside. The old phrase "a chicken in every pot" has been updated in the northland to "an oil pumpjack in every yard."

A good example – and there are many – is Rocky Mountain House, Alberta. This used to be a rather sedate town of a few thousand sometimes-impoverished souls who enjoyed life on the bluffs above the North Fork of the Saskatchewan River. The residents could take part in all of the outdoor activities one would expect in an area that rests in the foothills along the east slope of the Canadian Rockies and is surrounded by dense, mature pine forest with countless rivers and streams pouring out onto the prairie. Lakes of the purest water abound, as do grizzlies, moose, eagles, deer, wolves, various species of trout, grayling and mountain lions. For years, timber generated decent incomes for many, as did motels, restaurants and service stations that supplied occasional tourists with basic needs. Most everyone knew everybody else and crime rates were low. The population was perhaps a couple of thousand.

The town, originally founded 150 years ago because of the fur trade and the natural highway provided by Saskatchewan, is now an insane riot of oil rigs, logging trucks, related workers and the destructive craziness that comes from too much money deposited in a local economy way too quickly. Residents are now moving towards surliness, depression and anger caused by these rapid changes to their lifestyle. A recent trip up that way this spring revealed streets, even residential side streets, overrun with trucks of all sizes run helter-skelter to the oil-and-gas biz shuffle. Gas stations are constantly busy filling the tanks of industry vehicles. Beleaguered locals put on game but grim faces in the wake of this onslaught. A woman at a local bakery said, "I don't even remember what my town used to be. None of us knows anyone the way we used to. This place is frantic, like Calgary." Rocky Mountain House has more than tripled in population, and that doesn't include the countless oil and gas roustabouts, drilling maintenance crews, surveyors and the like.

What is happening to longtime residents of Rocky Mountain House and countless other towns scattered about the forests, mountains and prairies of western Canada is to be expected wherever extractive industry moves in and shoves locals out of the way. What was once home is now a corporate compound replete with out-of-control drinking, drugs, prostitution and the ubiquitous grifters plying a variety of hustles and cons—the ever-present tagalongs with this avaricious carnival. The townspeople don't know what's happening to them or their land. All that most of them see is the quick money fix that blinds them to the negative and long-term changes of this way of life.

Random Shots:
The Wanderings of a Montana Writer

In an interview in the *Edmonton Sun*, Suzuki said "We're all in a great big car driving at a brick wall at 100 mph and everybody is arguing over where they want to sit. My point is it doesn't matter who's driving. Somebody has got to say, 'For God's sake, put the brakes on and turn the wheel.'"

"In terms of greenhouse gas emissions the US is responsible for 25 percent and Canada two percent (of world emissions)," said Jim Fulton of The David Suzuki Foundation. "But Canadians are the largest per capita users in the world. We use more energy on a daily basis than the entire continent of Africa.

"The impact from gas and oil exploration, especially in the boreal forest of Alberta, is catastrophic," said Fulton. "Exploratory roads are laid out in a grid pattern that runs for hundreds of miles east-and-west and north-and-south. The combined impact of seismic exploration, then bringing in heavy equipment and constructing storage facilities is enormous. Then these roads are used by people on ATVs. This affects wildlife including migratory birds, bears and wolves. The terror experienced by caribou, deer and moose from ATVs cannot be overstated. If these animals are forced to flee even short distances they frequently overheat or lose pregnancies. Often they die. In some areas moose populations have vanished leaving indigenous populations without sustenance.

"The oil reserves in our tar sands are the largest in the world, larger than those of Saudi Arabia," said Fulton. "And the oil and automotive industries are doing anything *but* encouraging fuel efficient vehicles and conservation. Members of the oil industry are criminals of the first order."

The continual boom-and-bust cycle of the West is at play in Canada. Ten, maybe 20 years of feast, then complete collapse and all of the new homes and expensive toys go back to the banks while the oil, coal and timber companies are long gone, searching for the next valley to plunder. It's an old, ugly story that's been played out in Butte, Montana, Deadwood, South Dakota and in ghost towns with names like Garnet, Pony and Como. Now the routine is playing in Canada.

Millions of acres of land in these western provinces are being surveyed, mapped and then exploited by these extraction industries. And production figures in oil and gas, coal and other minerals along with timber are climbing rapidly and in many cases equal or exceed production totals in the US Forest trunk roads that used to wind serenely through dense pine forest and alongside unspoiled rivers along the Rocky Mountain foothills and now bustling muddy or dusty corridors conveying a steady stream of enormous trucks hauling huge machinery.

A couple years ago, a friend and I were traveling north from Rocky Mountain House on Forest trunk 743. We wore working on a book about the northern high plains called **Coyote Nowhere**. The late-June weather was warm but rainy and the dirt roads were now a muddy and treacherous quagmire. Even if there had been no other traffic the drive would have been a sporting proposition. We'd been warned by a forest employee the night before and a campground along the Pembina River to watch out for the steady stream of oil and coal rigs moving up and down these roads. "They don't stop or even move over for anyone. People are killed all of the time. Trucks, cars, campers—all of them sometimes crushed flat like empty beer cans. That's an extremely dangerous drive you're about to undertake." He wished us luck and then headed off down the road to check on another campsite.

At the time I considered his warning a bit extreme, but I was to find out differently. The next morning as we drove north a steady stream of enormous rigs roared past us, the tires on these machines taller than our GMC Suburban. The noise of the engines was deafening as they belched thick black clouds of diesel exhaust. While climbing a sticky hill a semi pulling drilling equipment moved well over to our side of the road, just missing us by inches and drenching the Suburban's windshield in a thick wash of slop. We barely made it to the top of the rise, driving blind, and barely managing to skid over into a slight turnoff.

Getting out to collect ourselves and settle frayed nerves, I looked around. On both sides vast open-pit coal mines stretched deep into the ancient pine forest. Tall metal stacks that rose above the trees were crowned by flickering flames of natural gas being burned off at several pumping stations. Oil company signs said "No Trespassing" at the entrance to every side road. In the pits, large machinery was scooping up and hauling away coal. Dynamite blasting roared in the distance. Far in the west the lofty crest of the Rockies flickered snow white between swirling openings in the cloud cover.

Fifteen years ago when I traveled this road on my way to the then-remote mountain town of Grand Cache (now overrun with the same madness as in Rocky Mountain House), I felt like I was in the middle of a primeval forest, that a grizzly or moose could appear from the edge of the trees at any moment. Now the atmosphere was more like a scene of some vast industrial park.

The rivers were running muddy along the road and the only wildlife I saw was an occasional raven gliding high above what remained of the forest. This vision of desecration continued for 60 miles before we turned off onto another road, but that one soon led past a mammoth coal mine where mountains on the eastern edge of Jasper Park in the Gregg River drainage were being carved down to nothing. The air was filled with the noise of heavy machinery and choking with waves of black dust swirling in miniature tornados as the wind whipped down from the remaining mountains. More than 800 miles north from my home and I felt like I was in Detroit.

Half of Canada is covered by either temperate forest (like that found in the Northwestern US) or by boreal forest (similar to that found in Siberia). The boreal forest is a 600-mile-wide band of timberland stretching from approximately 300 miles north of the US border to the treeline in the Arctic, and spanning the breadth of the country. Approximately 300 million acres of the country's forest are managed for timber production. This is an area more than one-and-a-half times the size of several Midwestern states. Two-thirds of Canada's estimated 300,00 wildlife species live in the forest.

The temperate and boreal forests along with the arctic tundra of these four provinces is extremely fragile. I spoke with a biologist at the Tombstone Campground Interpretive Center located on the Yukon's Dempster Highway. She pointed out that as few as 20 people walking the same line to a distant peak and back again would disturb the vegetation and soils of this boreal environment to the extent that it would take several decades to return to its natural state.

Less than two dozen people treading lightly, not thousands of pieces of machinery the size of houses, thousands more workers and thousands of tons of explosives, all ripping and digging away at some of the last wilderness left on the planet.

These figures give an idea of the magnitude of these extraction processes in Canada: The total timber harvest in Canada is near eight billion board feet per year, up from 2.9 billion in 1950. (In the US this figure is around four billion board feet per year down from 6.0 billion in 1980s.)

Canada's forests cover an area nearly three times the size of Europe. This is mainly boreal forest with some temperate forest including temperate rainforest. This represents 10 percent of the world's forestry cover. Only 5.5 percent of this forest is under some form of legal protection or constraint related to logging. This is the most productive forest in terms of biomass in the world. Grizzly bears, cougars the Baird Owl, woodland caribou and elk live there. Approximately 10.8 million acres of logged forestlands in Canada (an area more than twice the size of Wales) remain denuded. If present trend continues, all of Canada's suitable forest will be harvested within 30 to 35 years.

"Alberta is a very, very wealthy province compared to Montana, but that comes with its own baggage," said renowned Alberta guitarist Amos Garrett, who is also a devoted conservationist. "The provincial government is making millions in oil taxes and that just comes in the mail. Maybe there's $10 to $15 million coming in from sportsmen. That's paltry. So there are deaf ears in Edmonton [the provincial capital]. I don't think we have the programs that you have down there in the States. You do much more for the trout and upland birds than we do."

In British Columbia, ancient forests are vanishing at the rate of one acre every 70 seconds or 418,000 acres per year an area the size of 190,00 football fields. In the time it takes to watch a 30-minute sitcom on television, 26 acres of forest have been leveled. In the past decade an area eight times the size of Connecticut has been clearcut. Companies do not have to bid competitively to log public forests. Fees are typically set at one-fourth to one-third market value. The majority of logging in B.C. is in old-growth forest and the Canadian government estimates that the province is overcutting its forest by 20 percent. Clearcutting makes up 80 percent of all logging. In British Columbia, it is legal to log smaller salmon streams down to the banks, destroying aquatic life and leaving no protections against fine sediment and high temperatures that are lethal to salmon eggs and fry. There is no endangered species legislation to protect wildlife from logging, despite the fact that the Committee on the Status of Endangered Wildlife in Canada now lists 387 species of plants and animals at risk of extinction (eight percent of these species are shared with the US). This is an increase of 20 percent since 1992.

Coal production figures for Canada are similar. Alberta mines 27 million tons annually, British Columbia, 40 million tons. The Canadian oil and gas industry invested more than $20 billion in exploration and development in 2000, making it the single-largest capital investor in Canada. Oil production is not expected to peak for 10 years. British Columbia government officials have asked leaders in Ottawa to lift a decades-old ban on offshore drilling along Canada's Pacific Coast. Geologists estimate that there could be up to 10 billion barrels of oil and 1.2 billion cubic meters of natural gas in the area.

"We risk enormous damage to British Columbia's environmental heritage, all for a short-term dollar," said David Hocking, communications director for the Vancouver-based David Suzuki Foundation.

Much of the US from one coast to the other has been devastated by coal mining. Canada's western provinces are experiencing a similar fate and the pace of the industries is accelerating. Within perhaps as little as two decades the ecosystem damage inflicted upon the Yukon, British Columbia, Alberta and the Northwest Territories will make what happened in this country pale in comparison. At the present rate, most natural resources will be exhausted in Canada within 40 years. Even if Canada was exploiting its natural resources at only one half the rate of the US, which it isn't, everything would be gone within a century.

Some of the reasons that the mineral extraction industries have engendered the ire of both US and Canadian citizens is exemplified by some of these comments by the Canadian Minister of Energy and Mines, Richard Neufeld, in

Random Shots:
The Wanderings of a Montana Writer
his opening address for the 44th Canadian Conference on Coal held two years ago in British Columbia.

"We have eliminated corporate capital tax...reduced corporate income tax by three percent to 13.5 percent," said Neufeld. "Over 90 percent of our coal is exported, mainly to steel-making countries....The philosophy behind our actions is simple – increase certainty. Streamline regulatory requirements and make BC a better place to do business. We've changed the Coal Act to accomplish this for coal exploration and mining...As a result, coal exploration and development can proceed with fewer encumbrances.

"We will make dramatic cuts to prescriptive regulations under the Health, Safety and Reclamation Code to give companies more flexibility to focus on results not process. We have amended the Mines Act and we are developing related regulations to allow most exploration activities to take place without the need for permits."

This "philosophy" sounds remarkably similar to that espoused by the current administration in Washington. During a recent trip to the Yukon, I pulled over at a wayside that offered a spectacular view of the Klondike River valley and the seemingly endless sweep of mountains rolling north towards the Arctic Circle. The ragged, surreal peaks of The Tombstone Range ghosted in the distance. Looking to my left I noticed a large display sign touting a gold mine that was hidden behind a near range of mountains. Pictures and words graphically showed the huge scope of the operation, and extolled the operation as providing jobs and money for Yukon residents. Certainly, this is true, but what will the real cost to Canadians and all of us be when all is said, blasted and done in the not-so-distant future?

AN AIR THAT KILLS – CORPORATE GREED, GOVERNMENT APATHY, DEAD PEOPLE

The California Literary Review – 2004

I like doing book reviews. Reading closely and not purely for the sake of reading improves my reading and writing skills. I've done a number of reviews for the contemporary wave of publications called websites and e-zines that are found lurking all over the internet. This one was the first I ever completed and it was for a marvelous little site called the California Literary Review – now out of business. Excellent essays, interviews and, of course, reviews were found here including about a dozen of my own efforts. The books discussed range from best sellers to relatively obscure efforts by the likes of the late Max Crawford (my review of a brilliant Montana writer who can with the subtlest of humor make James Joyce appear as complicated as Tom Grisham). The Review doesn't pay much, but you get a free review copy, and if anybody had ever told me as a kid I'd get paid for reading free books, I would have thought I'd died gone to someplace like heaven.

AN AIR THAT KILLS; How the Asbestos Poisoning of Libby, Montana, Uncovered a

179

Random Shots:
The Wanderings of a Montana Writer

National Scandal is about small-town Montana and the devastating horrors visited on it by a vermiculite mine owned by those fun-loving corporate bastards at W.R. Grace & Co, and the Zonolite Company before it. The mining of vermiculite, used in products ranging from insulation to potting soil, led to exposure to asbestos that caused and is causing the deaths of hundreds of Libby residents. Grace knew of the dangers, but didn't tell the workers or their families of the deadly dangers associated with living in an environment where more than two and a half tons of asbestos were released into the town's air every day, when one heavy exposure or even one tiny fiber can inaugurate the downward spiral to the grave.

A third of the town received what one Libby resident accurately described as "the death sentence," possible lung abnormalities which could indicate early stages of asbestosis (a malignant disease caused by minute but lethal knife-like fibers of asbestos that cause hardening of delicate lung tissue, among other things, and makes breathing impossible in its final stages). Miners who'd worked for Grace or Zonolite were hardest hit. Almost half of these former employees had signs of the disease that would guarantee them a lingering and painful death. The national average for these diseases in a community is 2 percent or less.

I'm not known for impartiality. That's not my style. When it comes to writing about *An Air That Kills* by Andrew Schneider and David McCumber I don't have a chance. McCumber was my editor at Big Sky Journal when the magazine premiered oh so long ago. Before taking the job of managing editor at the *Seattle Post Intelligencer* he was my neighbor in Livingston, Montana. We're close friends. And one of the main attorneys representing the victims in this horribly revealing book is Jon Heberling, an individual who is not only a long-time friend, but someone I had the privilege of working with when we shut down the Flathead National Forest's lunatic Forest Plan of the late 1980s and early 1990s. He's also the godfather of my daughter, Rachel. And I used to live in Whitefish, Montana just a short drive over the mountains from where this book takes place.

I spent many days cruising over to Libby to fish the Kootenai River for rainbow and cutthroat trout, and the rare redband trout in little streams way back up in the timbered mountains that surround the valley. Not once did any of those I came in contact with, individuals that profited by living in the Libby area, mention the problem – not the guides and outfitters, not the local Chamber of Commerce, not any of the town's merchants, not a noted writer I spent a little time with who lives in the area. Nobody. And they all knew. How could they not have known when men, and later wives and children, had died and were dying hellish deaths from lung diseases caused by the mine.

"Hey, man, talking about death is bad for the local economy. Keep quiet and it will go away." Seemed to be the party line all too often.. Fortunately people like Libby residents Gayle Benefield, Les Skramstad and others would not remain silent, would not be shoved out of the dark picture, would not be intimidated. In a book of great sorrow, these are the heroes.

Hell, I figured the place was just another northwest Montana community that made its living from mining, logging, and tourism. A place that also had some pretty fair trout fishing in the bargain. I'll always regret not looking a little closer at what was going down in this part of the woods. Fortunately Schneider, McCumber and other members of the *PI's* staff did look and notice. What they found is awful, made all the more so by the knowledge that what happened to Libby, how Grace does business, is merely standard operating procedure throughout most of corporate America.

Random Shots:
The Wanderings of a Montana Writer

Just consider some of the following:

Millions of us are still threatened by asbestos in our homes, where we work. Most of us believe that using asbestos is now illegal. It isn't. The authors write "Nobody is sure how many homes contain Zonolite. Estimates range from 15 million to 35 million. But according to the EPA and US Justice Department's tally of W.R. Grace invoices the company shipped billions of pounds of tainted ore to more than 750 processing plants throughout North America. Most of those companies produced attic insulation."

Many automobile brakes are made with asbestosis. "About six million mechanics have been exposed to asbestos since 1940...those exposures are now resulting in 580 asbestos-related excess cancer deaths per year. Within 10 years, the expected rate of mesothelioma deaths alone will be 200 a year from exposure to brake dust."

And here's a big surprise. The Bush White House, through its Office of Management and Budget, blocked the EPA's long-awaited declaration of a public health emergency in Libby in April 2002, and an accompanying warning to millions of citizens that their homes and businesses might contain Grace's deadly asbestos-contaminated insulation. A drastically watered-down memo was finally made public. The authors' also reveal the Bush White House's successful campaign to cover up the asbestos problem in lower Manhattan in the wake of the 9/11 terrorist attacks. The authors write " Documents from the White House Counsel on Environmental Quality showed a repeated pattern of downplaying the hazard to health even when the sparse information available showed just the opposite – to the extent of ordering headlines of government news releases changed completely so no threat or hazard was ever conveyed." One asbestosis-stricken Libby resident said, "Twenty years from now, when those New Yorkers start falling over dead, some young government bureaucrat will get all choked up apologizing for what the EPA and others didn't do."

Schneider and McCumber look at the ongoing debate on Capitol Hill over legislation to create a mechanism for resolving asbestos claims outside the judicial system. The authors show how one bill currently under consideration, proposed in 2003 by Republican Senator Orrin Hatch, will prevent many current and future victims of asbestos from being eligible for compensation. They point out that jackals that infest the attorney profession are initiating class action litigation that offers victims small compensation while eliminating their rights to sue for future illnesses and wrong doings.

Schneider and McCumber aren't just run-of-the-mill journalists. Schneider's won a pair of Pulitzers, a National Headliner Award, a Society of Professional Journalists' public service award, and the George Polk Award. McCumber was a 1984 Pulitzer finalist at the Arizona Daily Star. He edited a Pulitzer-winning project there. He is a past winner of the Don Bolles Award for investigative journalism. His books *The Cowboy Way: Seasons of a Montana Ranch; Playing off the Rail; and X-Rated* are crystalline, poignant examinations of microcosmic aspects of American life that expand to reveal much greater truths.

So when these two talk about the link between the EPA's failure to follow up on its own reports detailing the hazards of Libby's ore, and the Regan Administration's "Private Sector Survey on Cost Control," which was headed by J. Peter Grace, CEO of W.R. Grace & Co., and in an interview with William Ruckelshaus, who served as the EPA's first administrator in 1970, and again during the Reagan years, the authors quote Ruckelshaus as saying " If Grace's company owned that mine in Libby or had any other major involvement with asbestos, (Peter Grace) shouldn't have been reviewing actions dealing with the regulation of the asbestos industry" – when Schneider and McCumber discuss these issues, I listen.

And when the two write about W.R. Grace's cynical strategy to reassign employees whose X-rays showed significant signs of disease to less dirty jobs so as to minimize their exposure to asbestos dust in order to keep them on the job until they retired, and preclude the high cost of total liability; or when they expose the company touting its "Libby Medical Program" for anyone in the town diagnosed with asbestosis, even as the program repeatedly denies coverage to applicants and refuses to pay for some of their medications and oxygen, when Schneider and McCumber write about these things and many other indecencies, I believe them.

If *An Air That Kills* just served the purpose of exposing W.R. Grace's criminal and barbaric treatment of the Libby mine workers and their families, the book would have covered its purchase cost going away. It would be an important title. As it is, this significant work serves as an example of how not only hundreds of companies in this country view doing business, but how corporate entities around the world callously make a buck. *An Air That Kills* is required reading for anyone who cares.

MONTANA'S DEPARTMENT OF FISH, WILDLIFE AND PARKS – THE INMATES HAVE THE KEYS TO THE ASYLUM

counterpunch.org – 2007

This little item speaks for itself. Following the trip below I e-mailed my long-time friend Jeffery St. Clair, co-founder of counterpunch.org, about whether he'd be interested in an opinion article about my experiences with the Montana Department of Fish, Wildlife and Parks closing off (gating) the state for its own personal needs and use. Jeffrey came right back with "Fire Away." So I did. The MFWP hierarchy became very upset and my wife Ginny even received a critical letter purportedly written by the governor. I also received a number of supportive communications from biologists within the department.

IMAGINE A GRASSY FIELD along a joyful brown trout stream in the west. The Crazy Mountains rise madly to the south. The Castle, Belt and Little Belt ranges hold the western and northern horizons. Every spring hundreds of sandhill cranes clack and chatter among themselves as they feed in the fields along the river before heading far north into Canada. This place is the Selkirk fishing access along the Musselshell River in central Montana – a place where

Random Shots:
The Wanderings of a Montana Writer

I've taken friends from places like Seattle, Cocoa Beach, Baton Rouge and Boston, and the place where I proposed to my wife one gorgeous October day when the cottonwoods were flaming electric gold-orange. This is a place I've been coming to over and over since 1972. Two weeks ago my wife, Ginny, and I decided to stop off here for a few days after an extended road trip around the state – decompress in familiar surroundings a bit before heading home to Livingston.

We never got there. In its imperious wisdom the Montana Department of Fish, Wildlife and Parks (MDFWP) installed a chain-padlocked gate across the narrow two-track access to the grassy plain. There was no need to do this. The land was not abused or overused. Litter was rare and always picked by others who used the place. The two-track was in good shape and its narrow nature prevented land yachts from accessing the area. We were looking forward to some spring fishing for the trout, watching the Great Grey owls that live along this fecund riparian corridor as do countless whitetail deer, black bear and kingfishers to name a few.

Of course there was always the option of going over the slight ridge ½-mile away and camping amidst a herd of motor homes. Perhaps even the maintained site alongside the two outhouse the MDFWP has installed perched atop six-foot earthen mounds would be available. High rise outhouses -great idea I guess, almost as great as taking out the spigot around here that used to pour out cold, clear water.

More and more when we travel around Montana we see signs of the MDFWP run riot.

The first one I observed was in 1984 when the Kokanee salmon population crashed in Flathead Lake in the northwest corner of the state. The reason for this turned out to be an inspired decision by those fun-loving boys at the venerable department. Flathead Lake is 28 miles by 15 miles with 185 miles of shoreline. It is pristine and the largest natural freshwater lake West of the Mississippi River. Up until about 1984 it had annual runs of Kokanee salmon of several hundred thousand fish that would migrate and spawn up the Flathead River which feeds into the lake. The runs of 14 – 20" fish would literally blacken the river. The salmon provided a quality fishery and a necessary food source for some people. The salmon runs crashed in a very small way from over-fishing but mainly due to MDFWP planting mysis shrimp in the ecosystem. Mysis compete for plankton that the salmon feed on. Lake trout numbers and size in the lake has dwindled because the loss of the kokanee feed source. Since the loss of the Kokanee the Lake trout have turned to aggressively feeding on juvenile bull trout and westslope cutthroat trout, both endangered species.

Another result of this misguided move is that the annual bald eagle migration that used to number in the hundreds no longer exists. The glorious birds used to feast on the Kokanee diving and swooping along the creek, tagging a salmon with their talons then gliding up to a tree limb to enjoy their prey. We used to watch this spectacle for hours. When the salmon population ceased to exist, the eagles went elsewhere.

Another example occurred last year when we drove down to the Tongue River in southeastern Montana to camp along the river at a very rough and rustic state campground, another place we had stayed at for years. In one year the MDFWP had turned the place into a zoo replete with manicured lawns and smoothed gravel parking spots that were inhabited by a flock of motor homes – loud generators, TVs, radios and the such tearing up the air. A manicured row of dwarf willows impeded the view of the river.

Random Shots:
The Wanderings of a Montana Writer

Needless to say, Ginny and I drove off for more isolated doings.

A side note here. MDFWP claims that they do not stock any rivers in the state with trout, that the populations are self-sustaining. There are hundreds of rainbow trout in this stretch of the river that are cookie cutter replications of each other. This in a system that is well out of trout country and more commonly associated with small mouth bass, carp and channel catfish. Those were clearly hatchery fish and unless the rainbows made a break for freedom absconding with a MDFWP tank truck, they were clearly planted.

With few exceptions, telling the truth to the public and media goes against company policy. One biologist in the Deer Lodge area was so well-known for his deviations from the truth, that any of us who interviewed the fellow assumed that the actual situation was 180 degrees counter to what he said.

The list of atrocities to Montana's natural resources is lengthy. The MDFWP, when it isn't busy gating off good country, is busy turning state lands into a ghastly Disneyland clone. An agency that is sworn to preserve the state's wonders and provide access for recreation to the public has become an isolated, self-serving monster – a paradigm for everything that is wrong with government.

My hat's off to the Montana Department of Fish, Wildlife and Parks. Keep up the good work, boys.

SECTION THREE

Big Sky Journal

When David McCumber first started this magazine it immediately became one of the best publications anywhere. After he left it steadily degenerated into just another spoiled trust-funder, dare I still say Yuppie?, money-obsessed advertising rag. Such is life ... sadly.

BULL TROUT

1994

In January of 1994 I received a call from David McCumber, who I did not know at the time. He said that he was starting a new magazine to be called Big Sky Journal. He wanted to know if I would be interested in contributing a story about fishing for the premiere issue. I said yes. We talked for some time about all of the places we'd fished in Montana and about our favorite species, finally settling on an article about bull trout, a species I've always been interested in. David has become a dear friend of mine in the following years. He moved on and is now the editor at the Butte Standard and at Montana Magazine. His vision for the BSJ was clear and good. Had he stayed with the publication, well, I've always wondered what it would be like now. If that first issue was any indication, incredible. Writers included my long-ago faculty advisor from the University of Montana, Bill Kittredge, Jon Jackson, Gary LaFontaine, Datus Proper, Diane Smith, Ralph Beer, Gary Ferguson, Michael Katakis and Greg Keeler. Andy Anderson, Will Brewster, Denver Bryan and Dale Spartus contributed photographs, and Parks Reece added his art. That's one hell of a lineup. After David left, the new regime turned the Journal into something of a vanity press. Editorial decisions were more often than not riddled with nepotism and politics. Since David has left the publication has been in a downward spiral reaching the depths described at the start of this section. I haven't contributed to the current disaster in more than a decade and have no plans of ever doing so again, I'm sure to the

Random Shots:
The Wanderings of a Montana Writer

great joy of the trust funder who owns the magazine. The following story and the others that follow it are an accurate reflection of my misadventures around the state in the past dozen years.

AFTER CASTING FOR OVER SIX HOURS without a hit, the fishing was starting to take on monotonous overtones. Standing waist-deep in a beautiful northwest Montana river is always a good time, but cold streams, even on hot July days, turn legs numb with hypothermic intensity even as the brain is slowly being sunbaked. The fishing was not only work, it was turning weird, surreal.

I had slipped over the edge, turned stone-dead goofy, and it was all because of my passion for bull trout. This was the third day in a row I'd been working to these secretive members of the trout clan and still no fish. I knew the bulls were stacked up in this fast, deep run along a short cut bank of gravel and sand. Earlier this morning I'd waded across the river down below here and then crept on hands and knees back up and above the stream. I could see the fish holding along the bottom, lots of them. They looked like miniature dark-green submarines. Some of them would weigh close to nine pounds. Their bellies flashed pink through the water as they moved side to side, adjusting to the shifting seams of braided current. They were staging below a small mountain stream that offered prime spawning grounds. One day soon they would make their move far from the main river and into isolated pools and riffles. To catch one of them, I'd need a good drift and luck.

Enough for now. I slogged back to the shore and pulled a cold Pabst from a miniature eddy I'd created with backside rocks. The can foamed when I popped its top and the beer tasted fine bubbling down my throat and felt cold in my gut. Maybe this was why I devoted several days each season to fishing for this species. I was after a heat-stroke beer high. At least that's how it seemed at the moment.

As I finished the beer, I decided to try one more hour of casting and then I'd call it quits for the bulls this year. Working out fifty feet of eight-weight, sink-tip fly line, I launched a large red-and-white saltwater streamer to the head of the run and quickly mended line upstream to facilitate the fly's trip to the stream bottom, and also to prolong the drift. I did this over and over again, automatically, like an obsessed fly-fishing robot. The river drifted by – or was I really moving unconsciously downstream, out of control, with little hope for redemption? The day was timeless. Even the sun stopped moving across the sky. The thing just blazed overhead with wicked intensity. I was gone, lost in the hypnotic rhythms of casting and working the drift.

Wham! The rod jerked into the water, pulling me close to the river's surface. Directly across stream, thirty feet away, a huge fish rolled on top. The creature's bright pink belly flashed in the light and I could see the white tips of its fins and a head that was as wide as it was long. My streamer was imbedded in the upper corner of the bull's mouth.

Then the fish sounded, heading downstream in a long, steady, powerful run that pulled yards and yards of the line from the reel in pulsing, ratcheting jerks. There was no choice but to follow the bull trout down the river and, from the looks of things, around the bend (appropriate considering my current mental state). Sinking in the loose sands near shore, banging shins as I crashed over and against downed trees and scratching my face as I ripped through bushes and pine trees – yes, this was indeed too much fun. North American bull-trouting at its best. Good sport. High drama. I wanted this fish. Not for killing. Those days were over. There were too few *Salvelinus confluentus* (Latin is such erudite bliss) left in the rivers and lakes of western Montana to participate in such atavistic luxury. I merely wanted to bring this fish to shore and hold it briefly in my hands. To marvel at its wildness.

Bull trout used to be called Dolly Vardon (named for a dress worn by a Dickens' character called Miss Dolly Vardon) until fisheries biologists determined that the two were different creatures. Dollies are still called *Salvelinus malma*, but the bulls are known as *confluentus*. The differences don't stop with the names. Once they hit a certain size, all trout like to eat each other. They turn determinedly piscavorious. But to examine the head and jaws of a big bull is to see evolution wailing away on its free-swinging course with feral vengeance and efficiency. Bull trout are the sharks of the fresh-water salmonid clan. Compared to Dolly Vardon, their skulls are flattened and wed to facilitate eating down-sized whitefish, ciscos, sculpins, other trout, rusted bumpers from abandoned Studebakers, you name it. They grow large, more than 20 pounds, and in the Flathead River system of northwest Montana those caught by anglers averaged over eight pounds a few years back. They rarely take a dry fly and those that do are often juveniles who have yet to find their true calling.

We're not talking eastern brook trout here, though they are related: bulls also have a good deal in common with lake trout and Arctic char. Bull trout thrive in pristine lakes and rivers in country that has not been hammered by logging (which usually degrades water quality to an unacceptable level for the discerning fish). There are not a lot of these char around anymore. In fact, levels have dropped so precipitously that the state Dept. of Fish, Wildlife and Parks has outlawed fishing for bull trout, until sometime in the hazy future when their numbers hopefully stabilize, in all but a few lakes west of the Continental Divide. This dreadful event occurred in 1992 and some of us have not been truly

194

the same since. (Being an ardent lover of the bulls I applaud any attempt to save if not enhance the species' numbers, but to penalize fly fishers, a conservationally devoted and financially well-heeled constituency, while taking a tepid stand on habitat degradation smacks of bureaucratic jive at its worst. There is also a movement afoot, spearheaded by several environmental groups, to get the bull trout listed in the Endangered Species Act. While I'm sure this is motivated by the best of intentions, listing the species may hasten its extinction as a pure, wild fish. Once taken under the auspices of the ESA, bull trout will more than likely be sucked into the federal hatcheries program, meaning that less-than-wild fish will be stocked in streams holding pure strains of the native, but I digress).

Those who wish to fish for the bulls may still so legally on some waters of the Blackfeet Reservation right along the eastern edge of Glacier National Park. And there are a few remnant populations scattered around non-tribal areas of the state east of the divide.

Actually bull trout are still taken legally in closed waters. I tied into a brace of them along a favorite Flathead drainage stream this past summer. After working large fly patterns for the bulls over the years and, in the process, turning up several very large rainbow trout, I realized (swiftly at that) that bull trout tactics take other species of size and distinction as well. So on this stream in question I worked the large streamers, hooking one nice rainbow, and two bulls of over five pounds each. I played the fish quickly and gently released them so that they might continue their mysterious spawning runs into creeks that can generously be termed "tiny." I certainly would never flout a well-conceived game regulation. I only wanted to catch a big rainbow. No laws were broken.

The first time I caught a bull trout was more than twenty years ago in a large lake in the Bob Marshall

Random Shots:
The Wanderings of a Montana Writer

Wilderness. I didn't even know what bull trout were back then. I'd heard the name, but figured this was a local euphemism for another trout species. I was quite wrong. Casting a large streamer (always large if success is a priority) along a rocky shelf at dusk, something big nailed the pattern. After fifteen minutes or so of watching my line knife back and forth through the still lake, I horsed the trout to my feet. It promptly made one last thrashing roll, snapping my rod tip. I pounced on the fish, grabbing it in a wet embrace, receiving some nasty scratches on my wrist from the bull's razor-like teeth in the process.

What an animal. Long, dark green with bright orange spots and a silvery belly, the fish looked primitive, almost dangerous. I admired it for a few moments and then it struggled free of my grasp and disappeared into the water.

I was hooked. Dead meat in an angling sense.

And that's where I was now, tripping and flailing after this big bull trout that was holding just above a strong run. One more lunge downstream with the current and he would be free. I inched the fish closer very slowly, praying for all I was worth that the frayed tippet would hold. And it did. I got lucky. The bull didn't make a dash for the faster water and a certain breakoff.

This one was lit up like a Christmas tree in spawning colors. The orange spots, white fin-tips and pink stomach glowed with procreation intensity. The greens of its back and sides shone like emeralds. The head was enormous, the mouth filled with mean-looking teeth. An eating machine. The lower jaw was hooked in a kype that is distinctive to males in the spawning phase.

Unhooking the streamer I pricked my thumb, drawing blood that swirled in the shallow water. The fish quivered, perhaps at the scent of this blood. I never lifted the bull from the water, but its heft, its untamed strength was palpable as I revived it with very slow back-and-forth motions. Holding the trout just above its wide, fan-like square tail, I could feel the energy returning and then the fish pulled loose from my grasp and was gone. In an instant.

Had it ever been here in the first place?

SOLITUDE, FREEDOM, ATAVISM ... AND ONE HUGE TURKEY

1994

I no longer hunt turkeys. I can't bring myself to kill one of this outrageously, magnificent birds. Grouse, Huns, pheasants, and chukar when I can hit them – shooting these birds is fun. It doesn't bother me nearly as much. But knocking down a turkey is a different matter. Their call, which sounds ludicrous in captivity, brings home the wild nature of the land I love more than any – the coulees and bluffs of southeastern Montana. That crazy, undisciplined sound, the internal vision it conjures of the turkeys moving secretively and swiftly across exposed sage flats, down eroding sandstone washes and beneath stands of tall Ponderosa, says it all for me. Thirty-pound birds that move with the swiftness of horses and the stealth of the night wind. To me they're special. I have a dry camp in the middle of not much at all down on the Custer National Forest in Tongue River country. When I arrive and after I set up camp, I like to walk to the edge of a bluff and sit on a downed tree trunk. I've done this for years. From this spot I can see across miles of broken and twisted landscape, across small valleys filled with pine trees and across rolling hills of native grasses and sage. Within a few minutes I normally hear coyotes barking and chattering away in the distance. They know I'm back often, it seems, before I do. And then, sometimes, I'll hear a turkey call, the

199

strange sound carrying and softly echoing through the land. And maybe another will answer the first one. I'll keep sitting where I am, smoking a cigar as I enjoy the ensuing silence. I'll watch the stars come out, the moonrise and perhaps the green glow of the northern lights will appear and shade the country in their unique radiance. The turkeys are a part of all of this and I can't kill them anymore.

I HAD ONLY THE VAGUEST IDEA what time it was. Very early, for sure. The Ponderosa pines were visible as towering, many-armed demons standing all around me in the dark. The stars were still out, shining intensely. The first suggestions of a false dawn glowed faintly on the edges of the hills and bluffs. Long needles carpeted the ground, covering patches of last year's dry grass. The spring had been unseasonable warm so far and dry. Scant moisture had fallen and the melting snow was long gone, soaked up by the thirsty ground.

My feet crunched on the duff, a brittle, hollow sound. Trying to find the roost tree I'd discovered yesterday was proving troublesome. The thick-trunked pine should be right around here only a few hundred yards from my camp, such as that was. No water, a small fire ring, the back of the truck serving as a kitchen, and my sleeping bag and tarp passing for a bedroom. Austerity has a well-remembered ring, one I'm comfortable with on the road or out in the sticks.

The drive over to this sparsely populated part of southeastern Montana was six or seven hundred miles, twelve hours, but this was one of the best places in the West for hunting the large birds. Back home in the Flathead you had to put in for a permit to hunt turkeys. There were less than 200 openings available and the odds were long. Out this way all you needed to do was walk into a sporting goods store in Billings or down in Sheridan and pay for the various permits and a conservation license, a total of less than 15 bucks this year (approximately $70 if you were from out-of-state) and an additional few dollars for an autumn license.

A friend had showed me this place years ago in what proved to be a hunt of heroic, slightly mad proportions. Now I come back every opportunity to spend a little time perched on this pine-forested bluff that looks out over miles of rolling hills and eroded coulees. The varying shades of green displayed by the native grasses, small cactus. Conifers and sage blended easily with the ochres, buffs and subtle pinks of the rock formations and exposed earth. This was wild, unspoiled country and I'd never seen another hunter in all the years, not even at the small store some miles distant that served as a post office and gas station. One pickup truck was the extent of human visitation during my undisciplined forays.

That was the main reason I drove all this way. To be alone, by myself. The turkeys were just an excuse, though a damn good one in my mind. I've not shot many Merriam's in this span of years, but I know where they are, to some extent. The tick is in the timing. Too early and the birds are scattered all over hell and back. Show up after the spring procreational soiree has completed its bizarre dance and the situation is similar. The turkeys have dispersed and even if they are trotting around in the trees or strutting in the grassy meadows, they are more than a shade reluctant to come to my calls, amateur efforts at best, but productive during the peak of the breeding season. In truth, when the birds are in full rut, so to speak, discordant notes bombed away from the belly of a tuba would work. Neophyte scratchings on a hollow cedar box sound like a symphony to the love-struck turkeys. At the first annoying notes, again if the timing is right, gobblings emanate from the hills in all directions. Pure lunacy. Lovely sounds singing through the air.

The roost tree I was trying to find right now was one of several I'd discovered in the area. Arriving in the afternoon, I set up camp, grilled a burger and sipped a few gin-and-tonics (no limes, Spartan trip). Around the time the sun started fading over the horizon, casting the countryside in an eerie orange-gold light, a series of "gobbles," "putts" and assorted other forms of Turkey madness issued from the coulee behind me. The cacophony advanced nearer finally culminating in thwacking sounds of wings beating and some disgruntled utterings from the birds as they settled into their perches for the night. What a crew. I was sure I knew which tree they'd pulled into. The other three roost trees were growing on a gentle slope a couple of miles away. Too far for the birds' racket to have sounded so close to camp. Tomorrow I'd shoot my turkey and then head to a small river running freely even farther in the middle of nothing where I'd try my hand at some untamed rainbows that ran to good size. Killing a couple of weeks in these parts was almost too easy.

Standing well alone in this country, looking away towards Wyoming in the south and then in the direction of Billings many miles north, the familiar feeling of loneliness descended. Not unwelcome, another reason to be out here and away from the smothering security of civilization where it seems I never have the chance to feel anything but what I'm told or programmed to feel. Do this. Think that. Buy into another administration con. Don't step out of line. That's where the loneliness comes in handy. The feeling is a means to connect with life, to turn briefly humble without being publicly humiliated. We all get enough of that trying to earn a living.

That's the power of this country, a place so foreign to most of us, alien to me at times, that we don't have a natural clue about what's taking place. Lightning strikes an exposed seam of coal and a smoldering fire starts, watched by no one. The coal may smoke and flare into flames, sizzling for centuries, until it is doused by heavy rain and runoff or burns its way through to the other side of the hill or runs out of fuel. The fire is so hot, mud and sandstone is baked rock-hard and kiln-cured to the color of dried blood. A fifty-foot seam of coal may cook two hundred feet of rock lying above. (What do the mule deer and the coyotes and the turkeys think about all this? Probably nothing at all. There's too much thinking going on as it is. Confused brain noise that is detectable, faintly, in the distant glow of Billings late at night. City rap. Disgusting stuff.) The clinker eventually builds up into huge beds of porous rubble storing billions of gallons of water that seeps down from the contributions of wicked storms raging on up above. Artificial wells naturally made. Trees and brush grow best in these spots and wild animals know them for their water. There are several such places near camp, wild drawing cards for the Merriam's.

I built up the fire and fried a fat pork chop and some onions in butter and garlic, threw together some salad that was liberally doused with Paul Newman's famous dressing. It was all I could find at a store some hours up the road. I was hungry and finished off the meal in minutes, then re-stoked the dwindling fire, ignited a cheap cigar from Connecticut, build a tall drink and enjoyed the night. Coyotes howled away from the surrounding ridges, talking to each other. They knew the turkeys were here, too. Earlier, I'd heard a few calls from the packs then some miles off, as the turkeys began to roost. I'd have some competition, but hopefully the boys weren't armed. After climbing into the sleeping bag, I tried to make sense out of the sky, but my mind faded to black and I was out until maybe four. Now I was trying to find that damn roost tree and then a place to hide.

Random Shots:
The Wanderings of a Montana Writer

The stars were disappearing and the sky on the east was actually turning to soft blue when I found the tree. The ancient pine, several feet thick at its base, gnarled and twisted from its long life, hundreds of years to be sure, loomed above me, its thick roots clinging to thin soil and crumbling sandstone ledges. Dark, lumpy objects, a lot of them, were hunkered down on limbs twenty and more feet up. As quietly as possible I crept toward a downed pine, its black bark and the exposed wood weathered grey. The cover was less than forty yards from the birds. Crouching down, I crawled back into an opening in the branches and situated myself so that I had a shot through a man-sized window in the limbs. Sitting on my butt, knees drawn to my chest, I rested the shotgun, an old Savage .22-twenty-gauge, in the nook made by my knees. I was afraid to move or make any noise, but cautiously practiced sighting in on where I thought the turkeys would land, hopefully in just a few minutes. They were notorious early risers.

Long moments passed and my mind wandered far into the coulees. I wondered what it was like living out here all years as a homesteader. The climate was extreme, fluctuating crazily between searing heat and teeth-cracking cold. Little wind in summer and fierce gales in winter. Sleet and dust choking the periods in-between. What a way to go. What drove men to leave the perceived safety of towns and cities to risk starting a new life out in this desolation? I knew the answer, for me, at least.

There was freedom in this frightening vastness. A chance to do what I wanted by myself with no one looking over my shoulder. Knowing that what happened, happened and the consequences be damned, was intoxicating. Yes, I knew why I would have taken a chance on this country and I could understand the unexplained drive in others a hundred years ago.

The sky was now a washed-out robin's-egg blue across

the horizon. The lumps in the old tree were stirring, making small sounds. Not clucks or purts or anything like that, more like the first sounds a person makes when he rides up out of a deep sleep.

I readied the gun and breathed shallowly. Then the turkeys started dropping out of the tree in the growing light. They sounded like sacks of cement hitting the ground and it was not a vision blessed with gracefulness. The birds didn't bounce, rather they went "thump," then tried standing on stiff legs, shaking their feathers and tentatively working big wings. I was reminded of a game where I saw a former Chicago Cubs' player, Dave Kingman, rounding second base, arms windmilling, long legs pumping as he gallantly tried to stretch a double into a leg (very leggy) triple. He slid and never reached third, tagged dead out by the length of a Rolls-Royce.

The crowd howled, then cheered at the unconscious audacity of the effort. A Chicago sports writer once described Kingman running the bases to the effect that he looked like an empty paint can being tossed from the window of a speeding car. As it raced along a bumpy road. I stifled a laugh. That's how these turkeys looked. Ungainly, not really with the program.

I sighted in on two males and tried to determine the largest. They were both huge, well over twenty-five pounds, with long beards, blue-white heads giving way to dusty-red wattles hanging from their chins and necks.

I knew the .22 would kill either bird with a head shot, but I was unsure of my ability to hit what I aimed at. I was excited and shaky. I flipped the selector to the lower barrel, loaded with a three-inch ("Magnooms" as a friend calls them) twenty-gauge filled with copper-plated No. 2s. Upland birds, yes, but more like big game. A lot of energy was needed to drop a Merriam's with a flank shot. The turkey on my left walked a few yards closer and gave me an angled profile. A regal bird now standing dead still. I sighted at an area just below the base of the neck and fired.

"Boom" The concussion rocked through the coulees and over the bluffs. The turkeys ran, leaped for the air and made sounds I'd never heard out of a bird before. Yelps, gagging gobbles and strained clucks. An avian Chinese fire drill. On the ground was my turkey, on its side, one wing beating a dying tune. I crawled out of my cover, stood up, almost falling back down, legs gone dead with waiting. I was wired, high on adrenaline and weaved my way the short distance to the fallen creature. The others in the flock were gone. Out of sight and sound. I'd hit this one with a number of pellets in the neck making a ragged, bloody mess. The shoulder and wing were damaged as well, though I doubted these wounds did the bird in. I set the gun in the grass and lifted the Merriam by the legs. It felt heavy, like a brace of very big channel catfish.

I let out a scream that had atavism written all over it and then just looked at the bird. That yell and all I could think was, "What a huge god-damned turkey." One of the highest things I'd ever done outdoors and all I could think of was, "What a huge, god-damned turkey." Moments of such profundity are stark, raving amazing, aren't they?

Walking back to camp with the bird slung over my shoulders, wings extended, I could feel the waning heat of the animal through my vest and shirt. Field dressing it was anticlimactic. I left both feet and legs attached for purposes of sex identification in case I happened upon a game warden. Fat chance. The tail feathers, large, mottled bronze, black and tan with a few hints of grey, were stowed carefully in a large freezer bag. Souvenirs for my children and potential wings for grasshopper patterns. I would tie for late-summer fly fishing. I hung the bird so that it cooled quickly in the morning air, then wrapped it in a couple of thick garbage bags before storing it in a cooler filled with block and cubed ice.

I made some dense black coffee, Golden Sumatran, added a dash or two of Jim Beam and toasted the turkey, the country, the day, and my good fortune. If only all hunts were like this one. Again, fat chance, but I was a happy boy at the moment. Coyotes were barking on the ridges. They must have winded the turkeys and I heard a lone gobble way off to the west of the pack.

I'd take a nap and then break camp. The rainbows were calling me now.

POWDERED CATFISH

1999

Catfish have been a part of my fishing life for as long as I can remember. From the youthful days in northern Illinois when I caught them on the Rock River to a brief stint is a sportswriter at the Beloit Daily News where I would catch them in Turtle Creek and now way out here in Montana where I look for them in the muddy waters of southeastern Montana. This is one of the first stories my wife and photographer, Ginny and I completed together. It is but one of many fine pieces of work we accomplished. Catfish are strong, much stronger pound-for-pound than trout, and to my way of thinking they taste much better out of the frying pan. After a lamentable gap of perhaps ten years, a time when I fished exclusively with a fly rod, I returned to this delightful angling down near Broadus. I'd forgotten the simple joy of flinging a glob of chicken livers in to a stream, setting the rod into a forked stuck in the bank and then waiting for that most magic of sights, the tip of the rod jerking up and down when a big cat took the bait. I've tried to convince several of my fly fishing friends to come down with me to fish for catfish, but they all beg off and shake their heads. They look at me as if I'm off my rocker or have gotten hooked on something as bad as shooting drugs.. They don't know what they're missing. Sitting alongside the Middle Fork of the Powder River watching the stars come out, the sound of a Coleman lamp gently hissing in the night, the peaceful solitude of all of this. I feel like I'm a little kid once again. It's great.

Random Shots:
The Wanderings of a Montana Writer

IT'S VERY DARK OUT, even with all the stars and the random drive-bye, fizzling-green meteor. 'Round midnight and songbirds are singing and owls are booming as they charge through the sky. A lone cow is bellowing pitifully, the sound cutting bell-clear through the muddy rushings of the Powder River. Wild, intact country. Whatever is at the end of the rod I am holding is doing whatever it damn pleases, runs up the narrow Little Powder River and boiling rolls along the far bank. Can't see a damn thing, but I can feel and hear the fish as it struggles somewhere out there. Flashes of far-off lightning illuminate jagged bluffs and dry hills that drift off in all directions. The thunder sounds much later, muffled by distance. This natural river system is so intact, so healthy, that the place is alive with life. Songbirds by the hundreds sing and chirp throughout the night. Coyotes howl. Owls hoot, and the catfish bite.

Finally the fish slightly reveals itself. An eight-to-ten-pound channel catfish swirling in the pea soup water and roiling the muddy bottom. Just a touch closer and I'll grab the sucker, but nothing comes easy for some us. A pair of curious muskrats motor upstream as though on a leisurely cruise. They circle the angry fish cutely avoiding my line. They look at the mayhem in the water thrashing beneath their paws, then up at us with an expression of natural disgust, before moving off into the night. The catfish is dragged up onto the slippery bank. Thick leather gloves are pulled on. This is man's play here. Chasing the noble cat is the sport of addled kings. The fish's fins can cause a most painful sting and I've moved beyond digging pain. Slipping and sliding to the river, I grab the creature by its tail and fling it up on the bank, knocking over a container of ripe chicken livers and another one holding treble hooks and lead sinkers.

Ah yes, the sport of kings right here on the Little Powder, in the depths of a late-April evening. We are wandering royalty indulging in regal pleasures.

Ginny photographs the cat as it rests on a huge, long-dead, cottonwood trunk. The silver greys, whites and black spots go nicely with the shades of weathered wood. How artistic. We hurry so that we can plop the fish back into the river. I'm not concerned, but my friend is. She worries about such things. Hell, if you're of a cruel mind you can throw a few of them in the bed of a pickup, careen and weave along dusty back roads swilling warm cans of Schmidt beer for hours as the cats bounce around with empty oil cans, Jim Beam bottles, rusted tow chains and Slim Jim wrappers, then return to the river and put the cats back in the water. They'll swim away. They're tough. They won't die, but I don't do this at all anymore. I only mentioned the possible diversion to give some idea of how hearty catfish are. I treat all fish, especially the ones I kill to eat, with respect. There are so many gods and esoteric deities chasing my soul now ... man, I don't want or need anymore running down my ragged ass, but I digress from the cat at hand.

Yes, we are using a fly rod and a spinning rod, too (just in case a local catfisher shows up). But delicate insect imitations, not even woolly buggers drenched in essence of chicken liver (and more on this later), are not being skillfully cast to rising *Ictalurus punctatus*. No way. Size 6 treble hooks loaded with gobs of chicken liver and weighted with several sinkers of marble proportions are heaved into the turbid Little Powder. The channel cats are on their spring spawning run and in this small stream that is no more than fifty feet wide at its most robust and the turbid gem is less than fifteen minutes outside of the town of Broadus.

Random Shots:
The Wanderings of a Montana Writer

Broadus is a small place of well less than a thousand cheerful souls who have always been nothing but friendly and helpful to us whenever we wander down this way, which is often. Cattle ranches are everywhere around here, so are pickups, cowboys and ranch women. The town is the county seat, features several bars, a damn good restaurant called The Judge's Chambers ("Finest Food In 2,000 Miles" says one sign not far outside of Biddle, population 6, near the Wyoming border a few cold drinks south of here), a couple of bars, motels, gas stations, a grocery store, hardware store, beauty parlor and so on. We once did a story on the restaurant for a magazine and the owner, Jean Hough, has always treated us like long-lost friends (even before the article was published). Hough comes from a ranching background and used to tend sheep far out on the prairie when she was eleven armed with a rifle and sheltered by an old wagon. She did this on her own. It was her chore. That's Broadus. People work. Take care of their own business. Help their neighbors and are kind to strangers like us. We've often thought of moving here and disappearing from all of it, all of the modern crap, but we don't. Broadus is these people's home and we're not ones to drop in permanently and uninvited.

We hook up (tarpon terms seem appropriate here) with fish from six to ten pounds steadily. Probably tons of them swimming past silently out of sight. There is barely time to set to the nine-foot, eight-weight rod into the crook of a stout stick before the tip is jerked towards the river. I dive forward out of my chair, grab the rod and reef backwards to set the hook. The catfish goes ballistic and runs up river. An eight-weight will at least slow any trout I've caught in Montana. Not catfish, and relatively small ones at that. Twenty pounds is not unheard of in this region. These boys power upstream in a wake of foam and indescribable detritus, the English reel screaming as though it is being subjected to some hideously obscene act, the rod's dainty tip pulled beneath the water's brown surface. Twenty minutes or more later the cat finally tires and is brought in. The hapless cat is tossed on the bank, photographed in a coating of dirt and leaves, then either returned to the river or put in the cooler for a deep-fried fillet dinner the next evening. Blood sport. The best of all behavior.

Earlier in the day the drive in on a sandy two-track was lovely. Huge, very old cottonwoods filter the light turning everything a soft blue-green. Last year's cattails stand tall and silver-gold next to the river. Whitetails bound away, tails brightly signaling our intrusion. Domestic sheep plod off into the trees bleating hoarsely. We set up camp and went off to fish in a mid-eighties, a hot, dry wind blowing sand and dirt in our eyes. I've never caught catfish in daylight, but someone in town said anytime is a good time, so I tried, for hours. Ginny sat on a log clutching her camera that was wrapped in a plastic bag to protect it from damage. Finally she said "Enough!" and went back for a nap. I hung on for awhile longer before giving up and deciding that a brief lie down would be appropriate.

Now in the cooling darkness I am covered with the blood of chickens, bits of the birds' livers and the slime of the raging cats, and I'm using a fly rod. At least my integrity as a consummate purveyor of marginally esoteric B.S. remains intact. In addition to channel cats there are also black and yellow bullheads and the most fearsome of all, the stonecat. Prior to this spring I'd only heard rumors of this specie's voracious appetites and fearsome power. To catch one of these was a dream, beyond imagining or comprehension.

The excitement was intense, palpable as we drove south on a red dirt road that wound through eroded bluffs and coulees worn ragged by wind and water. I'd often doze off only to be awakened as I banged my head on the dash when

Random Shots:
The Wanderings of a Montana Writer

Ginny braked for open-range cattle. Ponderosa pine clung to the sides of the hills. Antelope grazed on new grass. The Powder River described long, lazy curves as it flowed north. A shot-gun-blasted sign said "Welcome to Wyoming," so we turned around, dropped down a two-track that led to the river, opened a gate, drove through and set up camp above the water. The river was already rising from runoff and rain, slurping by more like mud than water. Thick stuff. Looking across the river I spotted a dead, bloated cow, legs splayed and pointing to the sky. The sign I'd been looking for. Dead Cow. Raging catfish. I could see the connection. This had to be the place.

After impatiently waiting for dusk, I rigged the eight-weight, pulled out an olive woolly bugger that had been soaking for several days in a plastic container of chicken livers, tied it on and launched the thing far across the river. As the pattern was slowly stripped in something jerked the line and I hauled back to set the hook, totally unprepared for the struggle that followed. A pale, flesh-colored fish that went easily over six inches soared past my head and landed in last season's tall, dead grass behind me. I knew this was tough fishing but I was not ready for the battle that ensued. Nearly thirty minutes were spent trying to find the fish in the grass, weeds and wild roses. When I finally found the thing, I lifted that catfish in both hands, held it high in the sky as an offering to the angling gods who once again shone down on me.

A stonecat. A lifetime dream realized, and on a fly with only oX tippet. More skilled anglers than I have spent lifetimes casting to these elusive fish, never connecting, let alone, landing one. And this cat measured seven inches. A trophy. (There are unconfirmed reports of foot-long specimens being taken in the 1890s, but I'm skeptical.) This fish was at least six years old and weighed three or four ounces. Ginny documented the event on film. I have friends who don't believe some things I tell them and her pictures would silence their rude doubts. The stonecat was put back in the river. The joy we experienced as we watched that catfish struggle down through the thick water to freedom was like nothing either of us had ever known. Hitting a steer with our Suburban outside of Roy, surviving the insane onslaught that is archery season in The Missouri Breaks, doubling on Western Meadowlarks last year up by Plentywood, none of those touched the magic of this stonecat. A special fish. We could only smile at each other. Beyond words. Then we returned to our fire and grilled a couple of pounds of Montana beef.

Noble catfish. The only true gamefish of the northern high plains. We'd finally come home again and it felt right.

JORDAN'S
HELL CREEK BAR
1999

There are parts of Montana that are still remote, even today. Jordan is one of them. This is wide-ranging, tough, dry land except for Ft. Peck Reservoir lying to the north, the place Ivan Doig wrote about so well in his book **Bucking the Sun**. *Our former landlords run a ranch up this way and when they saw a brief story about Ginny and I doing a story on the Hell Creek Bar in the local paper, they called and sounded very excited. Another friend of mine, a lunatic sculptor of fish, was raised on his family's homestead in the area. And I know a few others who make their living in this country. Every one of them might be considered a bit crazy by those who live in cities. Maybe it's the openness of perhaps the wind or the heat or the drought or all the stars or the antelope or the sage or the cactus or whatever. I really have no idea. They all seem just fine to me. They are all a good deal of fun to be around, upright, hardworking and, that rarest of commodities today, honest. The Hell Creek Bar in the following story is a gathering place for locals that live in the surrounding area, a space of several thousand square miles. Maybe this bar is crazy, too, but they pour a damn honest drink at the place. That counts for something in my book.*

Random Shots:
The Wanderings of a Montana Writer

WAY OUT IN NOWHERE, I guess that's where this begins and ends, in a place a New York radio station called "the lonesomest town in the world" back in the 1930s. In east-central Montana twenty-five miles south of Fort Peck Reservoir lies Jordan, Montana with a population of maybe 500. And if this is a lonesome place, the Hell Creek Bar on the town's main drag is not. All day and well into the night Jordan residents, ranchers, hunters, fisherman and peripatetic travelers wander in for a cold drink or a cup of coffee or a sandwich and always a little small talk.

For decades Hell Creek has provided a friendly place for people to relax, whoop it up or just plain regroup from the awesome vastness and relentless loneliness of the miles and miles of open spaces rolling off in every direction. Sage flats, coulees, bluffs, creekbeds that sometimes hold water but usually don't, mule deer, elk, antelope, coyotes, hawks eagles and lots of cows and sheep. That's Hell Creek country.

Charlotte and Joe Herbold bought the place four years ago and have done much to renovate and enlarge the operation. When you come in the door dozens of eyes stare down on you – pronghorns, mule deer, northern pike, sauger, walleye. They all glare at the new arrival with unblinking eyes from there mounted positions on the walls. And the patrons will turn ever so slightly from their bar stools, give you a quick appraisal and a smile before turning back to their drinks and conversation.

"What'll you have," asks Charlotte with a smile before we have settled into our places at the bar. We order cold drinks and she fills the order and asks how we're doing. We say "Just fine," and tell her our business, which is finding out more about her bar, and after a bit of give and take and checking us out to see if our intentions are what we say,

Charlotte opens up like we were old friends.

We remark on the craftsmanship and beauty of the cherry wood back bar and she tells us that when she and Joe were working on refinishing it she saw a picture of the bar and lighting fixtures at Chatham's Livingston Bar and Grill and away she went with theirs. The bar originally came from France a very long time ago. The racks to hold that country's fine wines are still in place. Once in this country it eventually made its way up the Missouri River from St. Louis to Ft. Benton by steamboat, sometime later by ox cart to Hilger and eventually to Jordan by truck over more than 100 miles of dusty two-track roads in the 1930s. All of this woodwork is accentuated by a tin ceiling that Char says she could sell for "beau coup bucks," but she won't.

She leaves us briefly to attend to a customer who just strolled in wearing work boots, dusty jeans, a denim shirt, red suspenders and a gimme ball cap. She pours him a shot of Jim Beam and opens a can of beer. "I need a puff," he tells Charlotte and she fetches his brand from a cupboard beneath the bar. Camel straights. As it should be. She and the old guy chat for a bit about someone and Charlotte adds "You don't have to be drunk to deal with him, but it sure helps," and there's a good deal of knowing laughter from the regulars. Another older gentleman, perhaps in his seventies, walks in and says "Where's my fish?" and Char goes into a room behind the bar and returns with a box of frozen salmon. He says "Thanks," with a smile and walks back out. That's the way it goes at Hell Creek. Friendly, seemingly happy and respectful people come and go here as part of their daily routine. And every few months area musicians, fiddlers, guitar players, banjo players, gather at the bar for informal jam sessions that last for hours.

Glancing at the top of the back bar I see a row of hats – New Orleans FBI, Memphis FBI, LA FBI, Kansas City FBI, Denver FBI, Chicago FBI, Atlantic City FBI and Cincinnati

Random Shots:
The Wanderings of a Montana Writer

FBI. If a person didn't know the recent history of the town, he might wonder just what in the hell kind of place he staggered into. And if he kept on scanning the hats above him he'd see CBS Sports, Fox News, ABC News, NBC News and on and on. "What gives here?" he might ask.

Well back in the spring of 1996 a group of individuals called the Freemen made the national and world news scene when their political views ran so counter to that of the various governmental agencies in the land that things came to a head and the predictable standoff with the Freeman, well-armed as is almost anyone in Montana or at least used to be before things went soft and West Coast, holding up in what the media termed a "compound" not far outside of Jordan. By the time it was all over and settled without bloodshed, unless you count the FBI agent who was killed when he rolled his car while driving pretty fast on the red-dust roads, literally hundreds of FBI agents, reporters, photographers and curiosity seekers had dropped in on the town and the Hell Creek Bar. Jordan was on the map thanks to the Freeman and everyone in town still talks about it.

"From March 26th when everything started until April 19th when it was over this place was packed with agents and media people," said Char. "And they were all well-behaved and nice. And they left good tips. We made beau coup bucks then," and she smiled.

"Joe finally started a media sign-up sheet so we could see who was who and who all was here," and Char hands me a sheaf of legal notepad pages filled with names and hometowns of reporters from New York, LA, Chicago, Australia, Japan and on and on.

It was a warm April day and the town was largely empty because the ranchers were still busy with calving and lambing along with working their fields, but everyone we encountered in Jordan was friendly and helpful, but the great thing about this place is the honest individuality of the people who live here. Like the editor-publisher of the weekly paper, the Jordan Tribune. Just before the Freeman story went ballistic she wrote an editorial saying that the Tribune would run no more news on the situation and it didn't. When I learned this I smiled, then laughed. Think about it. The biggest story that will probably ever hit Jordan and the editor decides for her own good reasons that she and the town have heard enough already. So, no news on the Freeman in the local paper. Fantastic. Great stuff.

Another story I was told by someone from the area is perhaps apocryphal and perhaps exemplary of the free-form life style swirling around Jordan and the high plains. Purportedly back in "the good old days" there was a guy who passed out in the mud on the street one night after a few drinks. The next morning he woke up to find his hair frozen to the ground. Some helpful souls passing by pooled their resources and pissed on his head until his hair thawed out. Well, tales like that out in the West are sometimes true, partly true or often weirdly mythical. Take your pick.

A lot of this attitude comes from the sere, wild, rugged landscape that shapes the people who live here and in a large part dictates how they live. And there is the remoteness, a remoteness that makes the Hell Creek Bar not just a great place to go for a drink and catch up on the local news, but an important part of the community. Jordan didn't have phone service until 1935 and back then the editor of the Tribune relied on his short-wave radio for world news. The nearest city with more than 1,000 people is Miles City and that's 83 miles to the south.

And now Char rejoins us and recounts the story of the FOX reporter from Los Angeles who asked her "'Can I have deli food shipped here?' and I said 'Sure. Go right ahead.' But then the Uni-bomber story broke over in Lincoln and he was sent there a half-hour before his food arrived. He called from Lincoln and said to 'spread the food out for everyone,' which we did, except for some deli meats and some kind of soup I can't remember the name of, that we sent to him in Lincoln." Char laughed some and went down to the other end of the bar to pour another round of drinks.

We finished ours and headed out the door saying "Thanks" and "Good-bye."

"Enjoy the rest of your trip and be sure to stop in the next time you're passing through," Char called out.

We said we would.

HIGH PLAIN'S SHARKS

2000

When fly fishers think of Montana, probably not one-in-10,000 consider northern pike. When you tell some of these individuals that northerns not only hang out here in many lakes and rivers, notably in the eastern half of the state, that they exceed thirty pounds on occasion, and then deftly drop in the fact, that unlike the rainbows and browns they so eagerly pursue, that northerns are native to some waters in Montana, most of these guys will give you looks ranging from disbelief to disgust to snobbish indifference. That's their problem. Northerns are incredible fish on a fly. Vicious predators that devour anything that moves in their waters. And a dozen-pounder is fine sport on a seven-weight. I've caught fish to fifteen pounds in creeks no wider than your living room carpet. I've stumbled onto a number of lakes, ponds and streams that flow through some of the most beautiful, serene grasslands in the world. Sparkling emerald waves of grass in the summer, golden seas in October. There is no one out here crowding my water or privacy. Everyone else is out making the scene on the oh-so-hip rivers like the Ruby or Madison or Missouri. Good for them. I've met ranchers who are both curious and amused by my driving all the way from Livingston way out to their country just to fish for pike. When I catch some, cut them into steaks that I fry up and share this treat with others, they all are impressed. So much so, that a few of them now let me camp on their land and even let me try and shoot a sharptail or two. They can see immediately that I'm no threat to either their fish

Random Shots:
The Wanderings of a Montana Writer
or bird populations.

HALF-WAY THROUGH APRIL and there's still snow on the ground. Old, dirty grey stuff packed and hardened into sheltered curves and crevices of the not yet green high plains here above Havre not too far south of Saskatchewan. And there's several inches of newer, white snow that is melting rapidly under the intense spring sun. The land is more or less lifeless, not awake yet from a mild but long winter. The water I'm fishing is little more than a series of shallow, scummy oxbows connected by long stretches of mostly dry rock runs, slight trickles of brownish water seeping downstream from between the oxbows. I've been casting a large chartreuse barracuda streamer (a saltwater pattern) for hours, turning absolutely nothing. Casts to rock and brush piles and into dead-reed shallows fails to move a single northern pike. Everything is more or less dead up this way. Way too dead. And the fresh water of a new year's spring runoff hasn't arrived yet. The pike are probably dozens of miles away hanging out in their deep-water winter sanctuaries along the Milk River. At least I'm out here beneath the sun out in the wind casting instead of reading another book, renting another predictable movie or staring zombie-like at the never-ending forecast on the weather channel.

Six months ago in a similar drainage a few hours east over by Plentywood I took pike after pike on nearly every cast in large bends in a creek that ran clear and tea-colored, small springs bubbling up through the clean sands and gravel. The northerns ran to a dozen pounds and hammered the bright green fly with a savagery uncommon to trout fishing.

In the past few years I've turned more and more to fishing for what are often termed either warm-water or trash species – catfish, goldeneye, smallmouth and largemouth bass, sunfish, bluegills and most invigorating of all, the pike. So many of my favorite trout streams are clogged with wading and drifting flyfishers, that what was once a solitary exercise in escape from the day-to-day madness of living has turned into a competitive, unfriendly riparian land grab. That's why I find myself wandering the dry, lonely coulees and wind-swept flats of the eastern third of Montana casting to the lesser lights in the fly fishing panoply of gamefish.

Over by Plentywood and up here by Havre and down near Chinook and so on the wind howls or the sun bakes or both, but over-dressed anglers are rare and the fish have often never been cast to. Streams on the Fort Peck Indian Reservation in the northeast corner of the state are virtually ignored, virginal from a fishing perspective. For many years I thought trout fishing was the epitome of fly fishing sophistication and joy. Now I have my doubts. I see things in the rapidly shifting light of relived experiences and the current, noisome commercialization of trout.

In the growing chill of this autumn day I make a seventy-foot cast into the wind, shooting the heavily weighted streamer to the deep water at the end of a grassy point. The pattern sinks swiftly and I begin a fast-paced, stripping retrieve. In seconds a copper-green torpedo rockets from nowhere and with a long-mouthed filled with millions of wicked curved teeth slashes the streamer in a raucous boil and splash. I yank back on the eight-weight and the northern pike goes ballistic, catapulting through the water in muscular undulations of its long, thick body. The pike then races straight downstream in the general direction of Glasgow and is into my backing in seconds. The rod isn't bowed from the fish's strength. I'm pointing the tip straight at the direction of its flight hoping to avoid a break off and a stress-induced explosion of over-wrought graphite. The pike sounds in ten feet of water that seems surprisingly deep in light of the fact that this little stream is narrow enough to leap across in places. I pull the pike towards me. Perhaps a mistake as the fish slams to the end of the oxbow to and hurtles over a dozen feet of clean rock and gravel only just covered by the low October streamflow. The northern drops down into another dark pool and I reel in line as fast as possible as I fast-step it downstream. The pike makes a series of circling runs before I bring it to my hips where I'm standing in the water. The wind is stilled now, gone for the evening, the sun is setting in a golden-orange glow filled with deepening purple shadows that stretch out across the open prairie. Coyotes howl as the stars come out. Hereford cattle low and bellow from their grazing positions on distant benches. Ranch yard lights wink on and cast their eerie blue-white glow on the land. This pike is about ten pounds and as solid as a well-trained athlete.

I return to camp, a simple setup as usual, of cooking area, sleeping bags arranged on the ground and chairs overlooking the stream as it winds its way through the swales, rises and bluffs of this country. As I sip a cup of tea I watch as a school of minnows leaps franticly from the water, some of them landing on the bank. A large pike makes a circling wake, dorsal fin breaking the surface, as it slashes its way through the terrified forage fish. Back and forth and then the pike is gone, returned to its deeper water holding spot.

Simply put, I love this fishing. No matching the damn hatch with microscopic flies I can't see or remember the names of. No delicate tippets and artfully presented delicate casts. Just a six-inch gaudy streamer, sixty-pound big-game tippet and long, slamming casts. If the pike see the fly, they kill it in a burst of speed that probably goes from zero to forty a hell of a lot faster than a Porsche.

I could do this forever. I used to say that about fishing the Madison or Rock Creek.

Just about every trout flyfisher turns his or her nose up at this fishing. Fine. Let them eat trout, except the blood part of my beloved blood sport is anathema to most of them. Catch-and-release gone mad in an elitist fashion. The northerns fish are native to Montana unlike rainbows, browns or brook trout. They've been practicing their savage search-and-destroy trade for thousands of years in these isolated, little-known or unknown streams. The other day while talking with a Daniels County deputy sheriff (and for once it wasn't because a member of the law enforcement contingent thought I looked like a felony waiting to happen) told me he'd taken an eighteen-pounder about a mile upstream of where I am holding the pike prior to release right now. And two friends of mine have caught a number of northerns of twenty-plus pounds in slightly larger watery doings less than a dozen miles south of here on the reservation. In fact one of the fish slashed one of my friend's waders with his rows of scythe-like teeth which in turn provoked a violent response from my friend.

"John when he bit me I had to stick 'em," he informed me over the phone. That was the trip where he also took out the driver's side window swinging on a turkey that chose to flee via the air waves instead of along the more conventional ground route. The copper-twos launched from my friend's twelve-gauge ventilated his rig. A few days following the slightly manic phone call, I received a series of color prints showing man and pike, both bloodied, next to a small, nowhere stream, the wounded (not mortally) van whimpering in the background. The sporting life as it should be. May it always be so.

The next day in this country was more of the same for me. From early morning when the sun first topped the gently rising hills drifting off to the east, the star's hot rays

Random Shots:
The Wanderings of a Montana Writer

lighting up the frost-cloaked landscape and turning the land into a motionless sea of glistening diamonds, emeralds, rubies and sapphires, on through the relative heat of an autumn midday on into another other-worldly sunset, I took northerns in water of a few inches deep in those grassy, reedy shallows where they held silently like freshwater killers only to blast thirty feet or more in an instant to attack my streamers. And I took the pike in the deep depressions of the oxbows. Fish from a pound to more than a dozen. And I lost streamers as the northern's shredded the thick leaders with their menacing teeth; and it was the most fun I'd had fishing in twenty years. I realized what I'd been missing since my youth when I used to hunt this species in the waters of the North Channel of Lake Huron in Ontario, and the pikes' cousin, muskies, in northern Wisconsin.

These are no bullshit fish. They live to kill and eat. Noisy presentations, large patterns, less than stealthy approaches mean nothing to these fish. Make the streamer, the bigger and gaudier the better, swim and undulate, hell, just make it move, and the pike explodes from out of nowhere in a murderous rush. Picky rainbows delicately sipping size22 baetis, I've had enough of that craziness. Finesse is not my style. The menacing voraciousness of the northerns is. I prefer the solitude, lonesomeness and straightforwardness of this fishing way out on the northern high plains. I'll take it any day (that is until I see twenty-inch browns smashing wind-blown grasshoppers on a river near Livingston).

So, that's why six months removed from the little stream over by Plentywood I'm up here not far from Havre casting and casting fruitlessly in the dying late winter that is lingering like a boorish house guest that just won't leave. The pike aren't here now, but they will be and their fierce, marauding energy will return as surely as the spring freshets will flush out this streamcourse so that it runs clear and sparkling once more. The big, nasty fish will swim all the way up here from the Milk and come October I'll be back catching them.

It's still way too early around here for the pike, but I couldn't wait. I had to at least give it a shot.

WYOMING'S OUTLAW TROUT

2001

Living in Montana makes it easy to become chauvinistic about the place. The state is a magnificent place to spend one's years, but there are lots of other corners of the world that have much to offer. In Wyoming I find that the northeastern quadrant is filled with wonder. From the Thunder Basin National Grasslands to the very twisted vibe in the Pumpkin Buttes and the Wyoming portion of Tongue River Country have captivated me for years and many hours. One of my favorite places is the Middle Fork of the Powder River Canyon. The place is like a down-scale Grand Canyon and there are trout swimming in many of the area's stream, a sure-fire magnet where I'm concerned. The place does receive more tourista visitation than one would expect when driving along and viewing all of the disturbed geology and the lonesome landscape. The reason for all of this can be blamed on Newman and Redford and their silly, inaccurate movie "Butch Cassidy and the Sundance Kid." The Middle Fork is where the real outlaws roamed, and they had to be tough son-of-a-bitches to hang out in some of the places they did. I'm fairly confident that 100 years ago they weren't riding bicycles with fair maidens or jumping their horse off cliffs in the country. If they did the latter, they'd have died. Last fall I was camped way up the canyon where only crazy ranchers go. An early winter storm blew up and took my Little Smoky grill over the edge

231

with it. The next morning I used my binoculars to locate the remains. The device which had cooked so many excellent pieces of meat for me over the years was lying broken and bent at the bottom of an 800-foot cliff. I was deeply saddened, but have since replaced the grill with one of its offspring that I found hanging out at the Bozeman Wal-Mart. Life moves on.

DREAMS CAN VANISH QUICKLY IN LIFE. I thought that I'd be enjoying a few days fishing in the high country of central Wyoming for browns and rainbows. Instead, I was hunkered down in my tent while rough winds blasted across this rocky plateau. Rain, sleet then snow knocked visibility down to near zero. I could not see my Suburban parked 100 yards away. And earlier, on the climb up this way, some ancient petroglyphs I'd been in search of for years, turned out to be ruined, destroyed by mindless graffiti and carelessly placed campfires. And moments earlier a mean gust had swept my little grill clattering across the stone and over the 1,000-foot cliff edge. Life was a bit ugly right now and I wandered back to memories of a warmer, more pleasant but still slightly crazy time...

...The guy was wearing a Hawaiian shirt and nothing else. His buddy was wearing even less. The two of us were them standing on a boulder that projected out into the clear stream, sunlight streaming down on both of them. A stunning though incongruous sight especially when juxtaposed with the rainbow trout making splashy rises right below the pair as the fish fed on medium-size caddis flies that are bouncing haphazardly in the air above the aquamarine water, flitting about the bankside willows and alders and casually swarming around the two sun worshippers.

Naked can be understood all the way down here in the

canyon of the Middle Fork of the Powder River, deep in the July-baking heart of Wyoming. This is Butch and Sundance Outlaw Trail country. Their cave is just downstream, a dark oblong hole fifty feet above the water. Their names, carved so long ago, scarred by more recent graffiti. A person struggles this far down the path to escape the hordes of people, not to mention his own demon herd, and a bit of naked free-play is expected, acceptable. But some things are not done. Decorum must be observed even when someone thinks they are alone. River gods do have a sense of propriety and this must be respected. The gaudy-colored – chartreuse, hot pink, electric blue, day-glo yellow pattern of palm trees and hibiscus – shirt was tough to take. Angling repercussions are a possibility. The pair spied us as we clattered up the rock and gravel bank after spending the afternoon catching browns and rainbows downstream around a steep-walled bend in the river. The two quickly vanished into a clump of pines and brush.

Years ago a friend told me that the fishing in this river was quite good for large trout, mainly rainbows with a few browns thrown in for variety's sake. He said the climb down to the water was steep and there were a few rattlesnakes. That's the main reason for my delay in following up on his tale. Snakes. Don't like them at all. The sound of that wicked hiss of their rattles, the alien, cold gaze of those reptilian eyes, and the flickering tongues make me do strange things, like dance the spastic ballet as I flee screaming from the coiled or slithering, venomous things. I don't like snakes at all. It's a visceral thing with me. Beyond control or a therapist's avaricious techniques. Much of the country I care for is filled with them, so I do the best I can.

So, more than a decade later, courage screwed to its low-level sticking point, we'd driven the several hundred miles south by southeast from Livingston and then the final ten miles to the rim of the canyon on a road that can only be described as rough. Signs at the beginning of the rock-ledged, loose rocked, red dust, sand blown-out, sometimes two-track warned those with campers and motorhomes to turn around because up ahead they'd never make it. The Suburban made it, but it was a grinding, lurching slog in. Knife-edged rocks waiting to slice tire sidewalls littered the way. I camped at the end of an even dustier road near the edge of the canyon. Late afternoon light was turning the thousand-foot walls deep yellow, bordering on orange. Early October and the temperature was in the eighties with not a hint of breeze. I could hear the roar of the river drifting up from the depths of the canyon.

But as I pushed through cactus and thick clumps of sage I heard that old, familiar evil sound that is more like a constant, nasty intake of air through rotten teeth than a rattle. To my left about ten feet away a coiled snake glared at me, his tongue tasting the air with flickering stabs. I spun on one leg, tottered backwards and stumbled away. I started to laugh but was moving pretty good, too. I circled far around the snake and ever so carefully picked my way to the canyon rim.

Far below me the river poured over boulders, formed large sapphire pools and long runs that glistened silver-gold in the oblique slant of the sun's rays. Ponderosa pines covered the hills and benches up above and grew precariously on ledges as the yellow, grey and orange-pink sedimentary rock walls plummeted away from us. Sage grew on slanted gully outwashes. Game trails coursed along these piles of rock and soil before ending abruptly where rock bluffs protruded only to begin again at the next outwash. I wondered how the mule deer made it from the end of one trail to the beginning of another. There didn't seem to be any way the animals could traverse the sheerness of the limestone. Goats would have a hard time. The river flowed far beyond us, finally disappearing around a crooked bend a mile upstream. Perhaps mountain lions could move around here. I'd spotted the tracks of a large one in the sand by camp. Cats were able to move through nearly all of this wild country with surety and élan. The water flowed downstream and then vanished again beyond a sharp right turn. The country was wild, unspoiled. Perfect. Turkey vultures soared far above, probably scooping out their next meal. Me. A bald eagle soared past at eye level riding the canyon thermals. Mule deer browsed in the dry grass on a slope a quarter-mile away. Not bad. But where was the trail? I decided to have dinner – grilled Rock Cornish game hens seasoned with black pepper, garlic, lemon and salt, steamed vegetables, rice and tea – go to sleep and kill myself tumbling down to the river in the morning.

I sat around a small fire watching a three-quarter moon rise between a gap in the limestone wall behind, watched as the stars, planets and galaxies turned on. The same old nighttime magic that is ineffable in its intense, perpetual nature. Bats swooped above my head and then beetles the size of pregnant half dollars buzzed in on me. They must have waited for the cool of evening to escape their sandy burrows. They homed in on me with loud, lumbering efficiency, crashing into my face, arms, the coffee pot, anything warm. I caught a flash of one in the moon light. Quickly pulling off one of my moccasins, I propelled the sucker into the next dimension with a reasonably adroit forehand. The whacking sound of beetle on worn leather echoed softly in the dark. I finished my tea and crawled into my sleeping bag to escape the winged invaders that were now banging off the lid of the stove, unwashed pots and the radiator grill.

Aside from a snake or two, some strange-looking spiders, slips, slides, strained knee ligaments and a graceful face-plant fall at the end of the trail next to the water's edge,

Random Shots:
The Wanderings of a Montana Writer

the stroll from camp to the river was a mile-and-a-half of uneventful toil. The sun was beginning to make its presence felt as it passed gradually above the canyon rim a little after 10. Shadowed escarpments, arches and large holes eroded in the rock gave way to shining cliffs that reflected the day's heat and light into the cool dimness of stream course. No caddis were visible yet, so I tied on a weighted #14 tan Hare's ear nymph and flung the thing about thirty feet upstream to the head of a deep run that issued from the base of an effervescent cascade that dropped through a gap between a jumble of rocks and logs. The pattern drifted for a few feet before the line stopped. I set the hook and a twelve-inch rainbow shot up through the surface, leaping and cavorting for several seconds before giving up the ghost. The trout was brightly colored with a tinge of green drifting through the black spotting along its shoulders and flanks. As I twisted loose the hook in its jaw, the rainbow appeared to stare at me. No big deal. They always do that. A bunch more casts turned more rainbows in the same size range. No browns, yet.

Climbing up a pile of boulders and washed up logs along the bank I came upon a riffle that bubbled over copper-colored streambed. There were streaks of white-tan rock washed clean, no doubt, by faster rips of current. I switched to a #12 Elk Hair as sunlight flashed across the broken water. Casts across the darker rock did nothing. The first drift over the lighter stuff and a brown tagged the fly, then ran back and forth in the current shaking its head and jumping a couple of times. I brought the fish to my feet, or rather it swam to me and wrapped line around my shins. Classic brown trout, golden browns, large black spots, lesser numbers of blood-red spots, creamy white fat belly. Sixteen inches, maybe more. The fish raced to the shelter of a shady rock overhang as soon as I released it. Working the strips of washed streambed produced browns all the way up

236

a mile of river.

A deep, emerald pool ran beneath some cottonwoods and overhanging willows. I could see trout rising everywhere, coming to the surface to sip baetis. I tied on some 6x tippet and a #20 fly to imitate the action. Superb eyesight and stultifying manual dexterity accomplished this act of angling artifice in a little over twenty minutes. The rainbows were still arcing in the smooth water. I cast to a decent one at the end of the run and it took immediately, leaping and cavorting across most of that end of the holding water. Other rainbows ran alongside the trout out of curiosity before spooking off beneath undercut banks. After turning the fourteen-incher loose I looked and saw that the rainbows were still long-gone frightened. I took two more as I worked up to the head of the pool as leaves, water and the canyon walls glowed in the midday luminescence.

Rainbows in the pools and deep runs, browns in the broken three to six-inch riffles and after enough, I sat in the sun and ate some fruit and cheese, guzzled water I'd packed down and then re-stumbled my steps back to where I am now. The scene of naked disappointments and garish shirts.

This was a true vision of gaiety as I came round the bend and said hello to the two fellows. They asked where the Outlaw Cave was and I told them that it was only a hundred yards away and a short climb up from the river. They decided to head downstream and check the hole out.

"We're from Las Vegas," they then said with wide smiles. The colorfully garbed guy, who looked to be about thirty but had grey hair asked how the fishing was.

"Not too bad for not too big trout," I said. "But I'm sure with an artful use of my consummate angling skills larger fish are on the near horizon."

The one in the vivid shirt said "That's great," and almost looked like he meant what he said. The other, now wearing jeans, white T-shirt, water sandals and wrap-around shades, applauded rapidly like a trained seal and said "Of course. That's the way it should be. Of course it is."

I suppose it's truly a case of different strokes for different folks in these electronically-compressed, frenetic times. I looked up to the sky and shook my head. I said my "Goodbyes," and then the three of us went our divergent ways. The Vegas boys down to the cave, and me back up the steep, hot, snaking trail...

...The wind and snow increased and the temperatures angled downward, but I eventually fell asleep. When I awoke it was already seven but still dim outside the tent. The snow and wind had stopped, but several inches of the stuff covered the rock, bunch grass and sage. Several mule deer were kicking at the clumps of grass and snorting among themselves about something. The animals' ears and tails flicked steadily like some nervous form of natural radar. I threw the tent and sleeping bag in the back of the rig, engaged the lock hubs, fired up the motor, shifted into four-wheel high and lurched out of what had passed for camp. I prayed that the road was not a morass of greasy gumbo and that I'd make it back down to the valley a couple of thousand feet below. Maybe I'd see the Hawaiian shirt guy and his friend. Who could say. It already had been one of those strange trips I've had so often before.

And as the boys on the corner on the street outside The Mint Bar in Sheridan have been heard to say, "No where to run. No where to hide," and one of them passes a bottle in a brown bag to another while sucking on a Camel straight before continuing with a crooked smile that reveals some cracked teeth, "Even at the end of the Outlaw Trail."

THE JUICE AT
MEDICINE ROCKS

2002

Not much to say on this one. Few people wander over to this part of Montana. Highways and lesser roads to the area are few and circuitous. What I remember most is that this was a magical, extended road trip that Ginny and I took together, and a really good time we shared. We've had many more since including trips above the arctic circle in the Yukon, but this voyage holds its own with any of them.

~ ~ ~

"The sun was just setting when we crossed the final ridge and came in sight of as singular a bit of country as I have ever seen. Over an irregular tract of gently rolling sandy hills, perhaps about three-quarters of a mile square, were scattered several hundred detached and isolated buttes or cliffs of sandstone...Some of them rose as sharp peaks or ridges, or as connected chains, but much the greater number had flat tops like little table-lands. The sides were perfectly perpendicular, and were cut and channeled by the weather into the most extraordinary forms: caves, columns, battlements, spires, and flying buttresses were mingled in the strangest confusion. On the tops and at the bases pf most of the cliffs grew pine trees, some of considerable height, and the sand gave everything a clean, white look. Altogether it

239

Random Shots:
The Wanderings of a Montana Writer
was as fantastically beautiful a place as I have ever seen."

- Theodore Roosevelt, circa late 1880's

OVER THE YEARS I've become uncommonly familiar with "the strangest confusion," a situation apparently exacerbated by several years of specious over-indulgence and a sometimes road weary, peripatetic existence. Not really along the theme of "If this is Tuesday it must be Rome," but more along the wavering line of "If this is 2001 can it possibly be Dawson City, Yukon?' or in this early October case "Is that really North Dakota over there?"

Ginny and I have wandered the southeastern corner of Montana many times, but we'd never made it to Medicine Rocks State Park located south of Baker and just north of Ekalaka on State Hwy 7. And yes that land of so many rude jokes was lying off on the short grass prairie a few air miles east of us – North Dakota, a much-maligned place of damn good country.

We drive in on a dusty, sandy road that was undergoing some serious construction by the boys from Baker. Twisting and turning through spacious stands of old Ponderosa the curious sandstone formations described by Roosevelt more than a century ago flash into view like large escapees from a twisted carnival traveling show then disappear just as quickly as we drop down an arc dip in the road only to be replaced by an even more fantastic shape. This geologic contrariness continues for perhaps a healthy mile until we break free of the trees and came upon a vista of dozens of the eroded shapes resting like long-ago wrecked ships on the native grass prairie that is glowing in autumn shades of yellow-gold, tan, purple-grey, still-brilliant green and rust. Beyond the formations the grasslands stretch for miles towards a horizon whose limits are marked by a soft blue sky that shimmers electric white near the ground. The day is cool, in the forties, and rafts of dark clouds sailed eastward.

We find a nice place to camp near a pair of the medicine rocks that had been heartily defaced with graffiti that ran to Jimmy adores Trish – 1996 and encircled by a crude heart. Some artiste has taken some serious time to carve a horse head replete with flowing main, but most of the scars are of the former variety. I wonder how many of these no doubt soulful relationships flourish to this day, but quickly turn addled with the enormity of the question, so I opt for a Jim Beam and ice. Coolers are arranged, sleeping gear settled, wood gathered and a fire built. We grill some brats and potatoes, have a few drinks and watch stars show up between the boiling masses of clouds. Despite the cold that threatens winter both of us feel energized, the lethargy and slight depression of living in town now vanished.

Medicine Rocks is a good, strong place and it's easy to understand high plains warriors and hunters of the Northern Cheyenne gathering here to draw on what this place offers. Hell, I was ready to jump in the Suburban, drive to New York and battle a few editors, but I fell asleep instead.

According to Roadside Geology of Montana the Medicine Rocks were originally part of a sea of ancient sand dunes. This is indicated cross beds in the structures and the fact that the sand grains are small and of uniform size. The rocks appear to be the remains left by wind erosion since there are no stream channels in the area and each of them stands in a small depression much like the hollow left around a tree in heavy, wind-driven snowfall. The area is located on the Ekalaka syncline which is a trough folded into layered rocks. As with much of this country, gas and oil is prevalent. We catch slight tastes of the stuff on the ever-present wind. Many of the rocks have eroded into a Swiss cheese-like appearance and a number of birds make their homes in these hollows, including a falcon that screeches, threatens with outstretched wings and puffed up breast and before eventually flying off somewhere each time we walk out onto the grasslands to be among the formations.

We had originally planned on heading down south of Ekalaka to explore the Chalk Buttes but wound up spending five days here. With the weather turned warm the second day and the sun changing the colors and textures of the countryside as it passed across the sky we just never move on. The more time we spend here the more the land opens up in subtle shifts of color, light, texture and sound. Basic green of grass becomes multi-hued. Wind moving through pine limbs grows from a single lonely note to chords of song. No one else camps here during our five-day stay. The only people we speak with are the guys from the road crew who come down to check us out, no doubt stunned by the fact that a couple of Bozos from the big city would like their piece of turf so much that they would spend a number of days here doing not much of anything but walking, talking, eating, and sleeping. Being an inveterate fisherman I query the men about fishing in the area and they say that many of the ranch ponds are filled with rainbows. Seeing my eyes light up, they offer to get me onto to some of the water. I noticed on the drive in that many of these waters are, clear, relatively deep and surrounded with cattails and reeds. Prime stuff. I say I'll take them up on the offer next time we are over this way and they smile, adding that the bird hunting for pheasants and sharptails was "not too shabby" either. Antelope, mule and white-tail deer live here, also.

Coming into Baker the other day we spotted a pair of Zebras, which caused a pair of triple-takes and a near collision with a tractor. We learn from the road crew that the owner of that land has other exotics and the guys refer to it as a "petting zoo." I have a vision of bringing a Vermont friend of mine who'd spent a good deal of time in Africa out this way, but wonder if the anomalous site will cause him a stroke. Some year I'll find out.

We spend long hours feeding the fire both during the day and night. We talk about not much of anything or just cruise in place surrounded by the peace and strength of this place. By the end of the third night I've regaled Ginny with enough scintillating anecdotes about my career as a sportswriter for a small-town daily in Wisconsin many years ago that I am forced to hide the Beam for her own well-being. And I never do get to tell her about that one infamous night with the Milwaukee Brewers' slugger Gorman Thomas at a place called The Pieces of Eight in Milwaukee. Next time.

One of my favorite books on the state is The WPA Guide to 1930s Montana. I learned that Ekalaka (alt. 3,031) was originally called Puptown and began as a deadfall (saloon) for cowboys. Claude Carter, the town founder, a buffalo hunter and bartender, was on his way to another building site when his horses balked at pulling his load of logs through a mud hole at the current townsite. "Hell," Carter said, "any place in Montana is a good place to build a saloon. He built the Old Stand, which in a newer incarnation still stands and now offers good burgers and decent drinks.

Ekalaka was named for a Sioux girl called Ijkalaka (swift one) who was a niece of Sitting Bull. She was the best at breaking camp and so acquired her name. In 1875 David Harrison Russell, the first white homesteader in the region, married Ijkalaka, and in 1881 brought her to the community that had sprung up around the Old Stand. She lived in Ekalaka until her death in 1901. The town is home to a museum that has on display many remains and fossils of dinosaurs discovered in the region along with samples of a long-gone swampland forest now preserved in the form of

Random Shots:
The Wanderings of a Montana Writer

petrified rock.

During the warm sunny afternoons we wander through the Ponderosa and among the rocks. I climb over a rusty barbed-wire fence and walk across about a half-mile of prairie to a large formation covered in pines. The rock stands by itself on the southern edge of the park. From the top I can see for miles. Ekalaka was visible. Timbered buttes with wide valleys twist away between them stretching to the south and east. The crests of the Chalk Buttes are visible as muted green and ochre in the haze of distance. Red-tailed hawks and a golden eagle ride the thermals. Black-capped chickadees bounce among the bushes. Wild roses hang with thick clusters of orange-red rosehips. Woodpeckers hammer on nearby trees in search of insects. A few late-season grasshoppers clack as they bound from grassy clumps to sun-exposed rocks. The clouds are gone now, replaced by a soft but deep blue sky. The multi-colored grasses move in the wind in waves of motion that flow eastward or circle along gentle rises that create large eddies of spinning air.

Thirty years ago this place probably would have bored me after a few hours. No classy trout streams. No jagged, snow-capped mountains. Just all of what I've described. Now Medicine Rocks seems like country I'd like to live near. A few good people. Good country. No cities.

Walking out onto the prairie and the isolated formations we watch as the sun sets cast a glow behind the rocks that moves from yellow to orange to blood red then fades to blue going indigo. A thin streamer of clouds reflects the last of the day's light in the same colors only fifteen minutes later.

The final night we grill a couple of rib-eyes and some corn-on-the-cob. Chocolate-chip cookies complete the meal. Then in the darkness we rebuild the fire to a decent blaze and sit back. I look at Ginny and begin "Did I ever tell you about the time Gorman..." She jumps up. Grabs both our cups and races to the picnic table. Builds a couple of drinks. Hands me mine. Throws some wood on the fire. Sits down. I don't continue.

Bright white light begins to illuminate the trees behind us. The Ponderosa and the Medicine Rocks cast deep shadows. We walk to the top of a nearby rise and watch as an enormous silver moon climbs above North Dakota. The light is intense, drowning out most of the stars. It climbs quickly above us, seeming to shrink in size but gain in intensity as it does so. The stars come back. A faint, green glow of Northern Lights moves up and down the horizon beyond Baker. Then a brilliant, bright green flickering startles us in the west. We turn and watch as a meteor low in the sky sizzles towards the Borealis. Pieces of the space rock break off in miniature replicas of dazzling green. I imagine the sound of the thing streaking hundreds of miles an hour towards an earthly impact. Then the meteor is gone leaving behind the moon and the stars. Coyotes break into excited yipping and howling. They liked the show, too.

The Medicine Rocks reveals itself over time. The longer you stay the more you see. A special place in nowhere.

PRISMATIC CURIOSITIES

2003

This was the first story I did following Ginny and I briefly going our separate ways the year before. Laura Hengstler, editor at BSJ, asked me to do a story for the fly fishing issue. After a winter cooped up in town with my son and daughter, I decided to make a break, much to the relief of all three of us. Heading down the road in the Suburban by myself felt odd after all of these years. I kept thinking I was back in the early seventies when I did much of this for the first time. A bit disorientating at first, but very fresh and alive. I'd forgotten how much I enjoyed doing the road by myself. The absolute freedom of staying up as late as I felt like, talking out loud or conversing internally with myself about the Cubs, fly fishing, books, whatever, and then rising before dawn without any concerns about making noise or what the next day would bring was intoxicating, addictive. And all of this spent during the first serious blush of a northern high plains spring with the little streams and the sometimes very little fish to keep me company. I'm a loner. I like it that way. And besides there are so many voices that have found their way into my head asking me to tell their stories...well...I can hold a sit-down dinner for eight with only one place setting. Saves on food and cleanup. As I said earlier, mad as a hatter.

~ ~ ~

"What is not brought to consciousness comes to us as fate"

Random Shots:
The Wanderings of a Montana Writer

- Jung

IF THERE'S ANY TRUTH to the observation above by Jung, I'm reasonably certain that I'm a futuristic dead man with only slight hopes for resurrection, never mind redemption. Long, cold, dark Montana winters spent grinding through stultifying days filled with television sports reruns (I thought the Ball State-Central Michigan game was particularly exciting even the fourth time I watched the thing), partially-written novels, and dysfunctional relationships, all of it without the mollifying influence of whiskey and, now, cigarettes, certainly obliterates much of what passes for consciousness in my life. So when the first genuine warm days of spring show up during the middle of May, the ones that threaten to pop the leaf buds and have all the little birds twittering well before sunrise, I hit the road looking for clear, running water, green grass and an isolated place to camp.

My teenage son and daughter are still in school, but I decide to take a risk and work without a net. I'm heading down to the Pryor Mountains and a little stream I've got going for a couple of nights. I decide to leave the kids home alone. I trust the little suckers, and even if I didn't, I'd go anyway. High time to flee the dirty, melting snow, wind and grit of Livingston, and harass the down-sized brookies and rainbows swimming in the brushy creek that flows behind a treeless campground at the base of the mountains down where nobody ever seems to stay. I bring along some rib eye steaks, club soda and Honduran cigars. It ain't whiskey and Camel straights, but I'm older and much wiser now. I'll make do. And if things turn ugly and far-gone lonesome, I'll run along some back roads that slice through wide open, desiccated sage flats holding some antelope and turkey vultures, down into small-town-liquor-store Wyoming and score a bottle or two of Beam and a few packs of smokes, and then run oh so swiftly back above the border into Montana where I've learned with exactitude how to diminish myself in complete privacy. No one will know but me and I've been kidding myself for decades.

So the Suburban was loaded, the kids warned to stay legal, and now I find myself rolling and lurching up a rough, gravel and dirt road that cuts between some old exposed rock on the planet, something like 48 trillion years old a geology book tells me with pedantic certitude – Triassic and Jurassic sandstone and shale atop the Pryor Uplift of Madison limestone. The air smells of new wild grasses mixed with wildflowers. Joe Jackson wails away on the system from an '85 Aussie concert about not getting what I want, 'til I know what I want. Cumulous clouds cruise by on a warm southwest breeze, and I know damn well what I want, but it's either illegal or has nearly killed me a bunch of times along the turbulent path that got me to this afternoon. If it weren't for the kids, and my love and responsibility for them, I'd probably get what I want and die a liquid, smoking death while derricking four-to-six-inch brook trout and rainbows into the tall bank side grass round sunset. Maybe I'd make it to the steak dinner or even all the way back home, but that's a touch of some of that unrecognized fate that the good doctor is talking about.

I artfully make the turn to the east that leads to the campground. The creek is full of early-season water and everything is very green. The grass already waist high. A few miles down the road, the campground is deserted and I pull into a place that has a weathered picnic table protected from the sun by a rusting metal roof supported by rusting metal pools. The fire pit is enclosed by a rusting circle of barrel-like metal. The grate is rusting, too. Outhouses are slowly leaning and sinking into the ground less than 100 yards away. I'm home.

Random Shots:
The Wanderings of a Montana Writer

I drag all of the gear out and arrange on and around the table. I put the sleeping bag and foam cushion in the back of the rig since it looks like rain. I've brought a delightful little fly rod for this water. A 6-1/2-foot, 1-ounce, 2-weight. The thing comes in a case about the size of a double corona cigar tube. Uncle Orvis gave me this one way back when he thought that connecting my name to his equipment was sound marketing. He finally came to their senses and disinherited me, and I miss him so.

The creek drifts, glides and bends through clumps of willow and alder mixed with dense grasses. The banks are covered with clumps of the grass along with prickly pear cactus and sage. A few small grasshoppers are bouncing around. One lands in the stream and a trophy brookie of perhaps 10 inches pounces on it before retreating to the shade of an undercut bank. Trout are rising everywhere, taking very small mayflies whose name, Latin or otherwise, I don't know. I tie on a small bug, about a #20 to a fine 6x tippet and work out about 20 feet of line. My initial cast lands at the base of a spiraling pool and my line begins to curl back downstream to me. As I take in slack, several fish, both rainbows and brook trout, rush the fly. A splashy take and the pattern is gone as I raise the rod and set the hook. A rainbow races back and forth arcing the slight rod. Then leaps across the seven feet of open water into a bunch of overhanging branches. The tippet tangles. The trout wriggles from the line as it dangles inches above the stream. I snap the tippet. The rainbow thrashes then drops into the water and is gone. Vanished. Other fish start feeding again. I tie on fresh tippet and a new fly, cast again and after a serious struggle of more than four seconds, ever so carefully work a husky five-inch brook trout to my feet. Cupping the tiny trout in my hand, I marvel at the intense coloration. The crimsons, indigos, sapphires, emeralds. The glimmering hard metal golds, silvers and bronzes, and especially the pure whites and blacks. The belly is flanked by a sophisticated shading of the deepest orange. The trout works its mouth open and closed in the water as it glides coolly through my fingers. Its gills flutter back and forth. Absolute perfection. As spectacular a fish as I've taken anywhere. Dropping my hand inches below the surface allows the trout to scoot free and race to the bottom where it becomes one with the shadows and gravels.

I continue fishing this way for hours until I notice that the sun is down behind the western hills and the sky is going pastel orange, red and pink. Back at camp I build a charcoal fire, cook one of my huge steaks, devour it, then light a cigar, sip some club soda and watch as an early-season thunderstorm flashes and rattles in the distance. The weather moves off towards Billings and the stars and darkest night come out and drop down over me like the gentlest quilt of dead-black fabric. Coyotes begin to riff and howl up the valley. I enjoy the peace, the cigar and the solitude. Maybe this is my unrealized fate. Then I climb into my sleeping bag and drift off.

This brutal regime continues through another day and night before I pack up, drop into Wyoming and make a call to the kids. I ask how things are going. They say great and ask after me. Sounds of large-caliber handgun fire, loud music, pop-tops and police sirens come through the receiver. Assured that all is well, that my children are following gleefully in my staggered footsteps, I tell them that I'm bound for another stream, this one in the central part of the state and will be back in two more days. Before hanging up, I give them my attorney's phone number. He's married to a writer. His father-in-law is a writer. He knows the score. He'll help the kids out if push comes to shove.

As I wander through Wyoming, I manage to eschew the Beam and cigs (there will be time enough for this foolishness once the children are off to college), but take time out to observe a backyard BBQ. Two hearses are parked in front of the house. Everyone is eating from plates piled high with food. There is a lot of laughter. The dead guys were either popular or hated I reason. Pushing on, I work my way up a very steep grade to through the Big Horn Mountains. Immense banks of snow wall in the highway until I drop down into Buffalo where it's spring again with temperatures near 80. I pick up the Interstate and run north pass Sheridan, then cut off the four-lane strip, zip through Billings, run north then east across a vast sage flat that is filled with antelope. The females feed casually on the new grass while the males survey their harems from reclined positions on overlooking swales and bluffs. Eagles and red tails work the thermals at close range with spread-winged elegance as they look for careless rodents and rabbits. A pair of coyotes with matted winter coats of thick fur working off their backs in ragged tufts, drops down into a gully. A dark purple and blue and black thunderstorm explodes tens of thousands of feet into the sky far off in the east. Shafts of manic lightning rip through the middle of the anvil-shaped cloud. Fierce rain stretches from the base and sweeps the land. A rainbow in fully-defined colors curves through the air in the wake of the violent system. Some small-scale species of yellow butterfly works up and down in the warm air. Millions of them in crazy waves above the native grasses that ripple like water in the afternoon wind. Man, Montana is alive again. Surviving winter brings this home to me with force as it does each spring.

I find the stream I'm looking for, cut up a dirt and slightly muddy two-track. I push along this for a few miles to a group of ancient cottonwoods that hold sway along a stretch of wonderful water. The leaves are coming out new and virgin green on the big, old trees. This is private land, but the rancher likes me and appreciated the bottle of whiskey I gave him a few years back. He's never said anything about the copies of some of my books that I gave him.

Setting up camp is the same procedure without the table. The tarped ground works fine. This time I rig a 7-6, 4 weight and tie on a brown woolly bugger palmer hackled with that most delightful of all feathers, Cree – golden tan, glowing brown and soft white hackles. The streamer is weighted with fuse wire, but I add a split shot at the head so that the bugger dips up and down as I strip it through current seams. I step into the water wearing wading boots, but no waders. The stream is fed by a warm spring. Lush aquatic plants flank the riffles and pools, their long, slender, glowing green tendrils waving hypnotically in the clear water. As I work my way upstream I kick up mallards holding in calm areas next to overhanging grass. Raucous quacks and palpitating wing beats pound the air. Bluebirds flit along an old, crumbling fence line of limp barbed wire.

As I cast the bugger slightly upstream and pull it back to me, smallmouth bass from 10 inches to two-pounds slam the thing. They jerk against the flex of the rod like charged bricks of iron. I take them on almost every cast. No one fishes here that I know of. I keep a pair of larger ones for dinner. Deep-fried in peanut oil, coated in Progresso bread crumbs, seasoned with sea salt and freshly ground pepper, some lemon wedges. This sounds good. I kill another fish. I take my knife and clean the smallmouths. Scales sparkle in the sunlight and scatter across my shirt and jeans. Next I slice open their bellies, and pull the guts out. The stomachs are full of crickets and caddis nymph casings. With bloodied hands I toss these into the grass for the various riparian mammals in the area.

At camp I round up some wood, build a fire that burns down to hot coals, fix a grate over this, heat the pan and oil, quickly cook the fish to just barely done, then devour them by pulling the flesh in white, moist hunks from the bones.

Random Shots:
The Wanderings of a Montana Writer

The sky is clear and once again filled with stars. The Milky Way is a thick white band arcing overhead. The coyotes raise some more hell as the Northern Lights flash in bands of instrument dash green for a couple of hours. In the spring this has always meant heavy weather often in the form of snow the next day.

I rise early to a raw wind from the northeast and an overcast sky that is already spitting snow. I toss everything into the back of the Suburban and race out on the two-track that is already turning to gumbo. The two-line state highway is covered with a few inches of wet snow and a spring blizzard is raising hell all around me. Three hours later I'm in a warm motel room in Lewistown. I call home and all is well. I order an anchovy pizza from Howard's delivered to my room. I finish the greasy mess, and realize that this has been one of the finest opening day road trips I've ever had. I wonder at the Jungian subconscious/fate number before falling asleep reading James Ellroy's *L.A. Noir.*

THAT'S HOW WE DANCE

2003

After being apart for several months, we decided to give things another shot, so we met in Whitefish in September 2002 and put together this number about Glacier National Park in autumn. The story turned out great, but that was about all that did. The constant bickering and fighting, the old and tired control games, all of the crap, resurfaced. We'd had enough. Couldn't take any more of it. I realize now that the reason I hung on so long (why she did eludes me) is because Ginny's talent as a photographer and more importantly as a friend is immense and unique. The work we do together is top-shelf. We've now been married for years and things are good and fine.

I AM DESPERATELY TRYING to find positive signs in any of this. A lucky penny I just found lying on the road. Those three ravens sitting on a cottonwood limb, the ones making the avian wisecracks about my dilemma. Anything. A few months ago life seemed bleak and that was probably an optimistic assessment. But for now at least, she is here, standing right next to me, and that seems like a hell of an improvement over how it was one July evening when she'd said over the phone that there was no hope and that she never wanted to hear from me again. Well who could have blamed her. I'd tuned her out for confused reasons uniquely my own months before and had begun focusing on the Jim Beam oblivion express again. Who could have blamed me.

255

Random Shots:
The Wanderings of a Montana Writer

She was telling me what to write and how to say it.

I look at the sunny sky, feel the warm temperatures, and wonder at the outrageous autumn colors that are truly Glacier Park's own unique fall palette – the glowing oranges, the startling crimsons and indigos, the electric yellows, and those last insanely-bright greens that radiate life's brief intensity before the approach of winter's cold death. I observe all of this with perhaps unwarranted optimism. I think that I still really like this woman and miss her and maybe even want to get back together, so I'm grasping at natural straws today, no matter how slim. And she did call one day in late August and even intimated that there was some hope, and as we managed to continue our conversations into September, I became cautiously, to the point of superstitiously, positive that this was the right thing to do. And when she said that since we'd already walked our relationship around in countless circles in the Yukon, Saskatchewan and Wyoming, so why not Glacier Park this weekend, I, of course, thought that this was a wonderful idea. Carving concentric circles in close proximity of each other, trying vainly to find ways to be close yet still individuals, that's something we both do together as well as anyone on the planet.

So, when I hear the slight, bordering on subliminal, scream and subtle hiss of the marten as it warns us of its presence, I desperately try to find a good omen in the animal's surprising appearance right beside The Going-To-The-Sun Road. The dark brown weasel-like creature glances at me, then looks over at her and her thick, red hair sparkling in the afternoon light, then back at me, then at her. The animal is no fool. It quickly senses our awkward confusion at being back together after all these months of painful separation, and the sleek mammal, with feral wisdom, determines that either love or hate or both is about to flash on the very near horizon. Then with a couple of rapid flicks of its bushy tail, the marten vanishes like a furry prop in a cheap magician's carnival act. I think, 'Damn. That's not a good sign,' and quickly look to see if she has disappeared into thin air, too.

She hasn't, but is looking at me with one of those at once curious yet pitying smiles that I used to associate with women flashing on starving, lost kittens or the terminally disturbed among us, but have lately come to see is truly reserved for those such as myself, those who are elaborately addled.

September and October in Glacier are perfect months. More often than not the weather is blue sky pure with temperatures in the mid-sixties. Sometimes dark rafts of stormy weather slice across the razor-edged peaks or at times the mountains generate their own miniature systems as they disrupt the high altitude gales and create boiling jets of downwind clouds that sizzle like angry smoke before dissolving in clear air. Distilled sunlight flashes off fresh dustings of white snow that is sprinkled across the severe faces of the ragged Garden Wall or along the tops of peaks like Mt. Saint Nicholas, Kintla or Clements. The number of visitors and their vehicles has declined to less than 10 percent of July's exhaust spewing, gridlock levels. Wildlife is on the move gorging on native plants, forbs and berries in one last feeding frenzy before all frozen hell breaks loose in the northern high country. Grizzlies, deer, goats, elk, hawks, my friend the marten, all of them are on the prowl and visible to the casual eye. She and I drive with the windows down on our '83 Suburban. The air smells of pine, fallen leaves, and new snow. We stop at small pullouts that cling to the sides of the cliffs so she can shoot some of the country. We hug each other and I look over her shoulder past the low stone retaining wall and down through the space of more than a 1,000 feet to McDonald Creek flowing sapphire through the distant forest. A rush of dizziness runs through me. Vertigo? Her touch? We watch for long minutes as shadows slide across hanging valleys and play games with slim waterfalls that shoot out from ledges and arc across space in moving rainbows. Trickles of water wash down smooth rock falls, the tiny streams the final remnants of this year's runoff generated from dozens of feet of accumulated snow that mostly melted with a rapid blast of kinetic energy under a tough summer sun.

We've lived together for years. Done countless articles and one damn good book together. We were working on two others, both of them about the Canadian north, that is until we blew apart. We've traveled above the Arctic Circle a few times. Fried ourselves senseless out on Wyoming's Thunder Basin Grasslands. Seen and heard some very magical things up in the Sweetgrass Hills. We've fallen in love with the rolling grass bluffs and small streams of the Poplar drainage in the northeast corner of Montana. And all along the way we've had some great times and a few too many wicked ones. Now we're here in Glacier in all its splendid fall quietude to see if we have figured out how to sneak past most of those hard, eternal moments when they show up. And we pause to look at each other, and laugh at our own shared madness and to wonder, often aloud, if we may have possibly learned enough this time around to make things work in a not-quite-so-savage-way between us. And we laugh again, because who the hell knows and as she says, we're a couple of bozos who probably deserve each other, even now after all these bad times and little cruelties to each other. Glacier is a fine place to begin finding some of this out.

We're staying at a mutual friend's outrageous home perched on a mountainside overlooking the Flathead Valley and the town of Whitefish. Her place is comfortable and relaxing. She offered us this hospitality in return for coming over to Livingston to stay at my place and visit with my two children. Seems like a fair trade. Both she and I feel like well-off, seasoned travelers staying in the sumptuous comfort we so richly deserve while all the time secure in the knowledge that we are at best somewhat talented and committed individuals working on a magazine article that will buy us, at most, a few weeks of financial freedom. But as we've learned, ride the highs, even the small ones, for all their delusional worth. We cook superb meals featuring top choice beef, selections of seafood, fresh fruits and vegetables and great breads, and then we sit in front of a fire and talk late into the night as we used to so long ago. We both know that we could wind up back together, that we both may take that risk and revive one last time with crazy feeling the Catastrophic Road Show. Though the eternal question floats in front of us, 'Will we be happy and have more fun this time around?' My head says not likely. My heart says, "What the hell. Give this a shot."

If today's easy hike up from the Logan Pass Visitor Center to the Hidden Lake Overlook means anything, all should fly well between us. Groups of cumulous clouds sail from horizon to horizon, spinning around wind-current eddies that swirl about the mountain tops. The dry sherry-colored sunlight of autumn gives the mosses, grasses and subalpine firs a rich, golden glow much like the tundra of the arctic north. The few people we encounter along the boardwalk and then the dirt and rock trail are all smiling, cheerful and clearly happy to be in Glacier today. From the overlook we watch as a band of mountain goats lazily graze its way down to the lake as they chew on the last of the year's green grass. A few hikers pause on their course up from Hidden Lake and watch the animals from a distance of only a few yards. The goats occasionally look up at the intruders before resuming their feeding. The wind cuts through the low trees and past the cliffs in a soft hum. The only other sounds are the muted voices of the other hikers, their

Random Shots:
The Wanderings of a Montana Writer

volume so low as to remind me of the ethereal humans on the intro to Pat Methany's long-ago *As Falls Wichita, So Falls Wichita Falls* album. Basically this is just another stoned Montana fall day in the mountains. Nothing unusual, but truly unique all the same.

We are enjoy the views while sitting on a rock outcropping having a lunch of seven-grain bread, brie, Tim's potato chips, apples and water; and we discuss plans on how we might finish those two book projects up north and how we re missing doing the road together this year, because, after all, our true calling is that of inveterate road bums. Then we both stop talking with an unnatural abruptness. Perhaps the rules of our current engagement demand a bit more restraint and tact. Skill and delicate maneuvers might be in order at this time. I have no idea, and I'm no damn good at any of this, but she is, and laughs while I, for some odd reason, think of the Cubs finishing a mere 30 games behind the Cardinals in the NL Central Division this season. I finally gave up all hope of making sense of any of it and fall back on a time honored phrase a world class manic depressive I'd once known used to say before disappearing into his bedroom closet. "Hoopy-toopy, ten-four, too much for me." He was a curious piece of work, and I miss him from time to time. I even manage to keep this line to myself while wondering where the boy is today. We load our daypacks and head back down the trail.

As the day begins to fade towards dusk the orange-pink alpenglow casually works its way up the western sides of valleys, cliffs and ridge lines. As the soft radiance glides upward it drags behind it a sheet of shadow that holds the slightest touch of deep blue and purple. By the time we reach the valley floor and are driving alongside McDonald Creek, a few stars and a planet or two are visible in the sky. She asks me to pull over so she can shoot the reflections of all this on McDonald Lake. I find a turnout and stop. She heads to the gravel shoreline to set up her tripod and camera. I walk some distance away from Suburban and out of the camera's view. Rise forms from feeding trout spread in those concentric circles, rippling quicksilver across the dark blue surface of the water. Dozens of large fish feed steadily on tiny bugs. The only sound now is that of the fish sipping insects that I can't see. I hear the shutter of her camera release in a sequence of three exposures. One stop under exposed. Properly exposed. One stop over exposed. Looking down to the moist sand at my feet, I see that I have made a circular trail that approaches the water then rises back up the shore towards the cedars, and moss and fern covered rocks. I look toward her and watch as she readjusts the focus on her lenses, stares through the view finder, walks off to her left and then circles back to the camera to take some more shots.

Nothing new here. The arctic. The northern high plains. The Powder River Canyon. Glacier Park. Walking in circles is one of the few things that the two of us do with style and panache.

DRIFTING THROUGH
THE PAST
IN REAL TIME

2006

This story also came about as a result of work on **Yellowstone Drift.** *It's all true, even the last section based on a slightly sodden experience while thinking about attending a hideous convention of more than a thousand outdoor writers somewhere in Idaho. Thankfully I never made it and cancelled my membership in that august organization shortly thereafter. Just as thankfully, the statute of limitations for this little bit of mayhem expired well over a decade ago, I hope.*

SHADOWED **FAMILIARS GHOSTING** within dazzling bright waves along a July afternoon's river that cuts through the Yellowstone valley in a timeless present. The wooden canoe moves through the uneven patterns with determined ease as eagles – bald, golden – and dozens of herons peer from limbed perches down through the entwined currents. Kingfishers plummet seeking small rainbows.

Hot. Breezy. Swift. Alone.

Trout, some big ones, slam and crush wind-blown grasshoppers whose only real mistake in life is or was an unconscious insect desire to soar over the always moving sapphire current with no particular destination in mind.

263

Random Shots:
The Wanderings of a Montana Writer

This is death on this alive afternoon. Thoughts of casting to these fish are everywhere – thirty-forty feet of line tossed on seams and in foam lines ahead of the canoe, watery variations that flash and disperse in light that sparkles golden-green through the rustling cottonwood leaves. Casual fishing with mixed results. Sixteen inches. One missed. Another. Seventeen inches. Ten. Broken tippet. Set the rod down on the canoe's braces.

The Yellowstone slaps and whispers against the cedar as the craft slices downriver. The paddle pushes through the river sometimes with no resistance or effect as standing waves shaped like loose-jointed pyramids appear to move upstream. These are crested as the tall sandstone cliffs block everything but the deep blue as the day slides along.

For a few days at least I'm on the run from my hometown that is the center of the western world when it comes to fly fishing. All the big boys come here, have been here, even Tiger, a few presidents, some actors – good and bad. Forget about Jackson, West Yellowstone, Manchester, anywhere in Colorado. Drift boats are parked in alleys, along streets like cabs in New York at rush hour. Guides, outfitters, fly shop owners bump into each other on every corner searching madly for misplaced clients that have usually found themselves in a bar – The Owl, Mint, Stockman's. There's a museum for this once arcane pursuit now spun big business just off Main Street. In these warm months, peak time, out-of-state fly fishers cluster along the streets like a blizzard hatch of whirling caddis or perhaps spinning mayflies – Vermont, Texas, Maine, Wisconsin, Washington, California, of course, Japan, England, Germany, Tasmania, Canada, of course, even Key West (foreign enough). Restaurants are filled in season with sports in waders, bonefish scrubs, vests, long-billed ball caps. The fish are all over the place, up in the Park, in the river, in lakes, drainage ditches. Within one-hundred miles

264

there are so many quality streams that learning all of them would take several lifetimes, lots of flies, plenty of gas, and a nothing job like mine.

By late March I'm wading some of these waters not far from home

with only a passing interest in catching anything, just happy to have survived another winter. Now I'm drifting along killing time with sandhill cranes. We clack and chatter back and forth with each other, our necks craning for a better view of each other. This silliness rattles onward for longer than it probably should.

One spring morning a couple of years ago while walking along the Yellowstone behind home I spotted a drift boat wedged among the rocks in fast water, partially submerged, abandoned, wrecked. An April outing gone astray with a lone Budweiser beer bottle still in its holder. Another year of angling madness that I take perverse pleasure in being a part of like now on this beautiful summer's day.

I've found that convincing the large ones to take is even harder than they tell you.

Matching the hatch jive doesn't really get it much of the time nor does artful casting over classic water with a dainty piece of pretentious fluff. The ones that matter, those worth the effort, rarely buy the obvious con of this artifice

Learning to see without looking, understanding how to chase without wanting because the trout know when they're being hunted, makes hammering an offering of substance tight to a sweet lie just barely possible with my laughable stealth and dark humor. Why would anyone want to do any of this to begin with I think sometimes, but accept that the primal urge and wonderful country and the crazy fish are answers enough.

I SEEM TO ENCOUNTER THE MOST INTERESTING SOULS in the most curious of places.

Random Shots:
The Wanderings of a Montana Writer

On an island a few miles below Big Timber I'd set up camp – sleeping bag and tarp on the sand, cooking area with small fire pit, folding chair and attendant cooler. I am sitting in my chair taking in the view of the river, green fields and distant purple Crazies when a bright red canoe comes into view – Mad River with the classic logo of a rabbit smoking god-knows-what in a small pipe. The guy paddling the craft appears to be in his late twenties, and familiar with canoes judging from the J-strokes and draw strokes he used to work the current for a smart landing in front of me.

"Mind if I stop and rest a bit," he asks in a cheerful voice. "I've got beer."

I'm easy and the beer is a sure come on, so I wave him in with the aplomb of an airport tarmac worker. He's tall, tanned and wearing ragged cutoffs like me and a white T-shirt, also like me. In fact he looks a good deal like I did twenty-five years ago. I brush my hand back and forth in front of my face to check and see if any residual effects from an abundance of late-sixties dalliances are making an appearance. No trails. No electric colors. I'm as okay as I get at this stage in the proceedings. Apparently this guy is legit and not some maverick hallucination. He hands me a cold Molson's ale pulled from a cooler filled with ice and brown bottles, then sits on a weathered, grey cottonwood trunk that's doing double duty as a windbreak.

We chat about the state of the river and the level of water – ideal for floating and high enough to be entertaining. And about the easy fishing for browns and rainbows on hopper patterns. Then Mike, that's the name he gives me – I tell him mine is Joe Graves – looks at me with an earnest and worried expression.

"I hope you don't mind this, but I've got to tell someone."

Confessions normally boor me, but what the hell? I'm not going anywhere – surprise – and I have nothing particular planned for the rest of the day other than some fishing in a side channel below camp, cooking dinner and working over a few drinks.

"Go ahead."

"I'm on the run," he said.

"Who isn't?" I said with a touch of cynicism, a rare state in my life.

"No really, from the Nebraska cops. I sideswiped a squad car in Hyannis out in the Sand Hill country. I wasn't paying attention. Well, actually I'd had several schooners of Grain Belt, four as I remember, cold and bubbling, at the Hyannis Hotel and when I went down Main to get back on the highway I swerved a little and hit a cop car. The door was open. Last I saw it was lying on the road. I panicked and took off down dirt and gravel roads then through a two-track next to a cornfield before working my way up through South Dakota, the badlands, Rapid City, then Wyoming, Yellowstone and down to the Rainbow Motel in Livingston. I don't think anyone followed me or got my license plate number."

I almost drop my beer. Parallel universes. Quaint coincidences.

I'd had a remarkably similar experience back in 1986 just up the road apiece from Hyannis at Alliance. I was on my way back from an Outdoor Writers of America Convention that had been held somewhere in Iowa. That was back when I thought being a member of that slap-happy group of hacks was of value. But I mean just how damn many camo-colored suede sport coats is one person expected to endure in a seventy-two hour span. I quit the bunch as soon as I got back home to the Flathead. Anyway, following a sumptuous meal and a pair of gin-and-tonics at the Porterhouse Chinese Restaurant (How can a person go wrong at a place with a name like this?) and with a meal of egg rolls, wontons, a porterhouse steak and the aforementioned cocktails, I continued on my lazy, leisurely backroad drive towards home, but before traveling one-

Random Shots:
The Wanderings of a Montana Writer

hundred yards I managed to drill a Box Butte County squad car parked in the middle of the main drag with lights and siren going loud, bright, insanely and the driver's side door wide open. The door, like Mike's, wound up lying mortally wounded in the street along with my side mirror.

Not wanting to take up the good officer's time and definitely not interested in a free-ride in the Box Butte County slammer, I high-tailed it through back country fields and along old roads until dark set in. I was out of sight before the officer discovered the damage to his squad. I hid in a dry irrigation ditch for a few hours before creeping and sneaking my way along nearly the same track my friend had taken all the way back to Whitefish. Stopped south of the badlands for gas at an old-time station, one of those numbers with the gas pumps that had the spinning glass-encased orange balls that showed that fuel was actually being loaded into your tank. Had a couple of drinks with an old boy as the sky turned black-purple and a trio of silver-white tornadoes played pinball with the rolling hills north of the station. Spent the night in my sleeping bag on his wrap-around porch. Demolished ham, eggs, biscuits and gravy and strong, strong coffee with the guy at sunrise and struck off for Potato Creek an hour or so northwest on BIA Hwy 2 on the southern side of the Pine Ridge Indian Reservation. I planned on reassessing my position at this Spartan location.

I'll never forget that little Cornhusker state road show and the adrenalin rush that resulted from acting the bit part of a small-time outlaw as I motored across the high plains and finally over the Continental Divide at Pipestone Pass.

I finish the Molson's and grab a pair of Miller longnecks from my cooler and offer Mike one.

"Thanks, Joe."

I look around then remember my new identity. Right. Joe. Nebraska. Battered cop cars. Lord, none of this ever goes away. What past? It's all the present to me.

"Don't sweat it. They aren't going to spend time, money or

energy on you. Nothing more than Hyannis bar talk by now for a few days, and off and on during the winter," I said. The banged-up, derelict sage holding court in the middle of the Yellowstone River on some nondescript island. "I've been there, almost the same road, so to speak."

We chatter away about this and my related experience and this seemed to calm him down a fair amount. We go fishing. Catch some trout. He stays for dinner – game hens, potatoes and onions wrapped in foil, same with corn on the cob, lots of butter, salt, pepper – a couple of more drinks over a modest fire and then off to sleep in an air mattress near his canoe and me in my bag. Earlier Mike told me that he'd rented the canoe from some goofy-named hustle joint back in town.

In the morning I help push Mike off. He waves his paddle back and forth in goodbye as he moves downstream and yells, "Take care, Joe."

Joe it is or was for the rest of this/that trip on the river. Hadn't thought about my great Nebraska squad car fiasco in years. Oh to be young and carefree once more. Never saw Mike again. Still, a little lunatic synchronicity along the Yellowstone felt good. I like things like that.

SO A LITTLE FURTHER ALONG that morning I am once again ghosting along with the shadowed familiars that have kept me company and given me so much curious pleasure over the years. Mayflies and caddis are floating, spinning and dancing in the pure light. Big trout are feeding on the bugs. Deer browse in the fields. The water pushes me along as I duplicate Mike's watery trail downriver following my own path within circular time.

I'm free again.

I'm not myself.

Or am I?

GOLDEN COUNTRY

2007

Perhaps the strangest aspect of fishing for me is when a tip about a great, unknown place to catch fish actually turns out to be true. This has happened when someone I was smoking dope with in Hyde Park in London in 1972 mention brown trout fishing in the Atlas Mountains of Morocco, a tip from a guy in a Manhattan, Montana bar about fine fishing for arctic char and browns in the Icelandic interior and the bit of information offered by a friend as described below. You never know about these things and I guess that's why some of us wander down so many back roads in so many out-of-the-way places, or maybe we just like seeing what's around the next bend, fish or no fish.

~ ~ ~

"There comes a time in every man's life and I've had plenty of them."
- Casey Stengel, manager of New York Yankees,
1949-1965

CASEY KNEW THE TRUTH about many aspects of life both common and esoteric. When it comes to fly-fishing I've had my times. Plenty of them. Often they revolve around trying to catch a certain species – grayling (Austrian and otherwise), bull trout (therapy and bizarre FWP regulations mostly cured this obsession) large browns each fall, and westslope cutthroat. These personal subspecies of manic behavior have been satisfied many times over along the watery road and will be again if I'm blessed in the coming seasons.

Unfortunately when the field of search turns to finding and catching golden trout there will never be any degree of satiation. There's something intrinsically intoxicating and, by all-too-familiar extension, addicting with this species. Perhaps the trout's riotous coloration – gold, vermilion, carmine, magenta, emerald, pure white, jet black, pink. The range of shades and variety of colorful shadings never seems to end. Each fish is unique unto itself and, being an addled child of the sixties, colorful visuals are part of my life along with music by The Finchley Boys, a lingering belief in anarchy and fond memories of those fun-filled Days of Rage at Chicago's Grant Park in October 1969 featuring the Weathermen and Mayor Daly's finest, but longing for the good old times is not really productive. Onward and upward. So back to the charming goldens and their heady attractions that possibly include the fact that the fish survive only in the purest of alpine lakes in stoned high country serenity far away from hordes of hikers, backpackers and others is responsible for the attraction. When in a cooperative frame of mind, they can be fun to catch, mainly on streamers, larger nymphs and wet flies in riffled current.

And on a grisly note, the smaller specimens aren't bad eating when fried with thick sliced bacon over a sedate campfire.

All of the above have their condign places in my golden fixation, but the real hook is the chase. Myth, slight fact and outright deception swirls around information and tales of golden trout locations. Are they really in those two lakes in the Missions? Will the water be ice-free in the Bridger Wilderness of the Wind Rivers in August. Are the trout cooperating and taking nymphs in the Beartooths? Could they be in that drainage ditch over by Peerless? "Not likely,

Sport," say the all-knowing boys who pass the time hanging out on the corner in front of Mickey's Liquors and Ollie's Pawn – Payroll Checks Cashed Here. How about the ones in southern Alberta? Are they still hanging out in that string of mountain cirque lakes?

To establish myself as a legitimate golden-trout-seeking nutcase I need to make a trip to the Golden Bear State and the trout's natal waters of the Kern River drainage in the Sierra Nevada Mountains. California scares me – Silicon Valley, Schwarzenegger, five-hundred-million residents (or as former Yankee catcher Yogi Berra would say, "Nobody goes there anymore because it's too crowded."), the Oakland Raiders, et al.

Yes, as always, it's the hunt, the insane expenditure of time, money and energy pursuing what is usually unattainable in life – solitude, the respect of one's community, sanity in D.C., and in this case, the elusive golden trout (*Salmo aguabonita* for those conversant with the esoteric Salmo dialect).

With the exception of the Peerless ditch, I've checked out all of the above rumors with child-like hope and vehemence. My faith has been rewarded in all three places. Enormous goldens in the Wind Rivers, some similar sized trout, but more often, much smaller fish in the Beartooths, and a few decent sized trout in the Wild Rose (the flower not the drink mixture of Irish whiskey, lemon juice, grenadine and soda water) province. The Beartooths are close to my Livingston home though many of the lakes require strenuous hikes, some I'm unwilling to undertake at this stage of the proceedings. I've only done the Bridger Wilderness once, and Alberta is only a day's drive away, so I've been there a few times. Timing is everything with goldens and a lot of other curiosities in life. Right after ice-out, often in August at lakes above 10,000 feet, is when the fish are accessible and casually willing to take flies. A couple of weeks past the disappearance of the ice and golden lakes often appear barren, lifeless. They've never exhibited wild, gluttonous surface feeding, but have had their moments with wet flies and streamers.

"When you get to a fork in the road, take it."
- Yogi Berra

THE TROUT IN ALBERTA COME AT A PRICE, a steep but righteous one. The trail into two of the best lakes is long and goes up and up forever climbing through some of the finest alpine country anywhere. This is the land R.M. Patterson lived within his heart and wrote passionately about in *The Buffalo Head*. The fishing can be good for strikingly marked goldens, but consistent cooperation on their part has proven the exception. Little matter. The trip is worth the effort for aesthetics alone. When younger I made this trip several times and was never disappointed. Never saw another soul. Sometimes caught goldens, and always promised myself that I'd return as long as I was able. I've permanently broken this promise now that a helicopter tour company has opened a flight service to these once isolated lakes. Throw lots of money on the counter. Take a quick fifteen minute hop to the water tearing apart the pristine silence with the whacking racket of whirring rotor blades. Fish for a bit. Dine on caribou pate, smoked inconnu and sip vintage wine – "I detect a faint taste of "tannin and a hint of licorice." Whizz back. Buy the T-Shirt. Check the place off some obscene been there-done that list and speed on down the road to the next hip, must-see location. Lovely.

When I lived in Whitefish my Australian Shepherd Rupert and I would make our annual pilgrimage to a beautiful lake tucked away beneath a severe ridge far up in the Missions. We did this the first week of October, staying for a couple of nights. I'd bring steaks for our evening meals, some dog food, a few beers and a bottle of cognac for sipping around a small fire build in a niche of granite where we camped. The goldens often were motionless in the clear water, ingots of precious living metal holding their positions with the gentlest of fin movement. Or they'd drift along the shorelines moving so slowly they almost seemed motionless. They always took woolly worms, not buggers. I'd cast one well ahead of the trout and they'd casually move over to the unweighted pattern as it hung in the water. The fish would congregate around the wooly worm and stare at the thing, often for fifteen or twenty minutes before one of them would break ranks and inhale the fly, the others breaking rank in a golden, all-directional flurry. Rupert would sit next to me and watch the drama. I think he liked bright colors, too. We'd keep two or three to go with our steaks. They tasted of the mountains, the cold rock, snow and ice, ancient lichen. Then we'd sit by the fire and its perfect heat watching stars come out and often a large moon rise over the Swan Mountains in the east. In the morning we'd repeat the simple, honest play. As nice a journey as I've experienced anywhere, anytime.

And years ago a friend turned me on to a lake that I never knew existed, a small item north of Whitefish. The guy owned a modest lodge on the western edge of the Whitefish Range, was trying to commercially raise brook trout, though predators and disease were decimating this costly venture. He knew the country around his place. Knew it well. While giving me vague directions, he added that he'd only been there once on foot by himself finding the little treasure by blind luck and that the walk in was a long rough one over deadfall, through brush and up and over large boulders. He concluded with "damn good country. Not bad fishing." When I pressed him further on the location of the goldens he said that "half the fun of fishing is finding places on your own."

Obviously this was an efficacious sharing of information on his part in terms of keeping me busy and away from Casey's Bar for several months. He preferred learning of my haphazard exploits in the hills to seeing me wander into that noble establishment, with I must say contrary to local rumor a fair amount of aplomb and panache, before 10 A.M. Walking out was possibly another story. That little tip of his pretty well killed off a summer and most of early fall that long ago season.

"I made up my mind, but I made it up both ways."
- Casey Stengel

THE QUEST FOR THE WHITEFISH RANGE GOLDENS began logically enough with the acquisition of several USGA topo maps of the country in question. Scanning these turned up three lakes within an area of several square miles in what I hoped was the right place. None of them were more than twenty or thirty acres and there were no marked trails to any of them. A good sign.

Parking on an old logging two track east of Olney I began my search. Days were spent wandering through brush, along game trails and side hilling beneath craggy slopes. Mosquitoes and deer flies were constant companions. By midday the sun's intensity made clambering and hacking through the terrain quite enjoyable. Heedless of giardia I drank deeply from tiny springs that bubbled out of cracks in the rocks, stone that was covered in lush moss. One day I found a nice mule deer rack shed the year before and packed it back down to the truck. Three-toed woodpeckers observed my futility with studied cynicism, small groups of them holding forth with weird cackling from the vantage points of pine tree limbs. Spruce and a few roughed groused rocketed through the forest at my approach in non-fool hen fashion. Blues tore across exposed ridges. Marmots whistled in derision from scree slopes and fresh bear sign kept me alert.

A month into this madness I topped a rocky rise and found one of the lakes. Fish were rising all about the surface. Quick casts produced even quicker results. Beautiful, garishly colored trout. Eight to ten inches. Brookies. At any other time I would have been ecstatic with this discovery, but gold was the quarry. The lake was only five miles from the two-track and stored away for future overnight camping reference.

By late August I'd succumbed to frustration, more crazy than usual, manic. Climbing farther up the flat-faced, gradually sloping mountain, farther along than ever before water sparkled through the bright green larch needles. The lake was rippled by a warm afternoon breeze. Casting from the trunks of large deadfalls that stretched out into the water I caught dozens of dark, nearly black-sided westslope cutts. Perfect trout averaging maybe fifteen inches, but no goldens. Another lake filed away. A gift.

Taking a break from the hunt, I floated the three forks of the Flathead River for a few weeks with friends. We caught many rainbows and cutthroat and enjoyed the fading days of summer in grand style. I returned to what now seemed to be just another absurd quest. My tipster laughed when told of my travails. Such are good friends.

The second week of October I tried once again. I forced myself through a dense patch of blowdown covering maybe a square mile, having avoided the mayhem earlier in the year out of innate laziness. Some of the timber was blackened from a fairly recent fire. By the time I was finished, clothes, face and hands were covered in soot. Streaked with lines of sweat-cleansed tan marked my arms and no doubt my face. A steep pitch through boulders, loose rock and brush was next then an easy stroll along a grassy bench marked with dried stalks of bear grass and some fireweed. The Livingston Range in Glacier Park blasted away in the eastern distance, jagged peaks covered in fresh snow. The North Fork of the Flathead twisted like an emerald snake beneath larch going yellow-orange and lodgepole still maintaining a rich green. Blue grouse kicked up on a regular basis. Should have brought the Beretta. Ahead the miniature plateau disappeared, dropping away from sight. Beyond this a barren rise climbed away to the sky.

Another dead end, I thought, but kept walking. The flat gave way to a gradual slope. At its foot lay a lake of dark blue surrounded by larch that blazed in the October wine light. Even from a distance the swirling rise forms of fish were visible. Sliding, stumbling and running down the gravelly incline, I reached the water. Trout were everywhere – close to shore, out in the middle. Sipping, splashing, cruising and flashing precious metallic shades.

I'd found my northwestern Montana Eldorado. Stunned and elated didn't quite cover the emotions. A small grey Elk Hair caddis on a 5x tippet turned the fish, on every cast. Groups of them raced for the fly as soon as it disturbed the water. These guys hadn't been fished for in years. Golden after golden. Not large. Up to thirteen or fourteen inches. Deep green, crimson, black and white. Orange and gold that were reflections of the larch surrounding the lake. I fished for a couple of hours, until I had a temporary fill, then sat back, and like my Albertan helicoptered nemeses opened a bottle of (due to budget constraints and a dwindling sense of outrage relatively cheap) wine. What's wrong with a screw cap, anyway, and watched as the goldens kept feeding in what seemed to be a combination of merriment and playfulness. The wine was cool and good:

and for once a tale of fishing brilliance shone with the light of truth.

This year's exertions were now defensible.

The day was mine.

"It's like déjà vu all over again."
- Yogi Berra

ABOUT THE AUTHOR

John Holt is the author of 27 published books including *Road Fish, Hunted in Paradise, Plain Crazy in Paradise, Blown Away Under the Big Sky, The Lost Patrol, Yellowstone Drift – Floating the Past in Real Time, Arctic Aurora – Canada's Yukon and Northwest Territories, Coyote Nowhere – In Search of America's Last Frontier.* His work has appeared in such publications as *Men's Journal, Fly Fisherman, High Country News, Crossroads, E – The Environmental Magazine, Big Sky Journal, The Flyfish Journal and Gray's Sporting Journal.* He and his wife, photographer Ginny, and Elmer live in Livingston, Montana.

ABSOLUTELY AMAZING eBOOKS

AbsolutelyAmazingEbooks.com
or AA-eBooks.com